THE LORD OF FREEDOM

PREQUEL

The Lord of Freedom

Prequel

The Way It Would Become

Amena Jamali

The Lord of Freedom

Prequel—The Way It Would Become

COPYRIGHT © 2023 by Amena Jamali

Edited by Mary Reid

Cover Art by Amena Jamali

ISBN

979-8-9859244-4-2 *Paperback*

979-8-9859244-3-5 *Kindle Ebook*

979-8-9859244-5-9 *Digital Ebook*

PUBLISHED BY AMENA JAMALI

www.amenajamali.com

This story of the mothers and the fathers of the Quest of Freedom
is lovingly dedicated
to my mother, who is as fierce as a lioness in defense of her family,
to my father, who is as gentle as a lamb in the presence of his,
and
to all those who cling to the Light at the approach of evil.

CONTENTS

AUTHOR'S NOTE AND MAP

Dear Readers:

My thanks for opening this book and perusing its contents. Your consideration means much to me, for the publication of this story is itself an act of gratitude.

While revising *The Bell Tolling* in the summer of 2021, I found myself consumed by curiosity about something I had never really considered before: the stories of my five heroes' parents. Lucian, Malika, Elian, Arista, and Kyros all have such vivid backstories, and it is apparent in *The Bell Tolling* that all five heroes respect their parents greatly. Their parents, from what the five of them say, made extremely difficult choices, from choosing exile to sacrificing one love for the sake of another, and somehow their hearts remained so pure throughout all these trials and troubles that they raised children who would one day receive the blessing of the Almighty and bring freedom to the world.

I could not help but be intrigued, and I began to wonder about what manner of people these parents must have been. What were they like, why did they choose the spouse they did, what motivated them to make the sacrifices they did, and... did they actually *know* what evil was coming? Did they *know* who their children would become? From Lucian's, Malika's, Elian's, Arista's, and Kyros' recounting in the opening fourteen chapters of *The Bell Tolling*, their parents' stories are marked with tragedy —and they seem to have borne that tragedy without complaint. So, did they *know*?

With such questions swirling in my mind, it is not surprising that, in May 2022, almost the moment *The Resonant Bell* was published, I began writing the first of these stories, *The Way It Would Become*.

The Way It Would Become is the first of five prequels, and it is the story of Malika's parents, Riqeta and Naman.

Originally, it was intended to be a more romantic telling of how these two wonderful people met, married, and raised the child who became the Second of the Quest of Freedom.

But, as I wrote, it became... more.

On its surface, *The Way It Would Become* is still a romance, sweet and endearing like chocolate.

Yet, underneath... it is the story of what it means to see evil when it brews in the world—to not turn away out of discomfort or fear of pain, to not remain blind out of a desire to maintain a good opinion of those one loves, to not ignore the coming of tragedy for the sake of clinging to happiness. To force oneself to acknowledge the destructive force of evil and witness the turning of the great cycle of prosperity even when no preparation can be made for the future. For no reason other than the agonizing truth that the truth must be known.

It is a painful story.

But it is a story that gives wisdom about our own world and our own times, just as much as it deepens our understanding of the world of *The Lord of Freedom*.

Thus are the reasons I have undertaken to write this book alongside the main series, and thus are the thoughts I urge you, dear readers, to remember as you read this book.

The Way It Would Become, as the first prequel, can be read before all other books in the *The Lord of Freedom* series, and indeed it is designed to transition seamlessly to the first chapter of *The Bell Tolling*. It does not require the context of the main series to understand. However, if you should so desire, dear readers, *The Way It Would Become* can also be read at any point in the main series without receiving any untoward revelations. You may also choose not to read it and not find your understanding and enjoyment of the main series spoiled. But, if you desire to know about the origins of *The Lord of Freedom*'s heroes and villains, this story offers the first portion.

As you begin this story, dear readers, I also urge you to remember this warning: because of the age in which *The Way It Would Become* takes place, many evil things emerge during the course of the story, such as depression, familial abuse, matricide, and violence of numerous forms, including harm directed toward children. No explicit language is ever used, but the implications still may be troubling to those sensitive to such triggers. Please care for your heart and your health, dear readers. Choose freely and wisely on your own behalves, and cherish your own dignity.

If you do choose to read this story, remember that eventually the Quest will come, with blessing and freedom spreading in their wake...

What follows hereafter is translated from *a'Makalle é a'Ambele é Fidaana Malika a-Haséalaah*, a preliminary to the volumes of the annals compiled by the Archivist under the wishes of the Lady of Icilia and the guidance of the Guardian of Names.

With Gratitude,
Amena Jamali
January 2023

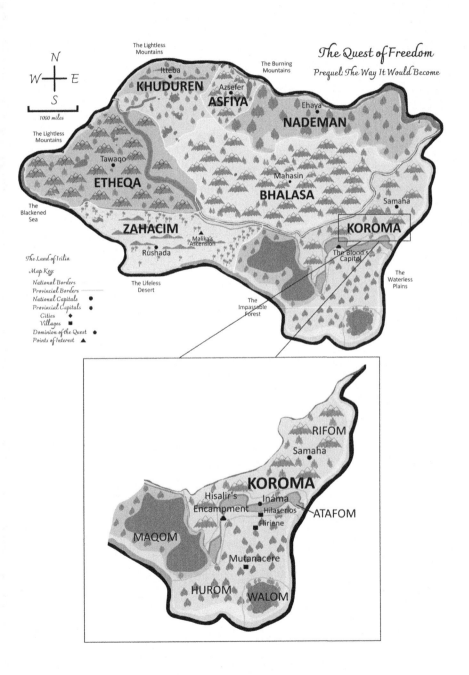

The Quest of Freedom
Prequel: The Way It Would Become

The Land of Icilia
Map Key:
National Borders
Provincial Borders
National Capitals ●
Provincial Capitals ●
Cities ◆
Villages ■
Dominion of the Quest ●
Points of Interest ▲

THE BEGINNING

In the beginning, nothing stirred. The divine cleansing of the land had left none who dared to move, for the memory of the purge haunted each breath. But with time, those who survived the purge believed themselves to be spared and then immune to any form of accounting. So, before many years had passed, the land devolved into chaos. Iniquity abounded, and no conscience whispered the truth. There was only darkness.

But then, amid the disorder, came Light. The Light entered the morass in the figure of a man, one who shone. Folding his sleeves up, he gathered a people, a few who were just a little less unruly than their neighbors. He brought them together, he healed them, he nurtured them. Dazzled by his light, they knelt at his feet and pledged to follow him and through him his Master the Almighty always.

The Shining Guide, as they revered him, pleased with this pledge, gave them civilization. He taught them the arts of government and writing, the sciences of farming and metalworking, and the sanctities of family and community. Eagerly they learned, and he smiled and called them Muthaarim, those who shone. He then showed them the treasure that blossomed in their country, the trees which bore athar, the most blessed substance ever known.

He taught them new disciplines, the ways of benefiting from athar and forming their natural magic. Thus, the people flourished.

Yet then came the day on which the Shining Guide bid them farewell. He had completed his task, so his Master called him to another land, and he would answer. The Muthaarim, his heart's children, cried and begged for him to not leave them amid the chaos. The Shining Guide, seeing their misery, smiled and promised them that they would not be abandoned. For one day, the land would unite with them, and, whenever troubles overwhelmed them, saviors would come. And with that assurance, he departed.

Much time passed, and the Mutharrim lost the fervency of their devotion. Thus was the first trouble that broke upon them.

But the Shining Guide's promise was not hollow. Four generations after he had first chosen the Muthaarim to be his people, the Quest of Light arose and fulfilled his promise and prophecy. With the dedication and effort of their lifetimes, three of the Muthaarim, Aalia, Manara, and Naret, spread the blessings of civilization to all the land, which they named Icilia.

So connected, the Mutharrim found companionship with the Areteen, the Ezulal, the Nasimih, and the Sholanar. Seven mighty nations formed, and peace reigned. And the land revered the names of Lady Queen Aalia the Ideal of Light, Graced Queen Manara the Exemplar of Truth, and Honored King Naret the Exemplar of Love only beneath the name of the Shining Guide.

But, as is the way of things, prosperity did not last...

THE PROPHECIES

In accordance with custom, the Guardian of Names delivered these prophecies at the naming ceremonies of two royals:

In Koroma, in the year 446 amid the Civilization of the Quests, C.Q.—

> Oh Father of Wisdom, may your gaze discern
> The haunting shadows and the sky's patterns.

In Zahacim, in the year 447 amid the Civilization of the Quests, C.Q.—

> Oh Mother of Prudence, may your hand nurture
> The truth revealed through you and light's structure.

Though the Guardian of Names was almost a divine figure, these prophecies seemed so odd and obscure amid that age of prosperity that they were soon disregarded, save for brief, ceremonial reminders to the children raised under their weight.

The enclosed is a prequel to the seven volumes which present the story of the Quest of Freedom and reveals the story of the mother and the father of Graced Malika the Exemplar of Wisdom, as drawn from their personal journals and memoranda, as well as those of her aunt, her uncle, and her grandparents, and the royal records of Koroma.

So writes the Archivist.

PROLOGUE: THE WAY IT WOULD ALWAYS BE

Perspective: Princess Riqeta sej-Shehenzahak, auxiliary heir to the throne of Zahacim
Date: Eyyésal, the twenty-first day of the fourth moon, Likberre, of the year 468, C.Q.

My fingers twitched toward my sword's hilt as the crown prince of Bhalasa tossed another smirk toward my cousins and me.

That blasted prince was convinced my family's agreement to this trade summit between Zahacim, Koroma, and Bhalasa indicated our weariness for war.

If he was not careful, my cousins and I would show him just how weary we really were.

On my left, Sholata tightened her fingers around the shaft of her spear. As the sister who had trained her, I knew the slight motions were signs that she was seconds from lifting that spear and throwing it.

I subtly brushed my elbow with hers. *Calm yourself*, I ordered in another cousin's mindlink. *Auntie commanded that this summit was to remain peaceful.*

How do you know what Mother plans? she retorted and

slammed her arm against mine. Hard enough to leave a bruise, despite my armor. Though she then relaxed her posture, resentment for me filled her presence in the link. Not the eager obedience she had once felt, that she *should* have felt, for her older cousin and commander, the second-born heir of our generation.

I suppressed the hurt welling in my heart. There was no sense in indulging how much her growing disrespect, nor that of the other cousins, stung—this was my life and my family, and they were all I had. There was no other way, no way out.

The four sisters standing to my right sniggered in the link, before turning, once again, as silent as desert sandstone.

I made myself silent as well and extended my senses as far as I could.

King Doman aj-Shehenkorom was speaking about the need for compassion in trade at the front of the small, brightly lit stone chamber, while both his family and the royal families of Zahacim and Bhalasa listened. Each family was given a wedge-shaped section of the room: chairs for the monarch, consort, and crown heir, and ample room for as many auxiliary heirs as were present to stand behind them. Zahacim was represented by six heirs in addition to the primary three royals, Koroma by the only other heir and the king's three younger siblings (who bore the titles of 'prince' and 'princess' but were not heirs), and Bhalasa by eight (half of whom were the children of the other four). Both Koroma's and Bhalasa's delegations spoke in quiet whispers among one another, but Zahacim's was silent. No one else was present, neither within the chamber nor in the surrounding area —the Bhalaseh king's requirement for a meeting.

My hearing was not quite as clear as it would be in the desert proper (where those of the earth-favored Areteen like myself were strongest), nor was my vision as sharp, but it would do. After four years of war with Bhalasa, frequent raids into her territory, and confrontations with her winged, fire-favored Sholanar warriors, I was well-accustomed to fighting with less than optimal senses.

Though Auntie had commanded caution and King Doman-korom had intended for this summit to resolve the conflict, it was difficult to believe that the Bhalaseh royals would keep the truce. They were the aggressors, after all, with their efforts to gain exclusive control over the central Anharat River. Even peace- and trade-loving Nademan had thought Zahacim's declaration of war justified—and Bhalasa's new ambition for ending any reliance on grain imports a reprehensible notion. It was why, despite their anger at not being invited, they had allowed a few of their trade scholars to aid King Doman-korom in negotiating a settlement in exchange for a portion of Bhalasa's trade.

None of it would have been possible without Zahacim's prowess. Bhalasa, with her obstinate king, would never have agreed to negotiate without Zahacim bringing her to her knees. That reality made the Bhalaseh crown prince's arrogance all the more irritating.

The queen reprimanded me for not ignoring his surrender and striking that mortal blow, I mused to myself, *but, quite apart from the laws of engagement themselves, even a boy should not have to lose his father as young as I did.*

As though on cue, the little five-year-old prince of whom I was thinking fluttered down from the ceiling perch on which he was supposed to sit. "Papa?" he asked in his high, singsong voice. "When are we going home?"

The crown prince gently wrapped the edge of a large silver-blue wing around his son and spoke to him quietly, his hazel eyes warming with affection. His entire demeanor transformed in the blink of an eye for his son.

I despised the man, but I almost smiled, remembering my own father, Prince Rettes Shehenzahak, who had treated me like the stars in the sky and the jewels in the earth. He missed his wife, my mother, who passed into the Almighty's reward mere minutes after my birth, but his grief only sweetened his love for me.

How different my life would have been if he had remained to cherish me and provide defense against his sister the queen's disregard.

Though perhaps even he would not have been able to protect me, and that would have broken his heart. It was indeed because I was a prince's daughter, not a princess', that such abuse had fallen upon me. Two of my cousins were not the queen's own children but were adored in so many ways I was not.

Yet even they did not care for me. The only sister who loved me at all, the only cousin to whom I was close, was Serama, one of the younger heirs. Though she had all possible privilege as Auntie's own daughter, enough to humiliate with impunity even an older cousin, she had always respected me. Always. Whether on the battlefield, in court, or in our private arenas, always.

In her absence (Auntie had not selected her for guarding this summit), I was all alone amid those who either did not want me or did not notice me...

Enough, Riqeta, I said to myself, crushing the pity and pain as I would an enemy combatant. *A warrior and a magician do not have luxury for such lack of discipline, and you are both.* Emptying my mind of errant thoughts, I settled back into the guard stance, a statue that only observed and did not feel.

As the Koromic monarch finished his speech with an appeal to the Quest for their favor, the young Bhalaseh heirs suddenly giggled and flew off their perch. Little wings flaring, they swooped toward the auxiliary heirs of the other nations in a move too like their parents' military maneuvers. But lacking all finesse.

Unable to control his flight, the son of the crown prince crashed into my sisters' backs.

They stiffened, their hands going to their weapons.

The crown prince flew to his feet.

I turned, dropped to my knees in front of the little prince, and gathered him into my arms just as he began to cry. Shielding him from my sisters' anger.

"My son," I cooed, "my son, do not cry, Prince Dinalir-bhala. Do not cry, little one." I stroked his silky blue wings and the soft, springy chestnut curls peaking from beneath his cap. "Do not cry, my son."

The boy curled into me and pressed his face, brown-black as the most fertile soil, into my neck, hiding from my cousins' glares. "I am sorry, Princess Riqeta-zahak!" he sobbed. "I only wanted to make you laugh!"

"I know, my son," I whispered. "I know what you meant. It is all right. I am not angry with you."

The boy only cried harder.

Murmuring more endearments, I settled him in my arms, holding him as I had held the children of my aunts and the nobles, and rose to my feet. Then, walking over to where the crown prince waited, I bowed and offered him his child.

The crown prince, an odd expression on his face, inclined his head and uttered his thanks as he took his son. Turning away, he cradled the boy and walked to the back of the room, where his brothers had gathered their own children, whose faces were also slick with tears.

Exhaling a sigh, dreading what I would have to hear from my family about this, I turned.

And my eyes caught upon those of the second prince of Koroma.

Lips slightly parted, he was staring at me, his expression even odder than the Bhalaseh crown prince's.

I frowned at him, then dismissed the strangeness as I returned to my post and my observation of the monarchs' speeches. There was a scolding in my future, as the glint in Auntie's eyes attested —though my action had actually prevented the speeches from being disrupted—so my attention would better be spent on preparing a stoic façade.

This was the way it would always be.

CHAPTER 1
THE MONARCH OUR PEOPLE NEED

Perspective: Prince Naman sej-Shehenkorom, auxiliary heir to the throne of Koroma
Date: Eyyélab, the eighth day of the eighth moon, Belsaffe, of the year 469, C.Q.

I crashed onto my back, expelling all the breath from my lungs and all thoughts from my mind.

The tip of a sword hovered over my face.

I blinked, trying to comprehend the sight of the silver metal point, capped with a dark wood block, that was dominating my vision.

"Yield?" a hard alto voice asked.

I was too winded to answer.

A laugh, the dramatic softening of that hard voice, filled my ears before the sword was replaced by a hand two-thirds the size of my own.

Looking upon that hand, despite the worn leather gloves that shielded red-bronze skin, one would never think it the hand of a warrior. The short fingers were so slender and dainty that they seemed better suited to the arts, to writing or painting or sewing, like the famed virtuosos among the Nademani, or else to the masterful politicians and treasurers among the Khudurel and the Etheqor. And, yes, the impression was not incorrect, for the mistress of those elegant fingers was adept in those areas as well. But first and foremost the hand belonged to a warrior without peer.

It was the hand whose support I would forever treasure.

A besotted smile played on my lips as I accepted it and let my wife pull me to my feet.

"Naman," she said, looking up at me over the twelve inches that separated our heights, "do you realize you have not improved a single degree since we met?"

I shrugged, still wearing that ridiculous smile. Only six months had passed since our wedding, yet I knew the smile was not likely to ever leave my lips.

"Naman," Riqeta said, placing her hands on her hips, "are you *listening*?"

I really was not, too consumed with enjoying how her eyes, a swirl of amber and chocolate, flashed at me, full rose lips pressed together, pert nose crinkled slightly, characteristic Areteen plates vibrating in exasperation. Tightly bound walnut hair, arched brows, high cheekbones, and hints of deep dimples completed the most beautiful face I had ever seen—

A right hook whopped my side, forceful enough to catch my attention but too light to sting. "Naman!" Riqeta exclaimed. "Focus on improving!"

Laughing, I raised my hands. "I am trying!"

A flash of pale purple light filled the corner of my vision before the rich, merry voice of my brother said, "You must forgive him, Sister." He bent at the waist and pecked her cheek.

A wry smile quirked her lips. "Must I, Brother?"

The kiss was chaste and entirely brotherly, as was his relationship with her, and the sight of it assured me that my family accepted her. Still, laughing, I exclaimed, "Leave us be, Raman! Do you not have crown heir duties demanding your attention?"

"Peace, Brother," Raman said, chuckling. "I come only to

assure my sister that the husband she chose is more smitten than obtuse—"

Both Riqeta and I swatted at his arms.

"—and to inform you both that Father wishes to speak with you," he finished, smile abruptly fading.

"Father?" Riqeta asked. "Is he not holding council with his advisors?"

"Your presence is demanded immediately in the throne hall," Raman said, turning on his heel to leave. "And, Brother, Sister, present yourselves well—the whole court is gathered."

Only as he walked away did I realize that he wore his full court regalia, shining silver armor atop lilac athar robes trimmed in gold that fell to his feet. His gold heir's circlet, embedded with polished pieces of purple amethyst, gleamed around the lilac cap, shaped a little like the broad, low cone of a mountain, placed over his chestnut hair.

Riqeta and I exchanged glances, expressing our confusion, before rushing to the side of the arena, where her maid and my valet waited with towels and our circlets. The moment we reached them, they began to wipe the dust off of our armor and helms.

"Will arriving without full royal dress be acceptable?" Riqeta asked as she held her arms out for the maid.

Startled by the unusual edge of nerves to her voice, I turned to her before my Areteen valet, Colan, hissed at me to keep still. I complied, but my mind whirled... then I remembered that Koroma's culture was still new to her. Though she usually seemed to know my nation as well as I did, Riqeta had only just begun to accustom herself to a court less formal than her own (not that Koroma could ever truly be considered *in*formal).

I smiled softly and answered, "Since the summons was so sudden, our circlets will do."

She exhaled quietly as she donned her circlet. "At h- in Rushada, we would be expected to change into full armor regardless of when we received the summons. Some of my cousins actually carried around their court armor, as a precaution."

My smile widened, though it hurt that she had almost called a place other than Samaha home. "Zahacim is frightening, my princess." As Colan put his cloths away, I removed my gloves and slipped my wedding ring onto my right small finger.

As I had hoped, Riqeta chuckled, rich as a forest river, as she donned her wedding ring as well. "Indeed she is, Naman. Koroma is quite relaxed and charming in comparison."

It was not quite the response I wanted. Though I knew only a few months had passed, how dearly I wished that she would consider my home hers. Riqeta's honor was legendary, and she was adept in the maneuverings of the court, but she rarely spoke of emotion... I still did not know why she had not asked me to defect from Koroma for her. I was the second heir for my nation's throne, yes, but her position was equal to mine, the second heir of the next generation. Once her aunt stepped down, she would have been her cousin's chief advisor and general, and I had been willing to forfeit my birthright for the sake of hers.

Yet she chose Koroma instead. Though she had not returned my declaration of love...

Colan gave me a sympathetic look, understanding well the weight of my troubles as he endeavored to woo Leoma, Riqeta's Nasimih maid.

I answered with a small smile and extended an arm to my wife. With words of thanks to our staff, we walked rapidly toward the throne hall.

Just as we approached the grand entrance, Riqeta tugged me into an alcove. Lifting both hands to my shoulders, she said, "Naman, use your farsight when we enter that room."

"Why?" I asked, even as I began to catalyze, concentrating on my conviction regarding the Almighty's purpose for all creation.

"Your brother called you for a reason," she said, golden brown eyes serious. "You know the machinations of your own court."

I exhaled a sigh. I was a child of the ever-manipulative Ezulal, but I utterly *despised* intrigue...

It was one of the few ways I was different from my brother.

Raman, my elder by four years, was the perfect Koromic crown prince, learned, skilled in war, an excellent judge in matters of rule, and a master of court intrigue. He understood the personalities and affairs of every noble so well that he could nudge them whatever way he wanted—which had, in turn, solidified their respect for him despite his youth. For the same reason, the people felt secure in his future accession to the throne, though they were not passionate for him in the way they were for my father. Or for me.

Unlike my brother, who had devoted himself to the court and to war, I had spent my childhood leaving the moment my lessons and duties were done for the streets of Samaha. There, with a curiosity matched only by my willingness to listen, I gave my days to whichever cause in which my fellow citizens most needed aid, from cooking for the elderly to teaching children the sacred tongue to comforting the sick. I passed along nails and hammers when houses were repaired, weeded gardens in the spring, and helped scrub filth when large amounts of sheets were laundered. Many families treated me like another son, and I found myself welcome at supper tables at which even my father would not be received.

This devotion to the people was the reason why, in my adolescence, my parents gave me increasingly greater shares of the duties of oversight in the Healing City of Ináma and of travel throughout Koroma to see to the welfare of the people. The experiences together had shaped my eloquence differently from my brother's—I was accustomed to the people, who wanted compassion for its own sake, not for furthering anyone's interests, whether mine or theirs. But while the people loved me for the honesty of my speech, the nobles disdained me for the same. For I like to speak only for the sake of others, while they reminded me at every turn that speaking for one's own sake was akin to speaking for the crown's. Yet such, such *selfish* thought for myself did not come naturally to me.

In the year before my twentieth birthday and my ceremony of

magical maturity, I had despaired that all of this rendered me an unworthy prince. But on the morning of that ceremony, Raman had held my shoulders and told me, in no uncertain terms, that, "I am what Koroma is. You are what Koroma is supposed to be, Naman." It was a sentiment echoed by our parents and by our aunts and our uncle. All of them together had promised to protect my back in court and had done so again and again as I fulfilled the duties that came with the rank of a fully mature prince these last three years.

Still, Riqeta's acumen for intrigue was yet another way our marriage benefited me.

And indeed I felt no shame in acknowledging that. I was well accustomed to listening to those of greater experience—for wisdom was wisdom, regardless of rank or age—and I knew well that strong women held the world together. Closer even than my brother, I had watched my grandmother, the second wife of my grandfather and so not my father's mother by birth, adore my father like he was her own son. She had never demeaned him in favor of the three children she herself had brought into the world. To her last day, she had loved my father without fault.

Equally had I witnessed my mother, one of the Mutharrim, born in Asfiya, a descendant of the first Quest, but neither royal nor noble, so smoothly manage Koroma's court that it seemed as though she were born *here*. Though her courtship with my father after his coronation as monarch was brief, she so fully accepted her duties as his lieutenant that she had entirely absorbed the customs and manners of a land not her own. In her was the grandeur of women.

So I was happy for Riqeta to lead whenever she knew better than I did. She knew so much more of the world, and I was glad to listen to her in everything.

Our marriage provided every benefit to me.

How I wished that she, too, benefited from it!

As catalysis took hold, my vision split in two, forming the

underlay and overlay in the use of which I had been trained since childhood. Both visions focused on her lovely face.

"Naman," Riqeta said, cupping my cheeks, "always remember that I guard your back. Let no one intimidate you."

Those were not words of love... but my heart warmed all the same. Even if she did not love me, her promise to stand by me... for what more could one of the Ezulal wish?

Perhaps glimpsing the contentment on my face, Riqeta offered me a pleased smile before twining her arm through mine.

Then the two of us, with my farsight beginning a sweep of the crowded hall beyond, approached the lapis-inlaid doors. We removed our boots, leaving our feet covered in only socks to revere the sacred space beyond.

The guards on either side dipped reverences and flung them open as they announced, "The Almighty's blessings and the Quest's favor upon his Highness Prince Naman sej-Shehenkorom and his consort, her Highness Princess Riqeta Shehenkorom!"

Despite how I strained to see in my farsight, I could not discern a hint of regret crossing my wife's expression—if I had defected and not her, she would have been the heir and I the consort, her silver circlet the one that was adorned with a jewel and mine plain.

On either side of the line of plum tiles leading from the doors to the dais, the advisors, the officials, and the nobles in attendance sank into deep reverences. At the front, my mother and my brother rose from their thrones on either side of my father, who alone remained seated.

My mind reeled at the full royal presentation, one usually due my brother and not me, but Riqeta expressed no surprise.

We reached the steps of the dais and bowed, waiting to be dismissed to the lesser chairs positioned on the right of the dais to face both the monarch and the hall.

"Kneel," my father ordered.

I suppressed a flinch at the unexpected command and obeyed, my wife beside me.

Satisfaction filled the faces of some of the courtiers in my farsight, while others seemed uneasy or displeased or openly shocked.

Boots tapped the ground as my beloved father, Doman, Koroma's treasured monarch for nearly thirty years, under whose hands prosperity reigned, came to stand in front of me.

"Praised be the Almighty, and beloved is the Shining Guide!" he proclaimed. "My cherished friends, I have summoned you to the hall of the Throne of Benevolence to bear witness on behalf of the people of Koroma to a change in the name of your future monarch."

What? Future monarch? Does he intend to change my brother's name from 'Raman' to something else? Mother named us so similarly, so similarly to Father as well, and Raman and I did use to jest that they would grow frustrated someday...

Father stepped aside, and Raman stood in his place. "Koromile!" my brother said, smooth bass voice ringing throughout the purple-ornamented hall. "Amid much prayer to the Almighty, I have considered with great depth the merits of my own character. I have judged the qualities of my soul and the testament of my actions. The fruit of that reflection has delivered me to this conclusion: I am not worthy of the Throne of Benevolence."

My head jerked up as both my sights focused on his face. Besides me, Riqeta muffled a gasp, while the court audibly inhaled.

A grim smile curling his mouth, he continued, "Though I have been raised to serve as your monarch, my heart is not made for the honor. I love our nation, but I do not possess the dignity and unwavering attention to duty that the rank requires. My heart longs for the thrill of battle, for the quiet solitude found only under the stars. I fulfill what is asked of me, but my actions are never more than sufficient, only ever just enough to meet the needs of our people. My qualities, I have found, meet every requirement—meet and never exceed.

"And, moreover, while I struggle to serve you as you truly need, there is one who excels in every area I fall short and in every area I do not: my brother, Prince Naman-korom."

I sputtered, trying to find the words to stop him.

Ignoring me, he continued, "His love for Koroma, the air of authority he carries, his quiet excellence in every responsibility... Koromile, he is the monarch our people need. The sincerity of his kindness and compassion far exceeds anything I could ever muster. For these reasons, I have made a choice as some among my ancestors have chosen and as our laws allow: I surrender every claim to the Throne of Benevolence, leaving the right in the hands of our king, and beg for that favor to be given to his Highness Prince Naman sej-Shehenkorom."

Bowing, he kneeled before our father.

Father nodded, a faint smile upon his lips, creasing the lines linking his nose and mouth. Pride twinkled in his hazel eyes.

Raman lifted the gold and amethyst circlet from his head and gently placed it in our father's outstretched hands.

Both of them murmured a prayer as their gazes met.

Light collected around their fingers before sparking in an explosion of blinding purple.

For a moment, both my sights were dark.

When they cleared, my father was offering the heir's circlet to me.

Behind him, my mother and Raman were wearing encouraging smiles.

My pulse pounded in my ears as I struggled to comprehend what was happening. I needed time to think and understand, but I did not have any, and delaying would be seen as a weakness, and I did not know if I could *do* this—

I cast a desperate glance, through my farsight, at Riqeta.

She gave me a single nod. Her expression was calm, decided, firm, as though she had already thought through and comprehended the immensity of what was happening. She defended my back, and she knew what to choose.

I inhaled deeply and removed the silver band I had worn since maturity, passing it to my wife. Then I lifted my hands in the gesture of fealty.

Father smiled. "In the name of the Almighty and by the blessing of the Shining Guide, I am King Doman aj-Shehenkorom, Monarch to Koroma. By what merit do you claim the throne of Koroma, my Son? What is the pledge you offer as Heir-apparent?"

My heartbeat seemed to halt in my chest. An heir's pledge, the one offered by a crown prince, required weeks of preparation! It was the personal plea of an Heir for the throne, why that person should be considered at all, the basis upon which royal claims were granted, and each Heir was supposed to compose her or his own. In Koroma, the more polished, the better. It was no idle custom.

"Naman," Riqeta whispered in my ear, "if it pleases you, I composed a pledge as your brother spoke."

As my consort, her words counted as my own... "Please, Riqeta," I whispered in return.

She gripped my arm and said, "Speak these words..."

Trusting in her promise, I raised my head and repeated, "In the name of the Almighty and by the blessings of the Shining Guide known through our Rulers the Quest, I plead for the chance to serve my nation. If the throne is granted to this servant of the Quest, I will pour of myself into my actions, proffering every kindness and compassion to the People of Koroma. I will meet sorrow and pain with solace, and answer anger and bitterness with understanding. Neither my adherence to the laws of the Almighty, the Quest, and Koroma will ever falter, nor will my compassion ever fail amid the trials of my future. Forever will I seek the kindness of the Divine. Praised be the Almighty."

Even as the words spilled from my mouth, I wondered at them. I would not have crafted their equal even with preparation... How well did my wife know Koroma!

Approval warmed my father's smile, and he gave a single nod

to Riqeta. Then, meeting my gaze, said, "With the prayer that my choice might bring glory to the Quest's name, I accept your pledge on behalf of Koroma and her people. I grant your plea for the Throne of Benevolence. May your reign bestow upon us the blessing of the Almighty."

Those ceremonial words uttered, he lowered his gaze to the circlet. A clear indication to reach for it.

My breath heaved in my chest as I stared at the gleaming gold. *This is the moment.*

Apparently sensing my anxiety, Riqeta squeezed my arm, and my mother whispered in one of her mindlinks, *It will all be well, Son.*

With the strength of their support, I touched my palms to the base of the circlet.

White sparks flashed from the gold and jewels over my pale skin. The cool, calming scent of a still, fathomless lake brimmed in the air, followed by the faint sounds of waves gently lapping at sandy shores. The taste of water, both fresh and salty, trickled over my tongue. Then those sparks swirled into brilliant beams of lilac, amethyst, and violet light that consumed my sights...

Gentle hands cradled my cheeks, and soft motherly lips kissed my forehead. Quiet words, unassuming drops of rain, reached my ears, whispered in a delicate voice, *Hallowed Father of Wisdom... Father of your people...*

Warmth rose in my heart, more blazing than love yet gentler than any passion... It was the unutterable kindness of a mother's comforting embrace, the irresistible softness of words spoken to the tormented, the inexpressibly open heart of the truly empathetic. And, as it filled me, soaking my soul like the first showers of spring, the tendrils of the bond settled.

Awareness sparked—awareness of the entirety of Koroma, every inch of land, every piece of flora and fauna, every single person who had pledged to the crown whose scion I had now become. The nation and I merged together until I did not know where I ended and she began... Unto the borders set by the Quest, I felt everything.

None of the histories of my ancestors had ever even remotely captured how it felt. And rightly so, for it was too much for my mind. Such awareness was the province of the divine, no mere incé prince, and as blackness crept around the edges of my consciousness, I begged for relief...

As though in response to my prayer, the connection lost depth and profundity, fading to a shadow, an echo... and yet I was forever changed. While this rank remained mine, my bond would ensure I always knew the circumstance of my nation. I would never meet a child of Koroma without learning something of her or his emotions. I would always be theirs, as they would be part of me.

I had never dreamed of becoming king. But, now that it was my path, a longing coalesced in my heart that someday I should wear the crown. For reasons beyond my understanding, the Almighty had decided to bestow this task upon me, and every part of me desired to serve.

CHAPTER 2
AS STRONG A RESPONSE AS THE CROWN CAN MUSTER

Perspective: Princess Riqeta Shehenkorom, consort of the Heir to Koroma
Date: Eyyéala, the twelfth day of the eighth moon, Belsaffe, of the year 469, C.Q.

I exhaled a charming laugh even as my fingers twitched toward the hilt of my sword.

Fooled by the pleasantness of my expression, Count Flirien continued, "His Royal Highness' lack of eloquence is a major concern, your Highness. I know spouses tend to believe only praise of each other—I certainly think my countess is the most brilliant woman imaginable—did you know she discovered a solution to the blights plaguing my village's cornfields for *two* generations within a *single* year of our wedding?—but it is always wise to be prepared. His Royal Highness will not hold the rank for long. He is a poor choice, and I do not know how we will be able to follow him." By the tone of his voice and the look on his face, he presumed my agreement to his slickly delivered words alongside the approval of all six nobles who stood with us.

Curling my lips into a sweet smile, I answered, "My husband is not fond of court, yes, but that does not matter, Count Flirien."

He blinked. "No?"

I let a hint of the bloodlust for which my birth-family and -nation were so infamous emerge in the cast of my gaze. "I will be present at his back to ensure every fool knows his place."

The nobles winced, unable to entirely control their expressions, while Count Flirien stared, pale skin blanching as horror mixed with the shock in his eyes.

I raised a brow.

He visibly swallowed and dipped a reverence, understanding what point I had made.

Retaining that ruthless expression, I inclined my head and walked away, easily ignoring the pressure of the nobles' gazes. Instead, my eyes caught on the approving smile worn by my mother-by-marriage as she and her elder son dealt with another group.

Beneath the façade of my unshakable confidence, the little girl desperate for parental affection that I still was squealed with joy. Particularly since the memory of Queen Edana's disapproval of me as her son's consort remained all too vivid. She had only begrudgingly agreed to let me marry him when she realized my skill in sorcery and weapons-craft compensated well for my being of a different kind.

It was not kindist sentiment, not entirely at least. Because magic was matrilineal, the identity of a person's mother determined what type of magic her children were likely to possess—whether wish or arms or no magic at all, and often the degree of strength as well. Queen Edana preferred her sons to marry from among the Mutharrim because such women were more likely to bequeath powerful wish magic to the next generation of Koroma's heirs, like she herself had. That was why only the news of my own powerful magic, and less so my prowess in battle, had placated her.

And now, it seemed, my defense of her son, though hardly Koromic in its execution, added to my prestige in her eyes.

I would always defend him. Always. For what he had done for me, there was no recompense.

Shifting my stride into a walk reminiscent of a lioness' prowl, I approached the next cluster of courtiers. Even as my mind dwelled, as it so often had these last months, on how blessed I was that he had chosen me.

My birth-nation held two reputations: the first, our war-craving nature, as seen in how we had incited half of all conflicts since the Quest of Light's founding, and the second, the fierce sisterhood of our ruling family. The matriarchal Shehenzahak house treasured their daughters over jewels, wind, rain, harvests, and the crimson drops of their rivals' blood. Even the daughters of the few sons born into the family were prized, like stars bestowed by the divine.

Or so was their renown. For, since my birth, that sisterhood had changed.

I was the daughter of a Zahacit prince and the eldest after the crown princess in my generation. By law and tradition, my rank guaranteed me the most glorious commands, the finest armor, and the highest prestige in court and on the battlefield, for I was meant to be the future queen's first lieutenant. But I was hardly treated like a royal, much less an heir of such standing. Insult, emotional abuse, and pricking acts of cruelty had been my lot since my parents' early deaths.

The only light in that darkness was Serama, who, as a younger princess, had hardly more control over her movements than I did. Too often we were apart, our spirits breaking, mine by bearing cruelty and hers by watching it.

All I had wanted since girlhood was to escape, to lessen the pain for both of us. There was no peace for me, nor would there be for my daughters. But, because of my skill on the battlefield, it had seemed impossible for me to ever leave. Though they mistreated me, Zahacim's crown found me too valuable to allow me to abandon them.

Then the second-born prince of Koroma had noticed me among my cousins at a trade summit in my twenty-second year.

Immediately enamored, he had pursued my hand with all the dedication of a tracker in pursuit until my aunt the queen acquiesced, his parents agreed, and my own heart lay in his possession. Using a cunning he rarely showed, he maneuvered everyone such that less than a year after our meeting we were wed and prepared to begin a life together.

It had been my chance to leave Zahacim, and I had seized it. No rank was worth remaining in that court, and I did not want my new husband to suffer its indignity. My birth nation was not worthy of a change in his allegiance, and Koroma needed him as the monarch's only spare.

How doubly glad I was now that I had asked him to not forfeit his rank. With the depth of his compassion, he would meet Koroma's ideal of monarchy. He was who Icilia needed as well, for Zahacim grew month by month more willing to push the boundaries of our laws.

Having delivered my subtle threats to the courtiers, I turned and searched for my next targets.

Hmmm. I tapped my thumb against the wedding ring on my small finger. *Judging by how terrified they seem, Mother, Raman, and I seem to have covered all of them... Excellent.*

A more genuine smile slipped onto my face as I walked toward where we had left Naman speaking with Father and his most trusted advisor shortly after the royal entrance into the chamber.

In moments, his lilac-robed figure was within sight.

Though the heir's circlet gleamed gold and violet atop his lilac cap and red-blond curls, he was deferentially lowering his head as he conversed with the old advisor. His leanly muscled form, although hard as stone, was relaxed, as usual not a hint of intimidation about him. The sword-belt buckled around his waist adhered to custom without rendering him threatening in the least. The straight, proportional lines of his handsome face were soft with welcome, bright-colored mustache and short beard framing full pink lips curled in a gentle smile, tanned cream skin aglow with health and compassion. The silver of his wedding ring, engraved with my name, glinted on his right hand.

Something knotted in my chest eased.

Perhaps sensing my gaze, Naman lifted his head. His jewel-bright blue eyes lit up when he saw me.

Warmth pierced my heart, as sure as an arrow, leaving my breath unsteady in my throat, head curiously light, feet dangerously close to stumbling. No strike by either blade or word had ever affected me so.

The smile on his lips widened as I came closer. The moment I was within reach of his arm, he grasped my hand, kissed my knuckles, and drew me close to him, holding my fingers as though *they* were what anchored him to the ground.

Consumed as I was by the sweetness of the moment, the most dangerous declaration of all nearly spilled from my tightened lips.

"My princess," Naman said, baritone voice warm, "Councillor Siniamt was wondering if you might consider drilling the Cliffside Army this week?"

Cliffside Army... the moniker for the army who patrols the southern province of Atafom... from who we will be choosing soldiers...

Remembering the news Father had given us in a private audience directly after the morning meal, I answered, "Yes, I will begin a round of practice tomorrow morning." This duty of military preparation was one I had received after our wedding, the Koromic crown's method of taking advantage of my skills, and it was all the more important now.

The advisor bowed in acknowledgment before leveling a piercing look at Naman. "Be careful, my Son. Your eloquence and appearance of strength must not waver."

Naman's hand squeezed mine anxiously. "I understand, Uncle." It was critical advice, and difficult for him to uphold, as one of his few weaknesses was that he was *not* as suave as the

Koromic court required. Raman refused to acknowledge such shortcomings—the reason for his entirely untempered praise in his abdication speech—but it was true just the same.

I returned the squeeze. "I will be by his side the entire time, Uncle," I said, using the princes' endearment for the old man. I would be his eloquence when his own ability failed him.

Councillor Siniamt sighed and gave me a soft smile. "Naman, marrying this woman was the best choice you have ever made. I am sure you have benefited much personally, but politically as well she is a treasure: no one is as frightening as a battle-ready Zahacit princess, particularly her, the Sword of Prudence. One look from her scares your opponents into politeness."

My husband seemed to actually glow with delight at the words.

While I had to struggle to maintain my composure. Despite all my abilities, I was a poor choice for him. Queen Edana had been correct but not for the reasons she knew.

I resisted the urge to press a hand to my belly. If only I had already conceived a child... No matter what he learned about my history and the darkness in Zahacim, Naman would never divorce me if I bore our child. I could only pray that I would be blessed with one soon. Though I preferred daughters, even a son would do.

The beat of a gong reverberated throughout the hall.

All conversation ceased at the summons, and everyone turned to face the front of the chamber, where the king and his consort waited with regal smiles beside the gong.

Prince Falan Shehenkorom, the king's youngest half-brother and the herald of Koroma's court, stepped forward and declared, "May the Almighty bless you, Koromile! In the name of our Rulers the Quest of Light, this servant of Koroma bids you welcome to the court of his Majesty King Doman aj-Shehenkorom. In accordance with our laws and customs, our monarch will speak of his concerns before asking for our voices. In all matters, speak in tones of praise and listen with the intensity of devotion so that all that we do benefits our Mother, Koroma, the land of eloquence." Bowing, he waited for Father's nod before signaling the staff to bring out tables and chairs.

In but a few minutes, the staff placed enough round tables and chairs for the entire court to sit, positioned in a large oval such that they faced the two royal couples—the monarch, his heir, and their consorts.

It is, I reflected as I bowed and took my seat, positioning my robes neatly around me, quite *odd to be seated with the Heir like this. In Zahacim, where consorts now have only secondary royal status, I was supposed to have been enthroned this way with Misleta... I can hardly comprehend how many of my rights Naman has restored.* My heart swelled with affection, though I did not dare to act on it. *How the Almighty has blessed me with his presence...*

King Doman leaned forward slightly, an indication that he was ready to speak, and I put aside my thoughts. When one's ruler or commander spoke, one listened with the whole of one's attention.

"Nobles of Koroma," he began, "I request your forbearance in commanding a meeting outside of the scheduled court sessions for a second time. But, in honesty, it was a necessary order, for the crown has received news of a troubling sort: there is discontent in the south. An insurgent. Something which our exalted Koroma has not seen in nearly half a century."

The chamber was as silent as an untraveled tunnel, half the nobles staring at him with open shock and the other half casting assessing gazes in Naman's direction.

King Doman deigned to answer that speculation: "One insurgency is not the reason that my firstborn chose to abdicate his birthright. Crown Prince Naman-korom's majesty is truly greater than such temporal necessity."

Naman cupped a reverent hand over his heart as his cheeks colored an unrestrained crimson—though the first reaction was traditional and respected, the second, as I well knew, would open him to further criticism from the nobles. Despite all his training, he truly was a little too artless for his own court.

It did not matter. With the cold, dangerous smile on my face beside him, none would dare to speak against him. Even in Zahacim I had been feared, at least among the nobles, but in Koroma—well, in Koroma, I was almost these nobles' worst nightmare. Though I would never break the Quest's laws of military engagement and raise my weapon against anyone without true cause, they treated me like a wild warhorse, likely to attack anyone who even approached her charge. It was an impression I intended to cultivate for Naman's sake, until he and his family tired of my impurely Koromic ruling style.

Like Naman, I could not match the calm, composed smiles on King Doman's, Queen Edana's, Raman's, and the other royals' faces—which, coupled with slightly raised eyebrows and tilted heads, conveyed such a sense of disappointment that the few nobles not cowed by me looked away in guilt. The product of a skillful manipulation of their emotions.

As well as a sign of how united Naman's family was. Unlike mine.

I pushed away that thought and the bitter pain it evoked as King Doman resumed his speech.

"The insurgent," he was saying, "from what intelligence the crown has received, is from Countess qia-Mutanacera's village, in the province of Hurom. The leader's identity is not clear, nor is his kind, but he seems to have some influence, and he has perhaps taken advantage of the hole left by Countess qia-Mutanacera's and her husband's deaths last year. It is likely not supported by the new count—though the county's heir has not yet presented himself at court, he has assured the crown's representatives of the stability of his governance. Still, this issue seems beyond his control, and regardless it is our matter to address. The insurgency still seems small, so it is an opportune moment to address it, before it can grow to a larger size.

"Considering what we have learned of recent insurgencies in

Etheqa, Khuduren, Bhalasa, and even Zahacim—" Father nodded in my direction— "a swift and strong address is needed. But, as to the specifications of the crown's response, I ask to know the opinions of Koroma's nobles, who will bear the weight of this decision."

The chamber was silent amid the reverberations of the king's words. Many of the nobles stared at their clasped or steepled fingers, while others read the notes they had written. A deliberative quiet.

I suppressed a mournful sigh. Such things no longer existed in Zahacim. The insurgency eleven years ago had been swiftly and effectively addressed, yes, but my aunt had not waited for a single moment of deliberation or allowed the slightest concern over her decision.

Some minutes passed.

Then Princess Basima qia-Kafalira, King Doman's half-sister and the countess by marriage of the most important county of northern Rifom, said slowly, "Your Majesty, I would argue for as strong a response as the crown can muster. Koroma has been strengthened by the trade summit of the previous year and by her Highness Princess Riqeta Shehenkorom's defection—" a nod to me— "but our refusal to include Nademan, while prudent, is an affront that has not yet healed. Nor has the far greater insult to Asfiya, Etheqa, and Khuduren. The second two may even fuel an insurgency to topple us."

The royals, the nobles, and even I flinched at that. Based upon Etheqa's refusal to send a delegation to Naman's and my wedding —considering we were both second heirs, a deeply inappropriate move even for wartime—they were angry enough to want to tear Koroma to pieces. Since the summit had threatened her control over the trade of grain, Khuduren was surely no less angry, even if she was better at concealing it. Only Asfiya would restrain herself, and only for as long as Queen Edana, a cousin of her king and once one of her citizens, lived.

"Indeed, strength is required," another noble, from the east, agreed. "But what form should that strength take? Sending an army is tantamount to legitimization."

"As is asking the king to travel himself," a noble from the western sea added. "We must be compassionate in listening to the insurgents' troubles, in trying to resolve the root of their discontent, but the matter must be ended quickly. There are other issues to address."

My spine just slightly stiffened at those words. *What could be a greater issue than an insurgency?* I wondered. But I did not feel sure enough of my place to ask through the queen's links.

"Then what is it that you propose?" Prince Falan asked. Like Princess Basima's statement, the question was intended to guide the deliberations in a specific direction...

Naman shifted his throne slightly closer to mine and anxiously took my hand in his.

"Asking the crown prince to go," Count Flirien stated, taking the bait as he had earlier, with a nervous glance at me. "His Royal Highness' presence in the south, should he deign to agree to this proposal, your Majesty, will carry the full weight of the crown without giving the villain credence."

One of the nobles in his group added, "His Royal Highness would be more than capable of listening in compassion and offering threat with intimidation, if necessary." He tipped his head toward me. "He would magnificently wield the strength Koroma needs to display."

I smirked to myself. *A little more overt flattery than this court likes, but it shows my plan is working.*

"Only a company should travel with his Royal Highness," a southern noble suggested. "I have heard enough of these stirrings that, though I did not comprehend them before, I would deem it likely that a large military escort would provoke an adverse reaction. The crown would not be seen as listening."

That is not many soldiers, I mused to myself, *but I would still be able to coordinate defenses and attacks appropriately...*

"That is reasonable," Count Flirien said.

A number of the nobles, including Princess Basima, wore expressions of agreement.

"Is such the court's full proposal?" Prince Falan asked.

The nobles murmured assent.

Prince Falan turned and intoned formal words of presentation to his brother.

Silence reigned once more as King Doman considered the matter thoughtfully.

Then Father glanced at Naman and me. "My Son, my Daughter, would you be willing to travel to the south? With only a company as escort?"

Naman's hand tightened on mine. "It would be our honor, Father. To deal with this matter in a manner that persuades the dissenting to return to our tradition of eloquent compassion, Princess Riqeta-korom and I must ourselves listen. Such would most completely fulfill the Quest's mandate upon us and yield true prestige to Koroma in the gaze of the Almighty."

I smiled with more visible serenity to show my agreement.

What the nobles wanted was exactly what the royal family had chosen to do. It was a victory. And with my defense of Naman's back, my darkness shielding his brightness, this journey would result in victory as well.

Even better, the journey would be a perfect opportunity to display Naman's skills to Koroma and my value to the crown. Another argument against the possibility of future dissent against his reign and against the chance of divorce for me. Perfect for both of us.

And, regardless, I delighted in confrontation, in war, in the spill of blood.

Then why was such a sour feeling rising in my throat at the thought of it?

CHAPTER 3
THE DUTIES THAT WOULD UNITE US

Perspective: Crown Prince Naman tej-Shehenkorom, Heir to Koroma
Date: Eyyéala, the twenty-sixth day of the eighth moon, Belsaffe, of the year 469, C.Q.

Though I *knew* the reason for this journey was grave, my heart was soaring on Sholanar wings at the sight of Riqeta riding beside me. Straight-backed, sharp-eyed, clothed in armor from her metal-backed boots to the helm (shaped much like the low cone of a cap) shielding her walnut hair, she seemed like she was on her way to war.

It was the most beautiful sight I had ever seen and almost the entirety of my focus. How I wished I had had the chance to see her glory on the battlefield... A few sparring matches and drilling sessions were poor demonstrations of her prowess. Though I did not want war in any manner, neither between Icilia's nations nor with the insurgent, I deeply desired to see her triumph over an opponent worthy of her talent. Which I would not find in Samaha—she had already soundly and easily defeated everyone there, including my parents.

But the hope of witnessing such a wonder was not the only reason this journey promised almost too much enjoyment: except for the fortnight immediately following our wedding and regular sparring matches after that, we had spent little of our days together so far. And since my coronation, nor did we spend our nights together, as Riqeta increasingly left our bedchamber for her duties before I woke and returned after I fell asleep. She had never actually fallen asleep next to me, but now I was not sure that she joined me even for a moment.

Indeed, it almost felt as though she were beginning to accept every duty she could to avoid me. As though she was starting to regret marrying me...

Perhaps these days together on the road and the nights in our shared tent would help strengthen our bond. I was desperate to believe that.

Though nothing had changed, at least not for the better, in the eleven days we had already traveled since leaving the capital— the distance between us only seemed to be growing.

I swallowed a sigh and reminded myself, *It is already unbelievable that she agreed after only a year of courtship to marry a man whom she had never met before—a man who is so different from what she likely wanted in a spouse. I cannot expect her to be passionate about me so quickly.* I ignored the part of my heart that fearfully questioned why she had even agreed if she did not love me—and whether, after more than a year of effort, it really was possible to earn her heart at all.

Instead, I nudged my horse closer to hers. "Riqeta, my love," I said cheerfully, taking her hand and kissing the metal-covered knuckles, "do you recall the tales told yesterday of the prowess of Atafom's premier master wrestler?"

She glanced at me, amber-brown eyes gleaming in the noon sunlight, but did not answer.

"Well," I continued, trying to not cringe at how awkward I sounded, "I truly think he must be dreading our arrival today.

Indeed, he must have lost sleep for many nights prior. If you challenge him, he will lose all his fame!"

Riqeta considered me a moment more. Then she finally deigned to smile, her lips curving up at the corners as though she were amused. But the amusement of that smile was rather the sort given to indulge a child than the bright affection bestowed upon a spouse. No glimpse of the dimples that showed she was truly amused.

I tried to not let my shoulders slump. *I do not understand! Is that not a compliment? Half of our conversations have been about war and weapons! How much do I want to hear her laugh... The trace of distance between us, which I thought would lessen as we lived life together, has actually increased. Could my new rank be what is pushing her away? If only the crown heir's bond would offer me some perception about a fellow royal!* That was the one limitation the bond had—while I was still a crown heir and not the monarch, the bond would not offer me more than awareness of the presence of a fellow magically mature royal, perhaps to offer a little privacy. For which I was actually quite grateful, even though I did dearly want to know what my wife thought of me...

As though taking pity, finally she chuckled softly. "Perhaps, Naman, though I would hesitate to claim that I could defeat such a master of a martial art."

I wanted to memorize those words. Not only because they showed she listened to what I said, but because they gave evidence to another aspect of her personality: she possessed the wisdom, born of her great prudence and extensive experience, to know her own mind and heart, as a true child of Zahacim should. It was knowledge to treasure. And I treasured everything about her.

Riqeta's smile widened (though it did not fully warm her eyes or flash her dimples) maybe, just maybe, at the adoring expression on my face. Then she dipped her head, murmured a brief "pardon me, Naman," and rode ahead.

I stared after her, trying to keep my heart from breaking.

The moment I had glimpsed her shielding Prince Dinalir sej-Shehenbhala, the child of her nation's enemy, from her own family had reoriented my entire world around her. Being around her, being with her, being *hers*, suddenly became the greatest of my ambitions, the fulfillment of the only wish I had left in my life, the dream of a spouse who truly understood me. All else, from a loving family to virtue, magic, and an honorable duty, the Almighty had already bestowed upon me—but longing for this one blessing had troubled my heart as I entered my majority and received my rank in full.

When I confided this yearning after my twenty-second birthday to my mother, she had counseled me to travel to Asfiya, as soon as the trade agreement that I was helping my parents negotiate was resolved. Looking forward to that journey, I had resigned myself to the tension that always came alongside dealing with Zahacim and Bhalasa, bitter rivals this generation, and glumly prepared myself to mediate between the two nations' auxiliary heirs. Raman would be preoccupied, so it fell to me to stand between the two groups, though I had never met any of them before.

Strangely enough, the calmest of all of these battle-ready royals was twenty-one-year-old Princess Riqeta sej-Shehenzahak, the Sword of Prudence, whose reputation preceded her as the fiercest warrior to stalk across eastern and southern Icilia in this age. A reputation she had achieved *before* magical maturity. Because of that reputation, her composure and restraint inspired my curiosity... but her compassion won my heart.

Only months of negotiation and courtship had won me my parents' cautious approval, her aunt's reluctant permission, and Riqeta's own wary acceptance. I had refused to leave western Koroma, met as often as possible with her aunt and her eldest cousin, and brought the customary Zahacit royal courting gifts—weapons made by my own hands—for her and her family. I prepared my most eloquent speeches and fought my best duels in the Zahacit court, even triumphing in a few spars.

But even this unusual and shocking display of political and martial prowess on my part had not truly earned me what I most desired. For what value did her hand possess for either of us if her heart did not follow it?

Oh Almighty, I sighed, *is my suit hopeless? Please, in the name of the Quest, let her love me!* I desperately clutched at the spherical locket tucked below the collar of my robes. Within its small silver shell was a strand of pure athar, harvested and preserved by my mother's mother as a gift for my magical maturity ceremony, and so it was what I held when I prayed. Perhaps if I was devoted enough in my prayers, the sacred substance would see them to fulfillment.

As the lore of the first Quest stated, athar was Icilia's connection to the Almighty. So it was my best hope for intercession.

Murmuring more prayers, I glanced up just as Riqeta returned from the front of our convoy (unlike many of the younger Koromic nobles, I refused to call it a caravan, as that was a nomadic village of the Areteen, not a temporary means of travel; I would not so insult the customs of another kind).

My heart swelled as it always did to see her, never mind that only a few minutes had passed.

"Naman," she said, reaching my side, "the city of Ináma is over the next ridge, and the citizens are already gathering for you. The captain and I have already secured the perimeter for you."

As I again kissed her hand, I blinked, startled, and glanced around. How had I missed the familiar, subtle changes that indicated our arrival at the cliffside city was nigh?

From the respectful but quietly amused expressions of the staff and the soldiers traveling with us, it was because I had hardly looked away from my wife for the last eleven days. Even my farsight, whenever I decided to use it, was focused upon her.

I smiled myself. I was not troubled by being seen as enamored. That was not an emotion for which anyone would fault me, and, even if it was, I did not care. Riqeta deserved a man unashamed of publicly adoring her.

"Naman," Riqeta prompted. "Do you have any orders?"

"No," I quickly said. Then hesitated but hurriedly added, "You do not need to see to these things, Riqeta, my love." It was not that I did not appreciate her efforts, but... she was my equal. My partner. Not a member of my staff or my guard. Those were the feelings I needed to speak, but my stupidly ineloquent tongue only mustered, "Captain bi-Himacer is more than capable, and I trust him entirely."

The captain, flying back to circle over the convoy, grinned and called out, "How complimentary, your Highness! Are those words meant to forestall your defeat later at my hands?"

Riqeta tipped her head back and retorted before I could, "You mean your defeat later at *my* hands?" Suddenly her expression was warm and her tone jesting, not merely polite.

My old friend laughed but quickly disappeared to attend to more of his duties.

While I stared in shock. Was she...? But, no, that could not be!

Riqeta glanced back at me and said more formally, "This is my honor, Naman. Please think nothing of it."

How could I think *nothing* of it?

"Now, if it pleases you," she continued, "the residents of the orphanage and the hospitals await you."

Holding back a sigh, I nodded and composed myself. Caring for those residents was my favorite duty, and they deserved better from me than a distracted mind. I needed to think properly about how to resolve the issues between Riqeta and me, not fret pointlessly while my duties required attending.

Breathing deeply, catalyzing for my farsight, I looked ahead.

As we had traveled south, the rolling, coppery mountains of central Koroma, some sides coated in forest and others exposed stone dotted by the occasional shrub, had gradually decreased in height, lessening degree by degree, until, suddenly, in a curve stretching from east to southwest, they met the edge of the great Hafébunna cliffs, where the land abruptly fell away like the border of an enormous table. Ináma, the cliffside city, the seat of the province of Atafom, was built on part of that edge and into the sheer wall beneath, arrayed on both sides by roaring waterfalls and steep but well-maintained roads that marked the passage south. Positioned so, the city was a center of trade—and, since the time of Asfiya's Prince of Virtue over one hundred and fifty years prior, the seat of healing education in Icilia. For that reason, my grandfather had also rendered it a center of childcare and education.

From all over Icilia, those children orphaned by war, sickness, or any other tragedy, from infants to those near maturity, were sent to Ináma and raised in the best manner possible, all at the Koromic crown's and court's expense. They were given not merely the basics of life, such as food, shelter, and medicine, but affection, education, and preparation for the livelihoods found in their home nations, as suited their interests and abilities. From soldiers to scholars the orphanage trained, and, as I had heard during my travels for the trade summit, the other nations, even Asfiya, highly valued those reared in Ináma.

It was small consolation for losing one's family, but the orphanage did much to return joy to the bereaved.

Thus, it was my favorite place to go. Since my parents had finally allowed me to travel without them in my fifteenth year, I had come to Ináma whenever I could. Indeed, so great was my passion for this cause that, even before maturity, I had been given the responsibility of supervising the crown's transmission of currency and resources to the orphanage and, after maturity, all of Ináma's institutions of compassion, from hospitals to healing libraries. And now, with my rise to the rank of crown prince, almost every project for the upliftment of the people of Koroma and of other nations was entrusted to me.

These duties were why I loved my new rank. If only Riqeta would as well!

As Riqeta's and my horses began the ascent up the final ridge, bits of sandy soil and rock tumbling from beneath their hooves, Lieutenant Gatiemt slowed his horse enough that he fell immediately behind us, while Captain bi-Himacer returned to hover over our heads. All three warriors moved their hands to the hilt of their swords.

I furrowed my brow. "Why is there so much security this visit? Usually you disappear before I reach the city's entrance, Captain, Lieutenant. Ináma is still the safest of Koroma's districts, is she not?"

The captain and the lieutenant of my guard glanced at each other but said nothing. Instead, Riqeta answered, "They remain at my command. I do not want to take chances amid an insurgency."

I deeply doubted that any assassin would hide in Ináma, the loyalest of Koroma's most loyal districts, but I well knew that my knowledge of war and combat was inferior to hers. Unlike her, I had never fought outside of the sparring arenas or ended a life. Even Lieutenant Gatiemt, the only one of my senior guards to have seen battle, had only done so as a page in Koroma's last war, with Nademan, in the early years of my father's reign. Riqeta was far more experienced, and I deferred to her judgment.

Yet another reason the marriage benefited me more than her.

We crested the ridge—to the cheers of the citizens gathered at the city's upper wall.

"Our crown prince!" many called, while others cried. "Long live the crown prince! Long live the Sword of Prudence!" And still others, mainly young children, simply shrieked with joy, their faces bright in my farsight.

My cheeks warmed with a blush, and I could not help the unrestrained grin that spread my lips. How I loved Ináma and her people! I always had, but now even more so for their welcome of my wife.

"Captain bi-Himacer," Riqeta called, seeming unaffected save for the slight curve of her lips, "send four squads to surround the city, from the wall edging the clifftop to the road by the lowest wall. The remaining squads will enter the city. Of those six, two will guard the orphanage, two the hospital, and one will accompany Crown Prince Naman-korom and me. Captain, take the final squad to clear the royal residence. Lieutenant, you will remain with us."

My guards scrambled to fulfill her orders.

I pressed my lips together, worried the soldiers' presence would disturb the children, but did not object. Riqeta knew better. Then I remembered something she had said. "Riqeta," I dared to ask, "will you be coming with me?"

"Of course, Naman," she said briskly. "It is my honor to accompany you."

How I hoped that meant she *wanted* to come with me! I had dreamed for weeks of showing her my favorite city.

"If it pleases you," she repeated.

I beamed at her and tapped the sides of my horse, spurring the stallion onward. Riqeta did the same with her mare, and, with the lieutenant on our heels, we both sped across the strip of flat ground before the cliff and the city's wall.

Ináma's citizens cheered again.

Using my farsight to sweep through the gathering, I selected the residents I most wanted to meet.

And, soon, we were among them.

Dismounting and tossing my reins to Lieutenant Gatiemt, I did not pause for the ceremonial welcome before I threw my arms around Duke Theriett.

The duke, a white-haired and -bearded man of the Nasimih as dear to me as my own father, laughed and returned my embrace. "Your Highness!" he exclaimed. "How am I supposed to demonstrate my loyalty to my future king if he does not give me the chance to revere him?"

I chuckled and briefly rested my head on his shoulder. "I do not need such demonstration from you, Duke Theriett."

He laughed again. "Perhaps, but I should offer it nonetheless." Withdrawing, he smiled fondly, oak-brown skin creasing with wrinkles formed by years of smiles, and bowed. First to me, and then to Riqeta. "May the Almighty bless you, my prince, my princess," he murmured, bending to kiss the knuckles of my right hand, his gaze resting upon the gold heir's circlet which Riqeta had had me don this morning. His own circlet was made of lightweight stone, and yet his gaze was adoring—the very emblem of why Koroma's nobles were so amazing.

Riqeta dipped her head, her smile formal, though not without warmth. "May the Almighty bless you, Governor Theriett. It is a pleasure to meet you again so soon after our wedding."

"The pleasure is all mine, your Highnesses," the duke replied. "If there is anything I might do for you, at any time, in any way —" his gaze intensified as he looked at Riqeta, a quiet meaning in his expression that she doubtlessly understood better than I did— "please, command me."

"Thank you," Riqeta answered, dipping her head again, and her posture relaxed from the more battle-ready posture of hand on sword-hilt to the at-ease one of clasped hands over weapons-belt.

I beamed, overjoyed that my wife and the man who had mentored me alongside my father had such respect for one another.

"Now, your Highnesses, if you please..." Duke Theriett began, then waited for my nod. Once I gave it, he gestured toward a man and a woman, who seemed a few years older to me, standing behind him. "May I present my grandson, Charan, and his betrothed, Barama. As I communicated to the crown last year, they are my chosen heirs."

The finely-dressed pair bowed and curtsied, and Riqeta and I murmured the appropriate responses.

Then came the moment for which I had traveled so far: "Please, your Highness," Duke Theriett said, as he had throughout my adolescence, and waved toward the city.

I beamed again, looped my arm through Riqeta's, and strode into the gathering.

Immediately, we were surrounded by children, both those I recognized and those I did not.

"Your Highness!" little ones cried and tugged on my robes. "Come play!" "See what I made!" "Look at what I can do!" Laughing, I responded, "Then take us to your house! Perhaps I have forgotten the way?"

Two little girls giggled and seized my free hand, and, with the unabashed enthusiasm only children could express, carried Riqeta and me away through the wide gate.

Beyond the gate was a marvel: carved into the thick brown clay of the cliffside was a series of tiers, flat shelves formed by earth wizardry that stretched deep into the mountain, comprising a city that was twice as much below ground as it was in the open air. Each building upon those tiers and within was made with the same stone, shaped by magic into copper cubes that gleamed like gold in the sunlight. The alleys that wound through those buildings and the steep stairs that climbed between the tiers were similarly molded from the rock with the precision only magic could bestow. Each tier was so perfectly vertically aligned that, save for the encircling walls that the Asfiyan Prince of Virtue had added nearly two centuries prior, only the faintest impression of edifices could be seen from above or below. And to make the city more welcoming to kinds other than the Areteen, the first Koromic monarchs had spent much wealth and energy in cultivating trees and gardens, placing perches, filling pools, and installing lanterns that shone like small stars.

It was a sacred city, the Healing City, forged within the view of the Quest of Light by earth wizards among the first Areteen to migrate away from Zahacim's deserts—wizards who were, according to legend, so favored that their efforts were aided by the first Quest Leader herself. Some of her blessed magic was said to pulse within the city's stone, rendering the people kind.

And beyond the city herself stretched plains so golden and so bounteous that their wealth rivaled that produced by the gold mines deep within Bhalasa's mountains.

"Is she not beautiful?" I whispered to Riqeta as the children led us both down the wall-lined stairway to the fifth level.

"Yes, Naman," she breathed, openly awed amid her iron composure, even as she gestured signals to the eleven soldiers of our guard, who were closely following our procession.

I grinned, loving the wonder in her voice for my favorite city. Perhaps here we would engage in the duties that would unite us!

The children tugged us inside the fourth building after the stairway, a monolith half the size of the Koromic royal palace and capitol—in actuality, the former palace of this city repurposed a century prior as the orphanage.

Within its courtyard, the children abruptly stopped and flung themselves at me. "Your Highness!" they cried.

Riqeta actually grinned, flashing her dimples, and stepped back a few paces.

Laughing, I disentangled myself enough to kneel and opened my arms for hugs.

Areteen, Sholanar, Ezulal, Nasimih—Koromic, Bhalaseh, Zahacit, Nademani, Etheqor, Khudurel, Asfiyan—noble and citizen—short and tall—toddlers to even those partway into adolescence—children from all manner of homes and circumstances flocked to my embrace, craving my affection as surely as I wanted theirs. Not one of them called me anything besides my reverential address, though I was not every child's future king. Indeed, even the children of Koroma's rivals revered me.

Until, when my arms were tired from hugging and my lips sore from kissing the little ones' foreheads, one final girl, perhaps six years old, emerged from behind a pillar.

Glaring, she stomped over to me and stuck out her tongue. "You are *not* my prince!"

Many of her peers, particularly those who had wanted more than one hug and asked for kisses as well, gasped and stared at her with huge eyes. Their caretakers, who had discreetly followed us from the gate to the orphanage and now stood silently in the corners of the courtyard, seemed ready to reprimand her.

Riqeta tensed beside me. The soldiers snapped to attention.

I examined the faint flush of Mutharrim silver on her pale cheeks, flecked with tiny chips of orange, and her Khudurel accent, and agreed, "No, I am not."

"You're not!" she yelled again.

"No, I am not," I agreed again.

The exchange repeated several times, until I held my hand out to her. "Do you want to know about your real monarch?"

She burst into tears and threw herself into my arms. "I don't have a monarch!"

With her mixed heritage, she herself was probably unclear on which nation was her home, and her status as the only one of the Mutharrim living at the orphanage likely worsened her sense of isolation.

So instead I answered, "Sometimes it is difficult to know where we belong, my daughter. The world is so big, so vast, that we often feel lost, our lives do not turn out the way we want, and sometimes our families do not love us as we need. We lose our friends, or we do not have any, and our loneliness only grows. We feel alone in the world. And, my daughter," I tipped her head back enough that her jewel-bright amber eyes met mine, "it is important to know we feel this way. It is always important to see our own hearts and know how we feel. But simply because we feel something does not mean that it is the only thing that is true.

"I say so, my daughter, because none of us are without monarchs. Even those without a home have monarchs. And those monarchs are the best and greatest of all monarchs: the first Quest, the Quest of Light, the Mothers and Father the Almighty gave us when we were all alone. They are always ours, always with us, and in them we should look for our home, whether we think we have one or no. The Almighty, my daughter, does not abandon anyone to slavery, as the first Quest Leader said, nor to loneliness. If you feel that you are alone, my daughter, believe in the Almighty and in the Almighty's Chosen. They are our family when our family is gone."

The little girl, her peers, the caretakers, the soldiers, even my wife, were all utterly silent.

Then another girl—a daughter of the Sholanar, who had stuck to my side until a friend reminded her to let others approach—asked, around the thumb she was sucking, "Does that mean anyone who loves the first Quest will also be our family?"

The youths, only some years short of their majority, most of whom had only smiled and dipped reverences to me, seemed almost to lean in my direction, eager for my answer.

I raised a hand from the first girl's back and cupped the other's dark cheek, not minding the drool. "Yes, in a way. It is good to try to love those who love the first Quest... but sometimes they do not stay our friends. Troubles come, and things change, and sometimes we can no longer love who we loved before. Or at least not the sort of love that is full of hugs and kisses." It was the best way I could explain the various sorts of passionate love, the love that was more emotion than reason, to small children. "So we have to remember that sometimes love means to understand that the Almighty has given them to us for only a short time."

"And sometimes forever?" the girl sucking her thumb asked, eyes wide.

"And sometimes forever," I affirmed. "Like my princess and me. We are together forever."

Riqeta's composure shattered at those words, as I saw in my farsight, her expression becoming a strange and unsettling combination of admiration, affection, agreement, contentment, and utter, debilitating fear.

Though alarmed and confused by her reaction, I clung to my outward calm and continued, "But remember, my daughter, that the Almighty and the Quest come first. Do not let anything, even love for someone or anger at their loss, tear you away from the Almighty and the Quest. In seeking to find a family, do not lose our first one. The Almighty and the Quest are our family, and no other is so good." I smiled gently at the Khudurel daughter of the Mutharrim in my arms and the Zahacit daughter of the Sholanar who had asked me questions. "So I may not be your prince, but we are the subjects of the same monarch, one people even when war divides us, and so we are not alone. Though, if I may be so bold to say, I would be honored to be counted among your family." I glanced at all of the children. "All of yours."

The Khudurel girl sniffled and snuggled deeper into my embrace. "Please don't leave me, your Highness." Words that were echoed on so many of the other children's faces, even the youths', even the caretakers', even the soldiers'.

Even Riqeta's.

I kissed her forehead. "Perhaps in body, but never in spirit," I vowed. Then, letting my smile gain a lighter cast, I declared, "So much talking makes me want more hugs! Does anyone want more hugs?"

Even the youths laughed, leaving whatever contemplation was beginning to occupy them, and a number of the younger pounced upon me. Then eventually carried me off to their playrooms and lessons, determined to make the most of my brief stay.

I smiled and laughed, exclaiming upon all the projects and improvements made since my last visit (a month before my wedding). I soothed many teary young eyes, counseled many older hearts, and lamented many losses. Then, in the evening, I met with each patient of the hospitals, mourning dire diagnoses and celebrating recoveries. All the activities of one week compressed into one day.

But throughout all of it, my farsight remained on Riqeta's face. Though her composure had returned, and remained as she accepted the shy adoration of many children and the open reverence of many adults (how I loved that they loved her, too! And that she cared for them in return!), a faint echo of the muddle of emotions that had broken her calm lingered in her eyes. And I could not help but fret over what that reaction had meant.

Admiration, affection, agreement, contentment—these made

my heart swell with joy—but fear? Why had she been *afraid*? What in Icilia could scare one of the most terrifying warriors to walk our land?

Was it my love that she feared? Or was it my leaving her?

How had she not yet understood that I was forever hers?

CHAPTER 4
TOO MANY SIGNS OF THEFT ABOUNDING USELESSLY

Perspective: Princess Riqeta Shehenkorom, consort of the Heir to Koroma
Date: Eyyéthar, the twenty-eighth day of the eighth moon, Belsaffe, of the year 469, C.Q.

L *ike my princess and me. We are together forever.*
Though more than a day had passed, those words, so easily spoken, were lingering in my ears, like the after-taste of sugar that quickly turned bitter as too much time passed. How I wished I could wash away those words as easily as I could such a taste. They troubled my concentration and interfered with the calm I needed to possess, a liability greater even than a broken limb. I wished he had not said them.

For he could not possibly *truly* mean them.

No, they were only sweet words to ease the minds of those children, words he would never have said if he knew how unworthy I actually was of him. Just as his frequent declarations of love were hollow without full knowledge of my history.

He would never have bound himself to me and promised me this 'forever' if he knew how deeply broken my heart was.

So, as much as I wanted the words to be true—oh, how *much*

I wanted that!—I could not allow myself to believe them. No matter how utterly persuasive they were.

Yes, persuasive, for the court of Koroma was full of utter fools. Complete idiots, blind imbeciles, ridiculously biased buffoons. How did they know nothing of the true eloquence of their crown prince? True, he rarely spoke well when speaking for the advantage of his crown or himself, but when caring for those entrusted to him... For them, his words could melt stone and cool molten earth. The world spun to the tune of his voice when compassion filled his heart. His every expression served his purpose so perfectly that he did not need to forge a single emotion. Indeed, he was truly magnificent then, limned by the love of the Quest.

Perhaps his caring was why he had spoken those too-wonderful words about me and why he had been compelling enough to win my hand. Perhaps he felt, though he knew nothing of my circumstances, that I needed his compassion, his sympathy... his pity.

From him I would accept even pity. I was too desperate for his regard to indulge in pride.

I did not want to ever lose him.

And that is why you must focus, Riqeta, I scolded myself. *During the insurgency in Zahacim, there was even an attack in the capital upon Auntie.* I brutally suppressed the memory of my first kill and the day my family decided that, despite not even having entered adolescence, I was ready for war. *You cannot let that happen to Naman. He should be protected from all violence.*

That final sentence, almost a hymn these last weeks, sharpened my mind, and I returned my attention to Naman's current activities.

Since we had only been able to spend a single day in Ináma, my darling husband had invited the caretakers and healers of the orphanage and the hospitals to travel with us and confer with him as he rode. Despite all the arrangements he had made before we left the capital, all the currency and supplies he had organized and sent ahead, somehow he still felt there was more need for discussion. And, of course, those staff members were all too happy to take more of the crown prince's time, not caring that they were delaying the undertaking of our primary mission. But, still, this was what Naman wanted. So I had made the necessary changes to guard the new members of our convoy, as well as protect him against any assassins or saboteurs infiltrating their numbers.

It was almost a torture to spend *this* much time with him, listening to his sweet voice and watching his lively expressions all day, but I refused to be more than the length of a horse away from him while those I had not assessed surrounded him.

The soldiers and the staff I trusted, somewhat—I had thoroughly investigated the ten staff members and the twenty guards dedicated to his service and protection before our wedding, and the other eighty soldiers temporarily assigned for this journey after his coronation—but these caretakers from Ináma I knew only from Naman's stories.

The risks their presence posed were not acceptable to my protective instinct. He was *mine* to protect. At least that much I could do for him, and I would do it well.

Protecting him was the only way I could show the depth of my admiration.

So, despite the thoughts and memories plaguing my mind, I listened carefully to Naman's and the staff's voices:

"...I can ask my brother," Naman was saying, "if any of his contacts in Nademan could facilitate the adoption. Some of those nobles have successfully helped us with more troubled children in the past, and the tension between our crowns should not affect this. Prince Raman-korom's receipt of the message may take a month—he traveled after my coronation to the northern border as part of his new military command, and my own staff are preoccupied—but certainly I will help however I can. Perhaps I will find an appropriate family of the Nasimih during this journey."

The chief caretaker, Koroya Gaira Etenama, a kindly-seeming

Areteen woman of about forty-five years, dipped her head. "Thank you, your Highness."

"For the child's sake," Naman answered. "Any other questions?" A smile curved his lips, as though he was excited to hear more.

Of course he is, I thought to myself, admiring the gentleness that emanated from him as I surveyed our surroundings. Thin streams of water and fluid gas, commanded through my catalysis of magic to monitor for threats, wove around Naman and the convoy like soft, imperceptible drapes of silk (at a magic-infused order, they would become shields capable of deflecting the sharpest and swiftest arrows). A final protection, Naman's contingent of soldiers, watched the land for two miles in every direction, supplementing their physical senses with the wings of the Sholanar, the speed of the Nasimih, and the spells and farsight of the twelve minor magicians among their ranks.

Naman, too, could have helped with his middling farsight—though his magic was not as copious as mine, he was still very skilled—but I did not like to burden him with such tasks. His duties of compassion were more important, for both himself and his throne, than any task of intimidation or protection I undertook. I wanted him to improve as a warrior and always carry his sword for his own sake—a precaution only, as I would always guard him.

Perhaps guarding could be considered a demotion from my previous role as commander of Zahacim's special forces and half of her army, but I welcomed the change. Naman did not spit upon my efforts.

The chief caretaker perused the documents in her lap. "The final case is that of a daughter of Zahacit warriors, your Highness. She has reached her sixteenth year but has expressed a desire to remain in Koroma. Her clan, newly reestablished, has requested her return, so Duke Theriett asked me to refer the case to you."

Both Naman's and her gazes flicked to me.

A jolt of surprise rocked my mind and heart—they wanted

my opinion on such a delicate matter? The opinion of a woman who was little more than a swinging sword?

"My princess," Naman said softly, using the endearment that I relished too much, "if it pleases you, what is your opinion?"

I hardly knew what to do with myself. It was one thing to smile and nod at the citizens' fawning in order to avoid embarrassing Naman; it was quite another to make decisions off of the battlefield that would irrevocably change another's fate. How could I render a judgment that would actually benefit someone when so much of my life was dedicated to death?

Little of that turmoil must have been evident on my too-stern features, however, for Naman sighed, seeming a bit disappointed. Returning his gaze to the caretaker, he inquired, "What is Zahasa Kheyata Ikhetamat's reasoning for such a choice?" The term for a daughter of Zahacim, alongside the girl's name, slid smoothly from his lips.

I could not savor that reminder of my birthplace in his beautiful voice as my heart spasmed with pain. My hesitation was yet another point against me in his eyes.

Koroya Etenama's gaze again flicked in my direction. She hesitated, nervous over whether she should speak. Then drew a breath and said, "She was inspired to choose so by your wedding, your Highnesses. I noted that she was too shy to ask directly, when you met her, but she seems hopeful of... well, joining your guard one day."

I felt even worse. I did not deserve the casual love of family, much less such admiration. Even if I did now recall the girl's face.

Naman nodded, thoughtful. He seemed to stare into the distance for a moment. Then answered, "I will approve her petition to stay. A girl of fifteen is no naïve child to know nothing of her own mind, and we can only teach her that her choice merits respect as a woman by respecting it now. She may remain a ward of the crown until her majority and thereafter apply for the royal guard, if she so desires." He gave a small smile to the caretaker. "The form, if you would, Koroya Etenama?"

The woman bowed her head and proffered a page on a thin slab of smooth stone.

Naman accepted it and dipped his quill in the inkwell I was holding in place with a stream of water vapor. When he raised the quill to sign his name, I assembled a mass of vapor to cushion his arms and torso, thereby lessening the vibrations that would shake his hand while writing on the back of a trotting horse.

He had not asked, but he did not need to do so. What was a guard's purpose save to anticipate her charge's needs?

Naman placed his quill in a pouch affixed to the pommel of his saddle. Then, flipping his hand over, he pressed the engraved amethyst of his signet ring to the side of his signature. A pale periwinkle glow (of magical catalysis) built around the ring and then dissipated into the paper. Leaving behind, when Naman lifted his hand, an image of the three-peaked crown symbol, bestowed by the first Quest to the monarchs of Icilia, embossed in purple.

As regal as that imprint was, my gaze was momentarily captured by his signet ring—fitted around the amethyst was a thin circle of silver engraved with my name, matched by the slim silver ring bearing his name that hung on a chain beneath my armor (the pressure of gripping a sword-hilt could cause a ring to tear skin). After our wedding, he, too, had worn such a ring, but, on the morning of our departure from Samaha, when the newly adjusted crown heir's ring arrived for him, he had switched to this little silver circle (as I would upon being crowned queen). Though the change was unexpected, I somehow preferred this circle—it felt like an acceptance of the vow I had sworn silently when he pledged, to always protect his throne no matter what our future would become.

A hint of satisfaction replacing his disappointment, Naman returned the paper to Koroya Etenama. "Would you have any more questions, Koroya?"

Koroya Etenama glanced again at her notes. Then she stiffened.

My hand immediately went to the hilt of my sword, and I readied magic for catalysis.

"Koroya?" Naman asked gently, seeing the same reactions but interpreting them differently.

The caretaker glanced at her subordinates, all of whom flinched and looked away. But apparently the discomfort on their faces somehow bolstered her own courage, for she turned back to Naman and bowed her head. "Your Highness," she said, switching from the formal, deferent tone of before to one more appropriate between aunt and nephew, "I dare to raise this matter to your attention in the hope that all the many years we have known each other will cool your anger."

I almost raised an eyebrow as I relaxed my posture. Even citizens far from the capital were eloquent in Koroma.

Naman chuckled softly. "I cannot imagine becoming angry with you, Koroya."

A strange heat lanced through my chest. Not at the emotion in Naman's eyes but at the familiarity in his tone. At the way both of them knew he would never be angry with her.

Koroya Etenama pursed her lips. Clasping her hands together, she fidgeted with them, before lifting them in the traditional gesture of entreaty. "Your Highness, my prince, we do not have enough currency to see the spring."

"What!" Naman gasped. "But-but- I sent you the requested amount! How can that be!"

I catalyzed and cast another spell, a subtle one that would use the movements of her blood to, through a complicated piece of design, tell me whether she lied. An invasive spell, but one I would not forego. No one lied to Naman, at least not without me knowing of it.

Koroya Etenama gave him a pleading look. "You did, your Highness, but we do not have enough. Half of my staff may need to resign, and the hospitals are in little better state."

The chief of Ináma's hospitals, a solemn-faced man, Koroyi Seharie, who had remained along with his staff after the end of his audience two hours earlier, nodded in agreement. "A number of the healers are now working without pay," he rumbled. "But, as we cannot afford to provide them with meals, they will soon need to leave."

I cast a second truth-learning spell upon him.

"But how!" Naman sputtered, lips spreading wide in a grimace. "The crown is giving you everything for which you asked! I have overseen every shipment personally for the last seven years!"

Rather than outraged, like any other royal would be, he looked so upset, so lost, so terribly *hurt*, that I almost broke the perfect alertness of my guarding position and held his hand.

Almost.

His safety was too important. And I did not trust these officials to not manipulate him if I was not terrifying them.

And I was.

The growing coldness of my expression, despite my earlier mistake, was causing shudders to rack the many subordinate orphanage and hospital staff around us, and the chiefs themselves repeatedly glanced in my direction, as though wary of what I would do next.

Still, Koroya Etenama continued: "Your Highness, please, we do not intend to imply you have done any less than what you have promised or impugn your honor." Deep concern brimmed in her brown eyes. "We only raise this matter because our position has become desperate."

"What do your words mean?" Naman asked, nearly pleading. "Please, tell me how I have failed you!" His blue eyes were starting to glisten with tears.

I barely checked the desire to remove the heads of those who hurt him so much that he cried.

A mirroring pain flashed across the two chiefs' faces. "It is not you, your Highness," Koroya Etenama said quietly. "It is your court. Most of them have reduced their contributions over the last four years to almost nothing."

"Only the crown and her Highness Princess qia-Kafalira," Koroyi Seharie added in an equally quiet voice, "continue to give everything they have promised."

They were not lying.

No one had ever fooled my truth-learning spells before—no one even knew they existed—and the lamentation in the officials' eyes matched their words.

They were not lying.

I had not lived long enough in the Koromic court to know independently, but... surely those nobles who doubted their crown prince, particularly one such as Naman, though they had witnessed his upbringing, could not be anything but liars.

That same comprehension was not present on Naman's face.

His teary blue eyes were wide, his lips parted in a small circle, his skin blanching until it seemed too close to the shade of bone. Shock, but not understanding.

Koroya Etenama and Koroyi Seharie exchanged a look laden with apprehension.

That is why they did not tell him before, I realized. *Not only to avoid causing him pain but because they feared he would not believe them. For many of the same reasons that Queen Edana asked me to not tell him of what the nobles really say about him behind his back. Their reactions match hers, and mine.*

From the frozen quality of his shock, the concern seemed valid. His expression did not change even as the silence extended to an almost rude degree.

He should not have an audience while he tries to understand this, I decided. Turning to the waiting caregivers and healers, I barked, "You are dismissed."

The staff jerked to attention, and the chiefs cast me almost defiant looks. As though asking what right I had to send them away when they had come for answers.

I ignored how that made me doubt myself. "If Crown Prince Naman-korom desires to act on these claims, it will be at his discretion, whenever and wherever he so pleases. Your audience is over."

They still hesitated.

"*Now*," I thundered.

At the dangerous edge to my voice, every single one of theInáma staff hastily bowed and, turning their horses, rode out of the convoy's moving formation in the gaps Naman's soldiers allowed. They then dismounted and returned the horses to the guards. Finally, shouldering their satchels and tucking away their papers, they began the long walk back to their city.

The lack of funding must be why they do not have horses, I noted. *And their trepidation over presenting this information is why they were reluctant to admit that they did not have any, until I relented and let them ride alongside us.* I watched their slowly retreating backs for a moment. *We have spent too much time, and their return is not my priority. We need those horses for addressing the insurgency.* I turned back to my husband and suppressed a sigh. *I do not know what to do about this.*

Naman hardly seemed to have noted the caretakers' and healers' departure. He was still staring straight ahead, eyes wide, lips parted, skin pale, heartbeat roaring so loudly that my streams of water vapor were swaying around him.

The soldiers and the staff around us, all dedicated to Naman's service and protection, gave him concerned glances but did not go toward him.

They were deferring to me.

I glanced to my right at Captain bi-Himacer, who was taking a rest from flying and sitting astride the back of his stallion.

The captain saluted and immediately jumped into the sky, his strong, sturdy horse enough accustomed to such maneuvers that he did not startle.

From the front of the formation, Lieutenant Gatiemt and his squad rendered more salutes.

Well, they will watch for now, I told myself. *So...* I nudged my horse closer to Naman's, removed my mail-backed gloves, and, hesitantly, so very carefully, took a smooth, slender cream hand in one of my callused, stocky brown ones.

His fingers seized around mine, and finally his expression eased. Though shock still filled his eyes, his lips pressed together, and he swallowed, color returning to his cheeks. His gaze dropped to our joined hands. And there it stayed.

Should I speak with him...? I did not bite my lower lip, that juvenile habit long since trained out, but my other hand itched the hilt of a hidden knife. *Perhaps he simply needs time to think. That is what I would want.* I wished I could be sure of how well I knew my own husband. *Oh Almighty, please let him have some comfort.*

The prayer seemed to go fulfilled, for, as the miles slowly passed, he seemed to relax further and further, slumping forward in his saddle as though the worst of the shock was behind him. Not that he seemed to already accept it but that he was beginning to deliberate upon it. But he still did not look up from our joined hands, or let mine go.

As uncomfortable as such contact made me—it was far sweeter than I deserved—I did not withdraw it. I had climbed cliffs and castle walls solely by the strength of my arms, both in training and in battle; holding his hand while on horseback was little trouble. And our horses, a mated pair (from a bloodline that took mates) gifted by his parents per Koromic tradition, certainly felt no hardship in riding so close together, as evidenced by their whickers and pleased neighs.

How I wish I could learn from their example, I thought, frowning as my mare lightly pressed her head against her mate's. Her liquid brown eyes were almost incé in their affectionate cast. *But holding his hand is already more soft touch than to which I am accustomed. Even Serama was not fond of hugs. It is one matter to kiss and engage in the passionate activities of spouses, but quite another to do soft things like* this. I suppressed a sigh. *Our marriage must already be quite a disappointment to him.*

But disappointment or not, he was mine to protect.

So, as the sun traveled on its westward journey, I set about organizing a full audit of Ináma's records. Summoning various staff members, I conveyed in whispers that I required Duke Theriett to send the originals of all of the city's accounting books to the capital, as well as his own. Once everything arrived, overseers of the crown's treasury were to carefully check every book against the royal records of contribution pledges. I hoped that, when Naman felt better, he would accept my plan to verify the caretakers' and the healers' claims before undertaking any action to support them.

As it was, he hardly seemed to notice as I arranged for the relay of these messages.

Once those arrangements were made, I called several soldiers and ordered them to ride and fly ahead to alert Count Hilaserie of our arrival at his caravan.

Those soldiers returned quickly enough and reported that he was awaiting our arrival.

And not long afterward we reached it.

At the top of a large hill stood a familiar sight: a ring of large conical tents, accented by laundry lines and cooking tripods, surrounding a central sward. If the grass and trees dissolved into sand and bits of tough scrub, it would be a sight of Zahacim. Even the presence of unhitched wagons encircling the tents and the nearby pen of oxen instead of camels did not lessen that familiarity. A piece of home.

Or, rather, what used to be. Home was the sweet man beside me frantically trying to compose himself as we neared the group waiting at the base of the hill.

The nobles, six in number, the count and his wife and their four adolescent sons, exchanged smirks as they watched us approach. Laughing at my gentle husband the way they always did.

Forcing my hands away from my knives, as soon as we dismounted, I stepped in front and placed Naman behind my right shoulder. "Blessings, Count Hilaserie, Countess Hilaseriat."

The sharp edge to my smile was as effective as an ambush in drawing their attention away from my husband. Stuttering in their answers, they seemed barely able to focus for fear, as entranced as prey snared in the gaze of a predator, as they ushered us up the hill and into the caravan's circle.

Behind us, Lieutenant Gatiemt took charge of the soldiers and the staff. Captain bi-Himacer and the chief of Naman's staff, an Ezulal man named Talan Iqrarie, followed on our heels.

Much as in Ináma, the entire clan was gathered to greet us, sinking into bows and curtsies as soon as Naman and I appeared.

Despite the expected reverence, there was a gleam of something unhappy in their eyes. But nothing violent or mocking. Save a few. And those few I quelled with a jagged glance in the minute it took to walk across the green and enter the count's tent.

Shaped much like the indent a sword made when twisted in the ground, the tent was nearly ten feet in height and thirty in diameter. Stacks of neatly folded blankets and low, sturdy wooden trunks edged the walls. A large table, also low, barely two feet high, with a top of polished wood inlaid with designs in enamel, dominated the center. On that table was a feast of a meal, from roasted and stuffed duck to pans of sautéed vegetables and newly baked loaves of soft bread.

It was a feast more costly than what I expected from the vocally selfless nobles of Koroma.

And the tent was more costly as well: glimmers of gold gilding accented the trunks, the fabric of the bedding was silk, the sort brought from Etheqa only a few times a year, and the enamel of the table was new, in a style the Nademani crown prince had sworn was freshly designed for Naman's and my wedding.

From the slight attempt at a smirk one of the older noble boys attempted, the presence of that table was supposed to be a slight against us.

I did not care about such petty antics. I was raised in a household where insult usually meant bruises, and I was commanding legions when I was this boy's age. Mischief like this hardly merited a blink from me. What I cared about was the flash of confused hurt in Naman's eyes as he, too, recognized the table's design.

But he still attempted to be kind.

"Count Hilaserie," he started, once the prayer was said and the meal begun, "how go your travels this year? Is there anything the crown might do to ease them?" From his too-open expression, it was clear that he had not even noticed the dark glances thrown by the countess when he had invited his guard and his staff member to join the meal, as was custom.

The noble's mouth curved in a sneer... until he noticed the casual way I used a war-worthy dagger, instead of the blunt knives provided, to slice my meat. "No, your Highness," he hastily said, gaze affixed to the gleaming steel of my weapon. "Koroma has been generous with her bounty this year, and many of our trades have been successful as well."

Enough personal success to yield such fine furnishings? I wondered to myself. *If my estimate of costs and trading value is correct, and they should be, as Great-Aunt Tilata does always say those who know their accounts are the true sovereigns of their nation... Caravans are usually less wealthy in terms of currency, for they count their wealth in the fruits of the earth... But... A full caravan's trade might be equal to this table and those trunks. How could he have saved so much while still purchasing necessities? Unless...* My hand squeezed the dagger's hilt as, again, I came to a damning conclusion. *Unless he stole the currency from his people.*

It was not too difficult to believe. The count and his wife were acting very differently from the critical but courteous couple Naman and I knew from Samaha. Each attempt they made at speaking had the potential for mockery but was only *not* mocking because I repeatedly distracted them from achieving their aim. Their children, too, were careless with the food, devouring only half a dish before discarding it as though it had rotted, and they glared at Naman's captain and chief of staff as though they did not also deserve to eat. The clan-sister who waited by the entrance flap of the tent barely glanced up, even when she was summoned. She certainly was not given a place to sit.

Naman saw nothing of this. His eyes were bright, his smile genuine, his cheeks rosy with artless humor, as he engaged every one of the nobles in conversation. He was so, so openhearted in his mannerisms, caring for them and giving them numerous opportunities to demand wealth and favors unfairly of the crown —opportunities they *would* have seized if not for my interference.

It was not that he saw these maneuvers and magnanimously chosen to ignore and forgive them—it was that he did not see them *at all*.

By the end of the meal, I was ready to stab someone. I itched to see my sword dyed red, preferably with noble blood. But this was not the place for such actions.

Still, I almost drew a blade as Naman spent several long minutes offering courteous words of farewell to the nobles and then wandered through the caravan, speaking with whomever dared to catch his gaze.

Most of the citizens rebuffed him, some hardly polite, or replied in low, shaking voices with what were surely lies. Their clothes were fraying and patched, their tents worn, their faces downcast, too many signs of theft abounding.

Naman saw nothing of it.

Indeed, he was still smiling as we entered our tent, which his staff had placed amid the ranks of his soldiers at the base of the hill. Still smiling even when I ordered, within his hearing, for his guards to be more vigilant than usual. Still smiling even when we found that Count Hilaserie had neglected to send any provisions to our convoy, as was custom, succeeding in insulting us despite my every attempt to prevent it.

He was still smiling... until, dressed in his nightclothes and his nightly washes complete, he said gravely, "Riqeta, my love, I am ill at ease about something."

I paused briefly as I brushed my hair, which was, in a most

irritating way, refusing to untangle. "About which part of this evening?" *Was I wrong? Did he truly see it as well?*

Naman sighed. "Riqeta... we should have met the nobles together when we arrived."

I whirled around. "*That* is what concerns you?"

"Well, yes," he replied, red-blond brows drawing together, "you are my equal, not my guard, and there was no need for guarding regardless—"

I threw my brush into the wall of the tent, which wobbled dangerously before regaining its balance. Then, remembering myself, I closed my eyes and counted, recalling the exercises every Zahacit princess was taught for reining in battle-rage.

"Is there something else that troubles you?" Naman asked, sounding worried and uncertain. "I know Koroya Etenama's claim was disturbing, but surely it is a misunderstanding—"

"How can you be so blind?" I whispered.

"What?" he asked, confused.

"How can you be so blind?" I repeated in a louder voice, opening my eyes.

Naman frowned, still clueless.

"How can you be so blind!" I yelled. "How did you not see the way they laughed at you and the way they are stealing from their own people? How do you remain so, so, so dashed *oblivious* to the way your own nobles mock you behind your back? The efforts your family undertakes so that none dare to mock you to your face? The efforts even your guards and staff exert so that no one spreads rumors besmirching your name? How do you not see it, Naman!"

"Riqeta, I—" he began. But his expression, too open and too artless, betrayed that he did not understand what I was saying.

"Do not speak further," I seethed. "How can you claim to be who your people need when you refuse to see the darkness in your nobles? You are as blind as a man who has willingly gouged out his own eyes." More harsh words brewed on my tongue.

But the world seemed to stop as a tear spilled down Naman's cheek.

His blue eyes, those kind, beautiful, so very precious blue eyes, were brimming with more tears. Tears that were slipping over the rim of his lower lids and sliding into the curls of his beard. His sweet lips, pink and drawn together in a knot of pain, trembled as more tears fell. And his shoulders shook with the sounds of barely-stifled sobs.

I caused that, I realized. *For all my words about protecting him, I am the one who made him cry today. Not the caretakers, not the nobles*—me. *I am the source of his hurt. I treated him just as my aunt and my cousins treated me, exactly as I swore I would never allow him to be treated.*

I did not deserve to be in his presence.

Sweeping up my helm, I jammed my loose hair inside, grabbed several weapons, and fled the tent.

Then, skidding to a halt after what reflex had prompted, I dismissed the soldiers for the night. And, ignoring their solicitous looks, I stood guard outside, alone, in a covering but thin night-dress that provided little barrier against the cold.

As the gasps of my husband's sobs reached my ears, I contemplated the edge of the sword in my hands

Noble blood would suit, but it would look best if it was dyed in my blood.

CHAPTER 5

A HARBINGER OF DOOM MORE POTENT THAN THE BOOM OF WAR DRUMS

Perspective: Crown Prince Naman tej-Shehenkorom, Heir to Koroma
Date: Eyyéthar, the fifth day of the ninth moon, Alkharre, of the year 469, C.Q.

I dearly wished it was acceptable for a man past the age of majority to remain huddled beneath his blankets all day. But escaping duty was acceptable for no man, no one at all, much less a prince. Much less a crown heir.

So, despite the way my eyes burned and my head ached and my heart throbbed, I was awake, in the saddle, wearing my circlet, and reading reports on the southern provinces. For the seventh consecutive day.

The words blurred repeatedly, but I kept my gaze upon them. The day was colder than expected so early in autumn, but I did not ask for a blanket. Arrows twang in my ears, but I did not inquire after what the guards had brought back for supper from their hunt.

The slightest glance risked a glimpse of Riqeta.

I could not bear to look upon her and see that she was not even disturbed by the distance between us.

She no longer even approached our tent at night, though I lay awake waiting for her, and in the day she rode either far ahead of me or far behind. She ate her meals with the soldiers, slept in the tent of the unmarried women among our staff, and spoke with everyone but me. Not a single word had passed between us since that terrible night.

It was not that she was avoiding me—for that, I would have to matter to her—rather, it was that my presence was irrelevant and my wellbeing another obligation to uphold.

How that thought hurt.

I hunched my shoulders and tried to focus on my papers—

"Sergeant bia-Donacera! Scout ahead," Riqeta ordered. "There will be heavy rain in the evening, so seek a sheltered spot for our camp."

Her voice was so calm, so composed, that it was clear she did not miss me.

My tears had not affected her in the least.

I suppose she really does not love me. I wanted to dissolve into the leather of my saddle and vanish. *Why did she marry me when she does not want me?*

The question swirled endlessly in my mind.

When we had met, my rank was equal to hers, and she could not have known what my brother would decide—from our conversations since his declaration, he resolved upon a course only after Riqeta's and my wedding—and becoming my queen was in actuality still equal to her previous rank, the second heir, which in Zahacim transformed into the monarch's lieutenant upon the accession of the crown princess, just as the monarch's consort did in Koroma. If she had remained in Zahacim, she would have become naj-Shehenzahak; in Koroma, she would someday be naj-Shehenkorom—in both nations, the monarch's right hand. But in Zahacim, her position, and all the attending privileges, would be hers in her own right and not at all due to her spouse's. Her rank there in Zahacim would always have been better than here in Koroma.

No prosaic reason impelled her to marry me. Much less to leave the nation she loved behind for my sake.

So, if not love or rank, what other reason could there be? What purpose did she have for my hand? What use did she intend for me?

And when would she exhaust it?

For if love or rank did not motivate her, all I could see for myself was divorce.

Looming closer and closer with every passing day.

If she chose to leave me, I would not contravene her will.

But the thought that such would be her choice...

My heart burned, scorched by thirst in a desert where no relief existed, set aflame by an unrequited love starker than anything even the most melancholy writers described.

And with every passing day, I fell deeper and deeper into torment.

For if Riqeta, a royal and a warrior of unparalleled honor, deemed me unworthy of love and called me blind, then there was no hope for me. I was defective, flawed, drowning in inadequacy —neither would I ever be a good husband, nor would I ever be a good king.

I wished I could dissipate like the vapor of one of Riqeta's spells...

But escaping duty was acceptable for no man, no one at all, much less a prince. Much less a crown heir.

Riqeta thought me blind, so I would at least try not to be.

Thus the reports in my hands.

I blew out a breath and managed a bit of focus.

The reports, written twice a year by the nobles of each of Koroma's thirty-six southern counties, detailed everything that had happened in these provinces from the first moon of Lushatte to the sixth moon of Kadsaffe in this year of 469. The copies I carried were finished only hours before my convoy's departure from the capital, and they were the only ones in the crown's archives that I had not yet read at the time.

After several weeks of sporadic attention and seven days of concentrated effort, the reports honestly seemed no different from the decades of files stored in the royal library. They detailed births, deaths, weddings, harvests, scholarly and magical triumphs, acts of compassion... the usual.

Nothing gave proof to Koroya Etenama's claim.

Or to Riqeta's.

Count Hilaserie waxed poetic about an abundant spring, the innovations designed by the young girls of the clan, and an enjoyable summer festival with plenty for all, and none of the contribution numbers for Ináma were any more or any less than what custom dictated.

Everything was normal.

But Koroya Etenama would never lie to me, and Riqeta could not be wrong. My wife's words hurt, but she would not have said them without conviction. It was not her way, or the way of her birth nation, to speak idly.

Yet lying was a dishonor of the highest order in Koroma. A noble who lied lost... well, everything was close enough. Every particle of credibility and every shred of reputation crumbled if an untruth was told. Persuasion without pretense was the only acceptable form of eloquence. Even the smallest child knew this, so it was unthinkable that the descendants of those families who had ruled Koroma alongside my ancestors for nearly two centuries would actually lie.

For that reason, the royal family trusted the nobles' reports wholly and relied upon them, and in return the nobles believed the royal family's every assurance—these were the pillars of Koroma's government.

But Riqeta had to be right.

So I bent my neck and read Count Hilaserie's report again. Then twice more.

And I found an error.

The noble wrote, "Your Majesties, the most wonderful part of this year has been the absence of illness. My clan-mates usually suffer much from fevers in the early spring and the late summer, but this year, gratitude to the Almighty, we have entirely avoided every sort of outbreak."

A memory flashed in my mind: an older man coughing miserably in a hospital ward. The man smiled wearily and attempted to stand when I approached, but I dismissed the reverence and sat behind a translucent silk curtain, which helped prevent the spread of disease. The man's elderly wife, also behind the curtain, jumped anxiously every time her husband's coughing worsened. Between bouts of coughs—ones I knew well to be characteristic of severe versions of the late summer fevers—the couple offered me a few respectful words but seemed reluctant to speak further.

There was something about their unhappiness in the crown heir's bond that matched the unhappiness of the Hilaserios caravan. Something that was not simply the usual unease that the autumn brought most clans.

Racking my mind further, I concluded that the accents also matched. As did what few details the couple let slip about their lives.

Count Hilaserie had lied. Someone from his caravan *was* sick. Very sick. Sick enough to be sent to Ináma, and his spouse forbidden to sit at his bedside.

The man was coughing blood, and the noble had not mentioned it.

Had not even asked me about his clan-brother's troubles, though he knew well that I had just come from the Healing City and that I often visited every patient there.

About what else was he lying?

And was it only him?

I read through the other reports again, this time calling forth whatever scrap of memory I could find of specific minor interactions with citizens from each noble's county.

Count Hilaserie was not the only one lying.

From the easternmost plains of the province of Hurom, Countess Nalimeria proudly informed the crown that the last brutal blizzard had not resulted in a single death—there were orphans newly come to Ináma from the hills her caravan frequented. From the western sea of Maqom, Count Mizaqett crowed that his village had experienced a record fishing season— when another noble from the same part of the sea noted that the population counts for a number of fish types were lower than usual. From the eastern sea of Walom, Countess Sharetama boasted that her town had been blessed with twelve births—in Ináma, a woman of her town had sobbed in my arms that her child had perished in her womb. From near the Hafébunna cliffs of Atafom, Count qi-Taraser exulted in the six weddings his aerie had held in the spring—before midsummer, one of those couples had petitioned my father for a divorce on the basis that they were pressured into marrying.

Falsehood. Omission. Distortion.

Lie.

These were only the most obvious lies, the ones I could discern based on my extensive travels throughout Koroma and my many readings of the crown's archives. There were surely many more untruths, little blips of unease woven into the web of subtle and skilled persuasion that comprised these reports. Numerous things for which it would be impossible to gather proof.

If the nobles had lied this year, what was the likelihood that they had not lied last year? And in the years prior as well?

If the nobles of the south lied so easily, what was the likelihood that the nobles of the north were not fully truthful as well?

If they lied in these reports to the crown, what was the likelihood that they did not lie to my family's faces as well?

How many lies had I missed?

And what *else* was I missing?

My belly roiled, nausea and bile rising up my throat, and I clapped a hand to my mouth, trying not to retch.

How many of my people suffer because of my blindness?

A cry erupted from my lips, and I yanked off my cap and circlet and flung them toward an open pouch. Digging my fingers into my beard, I tore at the short curls, then slammed my fist against my forehead.

What have I done! What have I done! What have I done!

I slammed my forehead again, then began to sob into the mess of reports on my lap.

I promised to serve Koroma, yet I did not listen to her! I promised to please the Quest, but I failed them so completely...

How many times even in this last month had unhappiness welled in the crown heir's bond and I had ignored it? What was the point of being able to discern the emotions of my people when I dismissed what I learned? What use was I as crown prince?

No wonder Riqeta thinks I am blind...

A hand touched my head, paused a moment, then began to brush back my hair with rough, uneven strokes.

My sobbing faltered. *Riqeta...*

A tug on the reins coiled loosely beneath my papers brought my stallion (who was oddly placid) to a halt.

Around me, the entire convoy stopped in a clatter of hooves.

The hand, hard and callused even through its glove, replaced the cap on my head and moved from my head to my back, patting it in stiff, uncomfortable motions. Not with a gentleness such as she had bestowed on little Prince Dinalir-bhala, our quarrel coming between us, but still possessing the compassion with which I had fallen in love.

Gratitude to the Almighty. I sighed and quietened, melting beneath her touch. Whatever the reason for her pity, I savored it, the comfort I most wanted.

Her powerful hand offered a few more awkward pats, before she said, "Naman, what is it that would please you?"

Still calm, still composed—but now she was speaking to *me*. No longer deeming me an irrelevance, a burden to bear until fulfillment.

I dared to raise my head a little.

Her beautiful eyes were warm, concerned, *affectionate*.

For just one moment.

When my gaze met hers, they abruptly shuttered, as guarded as they had been when I had first come to Rushada to try and court her.

But that one moment gave me hope.

Even as the words, "I am sorry, Riqeta!", spilled from my lips.

She regarded me expressionlessly. "A storm is building on the horizon, and Sergeant bia-Donacera has found a shallow cave in the lee of a hill. If we make haste and reach it soon, we can prepare an adequate shelter before the rain's fall."

I startled at such practical considerations but then nodded. I should have expected them. She devoted much of her energy to the wellbeing of everyone under her care—my hope-stricken heart wanted to believe I was special among that number—and I loved it. Only... "Could we then speak?" I ventured hesitantly.

Riqeta regarded me a moment longer and allowed a dip of her head. Then she turned, tucking something that gleamed gold and purple into a saddlebag, and issued more orders, the strident tones of her voice urging the convoy into movement as the storm charged toward us.

At one of her commands, Colan, my valet, gathered up the reports and stowed them away, and Talan, the chief of my staff, brought a salve for the bruise on my forehead. Lieutenant Gatiemt brought me a flask of water and a few slices of buttered bread, and, once I had drunk and eaten, Colan wrapped a blanket around my shoulders.

A few drops of rain spattered on my brow before Talan raised an umbrella over my head.

Their careful attention and concerned looks warmed my heart, but the best solace of all was the thought that Riqeta cared about me. She was not at my side, instead riding back and forth as she led our staff's and soldiers' activities, but she did consider my needs and hurts.

I needed every drop of reassurance, every hint that I could be redeemed as crown prince and as her husband.

Moments before the rain began in earnest, Riqeta ensured our arrival at the cave and the setup of our camp, which included several thick tents to extend the natural shelter so that all of us would be protected. Though a number of us were from among the Ezulal and so did not mind the rain, the wind was quickly becoming bitterly cold, and the rest, of other kinds, were rightfully wary of exposure. An early autumn storm was no light matter.

I sighed at the thought. *I will need to ask Father to open the treasury for any of the southern counties who lose harvests to these conditions.* I shuddered. *How can we even organize that if we cannot trust their reports at all?*

"Naman." Riqeta crouched in front of where I sat, my back against the wall of the cave.

At her direction, I was in the warmest position (despite my attempt at a protest), surrounded by the huddled figures of our staff and soldiers, who were arranged outward from me in order of susceptibility to the cold, from the most vulnerable Nasimih to the least vulnerable Sholanar and from the youngest and most elderly to the most physically strong, all bordered at the farthest edge by everyone's horses. Only the least vulnerable and the horses were under the tents; the rest of us were bunched inside the cave. With such efficient conservation of heat, in minutes we were all well on our way to becoming warm.

Riqeta seemed the only one entirely unbothered by the cold. Indeed, while everyone else donned coats and shivered under their blankets, she added nothing to her armor and moved easily amongst us.

Even as I scrambled to try to voice my apology, I wondered just what she had needed to withstand in war that such chill felt trivial to her.

If she remembered anything distressing, there was no trace of it on her face as she waited for me to speak.

I swallowed sharply and, praying I would say the correct words, managed to whisper, "I am sorry, Riqeta, for my blindness, for leaving so much to be your burden, and for questioning your judgment."

She blinked, amber-brown eyes disappearing momentarily behind bronze lids.

"Please," I hastened to say, "please, *please* help me in remedying my mistakes. I-I cannot let this continue."

She blinked again. "Naman, please explain what is it that has disturbed you so."

A flush heated my cheeks—of course she needed to ask, as I had forgotten to tell her of my findings.

So, aware that everyone among our staff and soldiers was listening—they deserved to know of the failures of their future king, did they not?—I described what I had discovered in the reports.

When I had exhausted my eloquence, Riqeta pressed her lips together and exhaled quietly. "This is much more than that to which I was referring." She grimaced slightly. "It is I who must apologize, Naman. Please, if you would deign, forgive me." Cool, stilted, formal—but anxiety and guilt underlay her words and flashed briefly in her eyes.

A sincere apology.

And one that was entirely not necessary.

"Oh, my love!" I exclaimed and tugged her into an embrace. "Please do not say that! You wanted to alert me to something I never should have missed! You did nothing wrong!" Happy that she was not refusing the affection, I pressed my cheek against hers, not minding the stiff way she sat on my lap. "I love you so much, Riqeta."

Something about the declaration seemed to relax her, for once, and she leaned into my chest. Raising both arms, she rested her hands on my back and patted it as she had earlier. Until, at last, she wrapped her arms around me and tucked her head beneath my bearded chin.

I pulled her closer and beamed into the smooth surface of her helm. Her armor poked my limbs in multiple places, but I did not mind. Too many days—too many *weeks*—had passed since I had last held her, and, although our wedding was not too long past, holding her was already the best feeling.

If we had been alone, I would have dared to ask for a kiss. Perhaps more.

But, for now, our embrace fulfilled all of my desires.

And, from the grins and muffled giggles around us, our staff and soldiers were delighted as well, their horror at my answer exceeded at least momentarily by happiness.

My smile spread wider, and I closed my eyes, contented...

"Naman," Riqeta said, "what remedy do you want to pursue?" She drew back just enough to meet my eyes and arch a brow. "You do realize that much of what you concluded cannot be easily proved."

I sighed, appreciating the reminder of our conversation even as I wished we could have simply hugged longer. "I know, and I cannot yet comprehend what step is required to obtain that proof. Just..." I looked into those golden eyes and hoped she would understand me. "I-I- I *must* see it for myself. It is simply... just, well, too much to digest otherwise."

She raised both brows. "What is it you want to see?"

The affirming question soothed away the fear that she would think me foolish even as it pushed me to think.

There *was* something I could see for myself, but...

"Naman," Riqeta prompted, "tell me."

I took a deep breath and rushed out, "I want to see Count Flirien's lands! Today!"

"Hmmm..." Riqeta pressed her lips together again. "Count Flirien is an excellent choice of target, and we have three more days to spare for such a detour. However, I would not advise traveling there today. His village and farm are only a few miles away, off the road, but that is quite a distance in such a storm."

Encouraged that she had not outright dismissed me, I argued, "But this is the perfect circumstance! He did not invite us—"

"Conveniently," Talan muttered dryly nearby, before Leoma, Riqeta's maid, hushed him.

"—so he would certainly object if we came," I continued (though I had to now wonder if, like Count Hilaserie's forgetfulness in sending provisions, the omission was purposeful, as Talan implied). "In full daylight, our presence would be easily noticed—or at least mine would be—but in a storm, even I could manage more stealth. It is a perfect opportunity!"

Riqeta cast me a wry look (finally, more emotion again!). "A perfect opportunity to risk your health ahead of the confrontation we will likely have with the insurgent in Mutanacere, you mean."

I winced, seeing her point. "Well, yes, that is important, but," I sighed, "so is this. We must understand how deep the rot spreads. The issue in Mutanacere affects Koroma's stability, but so, too, do these lies. And," I wet my lips, hesitant to attempt this argument in case it made my request more of a burden to her, "I know you could shield me, from both the rain and any attackers."

Riqeta considered my words, her lovely face thoughtful. One gloved hand shifted to the other forearm and played with something beneath the metal-backed leather sleeve there—likely a hidden dagger. Then she nodded decisively. "We will undertake this operation, with two conditions."

I beamed. "Whatever you like, my love!" I really had not thought she would say yes!

Our staff and soldiers chuckled softly.

"One," Riqeta held up a finger, "you will stay behind me at all times."

I nodded eagerly.

"Two," she raised another finger, "Captain bi-Himacer will accompany us."

Sitting near the front, my old friend jolted and glanced nervously at me. "Your Highness, maybe I should not—"

One of his soldiers jabbed an elbow into his ribs, and the captain fell silent.

While I bit my lower lip, wondering why she would want him to come—

"The captain will provide aerial surveillance," Riqeta stated, "and he will be supported by a grounded squad of ten traveling in pairs." She proceeded to instruct the company on exactly which soldiers would come with us, what they would do, and what the rest of the convoy would accomplish in our absence.

Despite my lingering doubts and the horror of my discovery, I could not help but grin like a besotted fool. How I loved the way she took charge. Her protections and defensive measures made little sense to me—lying was not the same as an inclination toward violence—but her command was beautiful.

From the reverence glowing in their eyes, our staff and soldiers felt much the same.

Riqeta concluded her orders and, with characteristic efficiency, organized her detachment and cast several spells—the true wonder of which we only understood when we stepped outside the shelter into the storm-dimmed afternoon.

The heavy, blinding rain slipped away from our forms as though we wore oiled cloaks, allowing not a drop of moisture to wet either clothes or skin.

Anticipation lighting his hazel eyes, Captain bi-Himacer spread his wings and, with the flash of a grin in my direction, jumped into the sky. Abandoning all military restraint, he whooped loudly. "Hail her Highness!"

Following their captain's lead, the other ten soldiers cheered as well and jumped up and down in the cold rain.

I could not help an answering laugh, even as the weight of the worries on my heart prevented me from joining them.

Only the twitch of her lips revealing her own amusement, Riqeta allowed the childish antics for a few moments. Then she called, "Return to your posts!"

Our soldiers immediately organized around us, quickly controlling themselves back into a proper level of composure.

Riqeta glanced back at me with a considering look. After a

deliberative pause, she reached out and seized my left hand and guided it to the pauldron covering her right shoulder. "Do not let go," she warned.

My cheeks flushed, and I beamed again, savoring her touch and concern. My fingers tightened on the cold armor.

Riqeta nodded once, faced northwest, and set off into the darkening day. Our soldiers scattered around her, prowling the rolling plains, and I moved as quietly as I could in her wake.

The wind howled overhead, the rain thrummed on the grass, puddles of mud squelched beneath my steps, and slowly the sun's light faded as the hours waned.

It was not the first time I had been outside in a cold autumn storm, and certainly this was the best of those experiences, with Riqeta near me and her spell sheltering my body, but... with the morning's revelations fresh in my mind... the dimming light felt ominous, a harbinger of doom more potent than the boom of war drums.

The ice of the thought chilled my bones more deeply than the wintry wind could ever penetrate.

What do these lies mean for the future of Koroma?

Too soon, Riqeta held up her hand, signaling a halt. She tilted her head, appearing to listen closely, and then led me in a different direction, northeast instead of northwest. Pungent scents, reminding me of the hospital and the kitchen, pooled around us in a stream of sharp, fresh smell.

When we reached a copse of straggly trees, she halted us again.

"Have we reached?" I asked, confused. From both my maps and my memory of previous travels, Count Flirien's farmlands began another half mile to the northwest. But the scents were sharper than ever.

Dropping lightly to her knees, Riqeta grasped my hand and drew me alongside her. "Yes," she replied quietly. "Can you hear the sounds of voices?"

I knelt beside her and concentrated, catalyzing for my farsight and sending it ahead of us.

The world flashed several times in my vision before I could adjust the force of my magic to the dim light.

Then the land ahead became clear.

Beyond the thin screen of trees lay vast acres of crops.

Herbs.

Grown large, not the familiar, small clumps in healers' gardens but big plants capable of fueling grand harvests. Thick bushes of rosemary, thin fronds of thyme, and many others I could not name in this form spread as far as nonmagical eyes could see.

My magical vision counted five square miles.

Twice as much area as the count had claimed in his last reports.

None of it was food. No corn, wheat, barley, oats, quinoa, or *anything else.* No ranchland for cattle, sheep, or goats.

Only herbs.

And amid those herbs...

"Riqeta," I whispered through numb lips, "the harvest is beginning in the *rain.*"

Riqeta actually startled. "There are citizens working currently? In *these* conditions?"

"Yes," I breathed, watching the distant figures toil, shivering in the cold. "They are of the Nasimih and the Ezulal primarily." Their vulnerability tinged their skin, both coarse brown and ashen white, blue. "And they look so thin..." Tears welled in my eyes as a gnawing melancholy spread in the crown heir's bond. "So hungry..."

"Hungry?" Riqeta asked sharply. "Do herbs not replenish the soil?"

I shook my head. "They do, but... I cannot explain it. I only know what I feel in the bond."

Riqeta remained silent for a moment, her hand flexing around mine. Then she whispered, "I can explain it." Her voice sounded hollow, in a way I had never heard her speak before.

"How?" I begged.

Riqeta exhaled a sigh. "You mentioned when you first introduced me to the nobles of Koroma that Count Flirien has started in the last decade to diversify his crops with herbs, and I have heard allusions to this change, described as a way to prevent blight, from the man himself. The trade agreement with Bhalasa and Zahacim included a provision for his herbs as well. Koroyi Seharie mentioned that the Ináma hospitals have increased their purchases of herbs from Fliriene. While the nobles have reduced their contributions and lied to the crown about it."

My gaze fixated on a young woman's hand slipping on her scythe as she rushed to catch up with her peers. Before she could control the motion, the tool's sharp blade lacerated her palm, and she doubled over, screaming. The overseer snapped at her to stop dawdling, and her fellow workers looked away.

"What I think has actually happened," Riqeta continued, "is that Count Flirien has sought to dominate the nation's trade in herbs, both within and without. He cultivates massive quantities, sells them to our counties and our allies, uses the roads to transport them in great quantity, and..." She clenched her other hand into a fist. "He does not use his profit, or at least enough of it, to buy food for his people." A bitter laugh. "He avoids blight by not growing corn at all. Since your last visit six years ago, he has massively increased his operation, and this is why he did not invite us."

"There are no longer any grains or animals," I mumbled.

"He seeks to produce the maximum," Riqeta said simply. "There is no room in that for the wellbeing of his people."

There was something in her voice that rang of personal experience...

The young woman seemed to come to her senses a little and, tearing off a piece of her rags, began to wrap it around her bleeding hand. The overseer, however, appeared to have grown frustrated beyond his limit and stalked toward her, pulling a strange, lengthy supple object from his belt.

My breath caught.

That is a whip!

I surged to my feet.

No, no, no, no—

"Naman!" Riqeta snapped. "Get down!"

"He is going to hurt her!" I exclaimed, darting toward the treeline—

A harsh pull on my hand yanked me to a stop. Before I could tug loose, my hand was pushed up, and a strong arm wrapped around my torso, holding me in place.

Then a voice snarled beside me, "That will not solve anything."

As much as her nearness and embrace were welcome, I tried to wriggle away. "She is going to be hurt, Riqeta!"

"And your charging in there would have only made it worse," she growled in reply. "You both would have perished."

I stilled. "What?" *Surely that is not true! Will my title truly not stop the whole disaster? All of the abuse?*

Riqeta rose onto her toes and leaned closer to my ear. "Naman," she said tightly, "if you interfered, Count Flirien would try to kill you, all of us who came after you, *and* that woman. On his land as we are, the margin for my success would be too thin to ensure your and everyone else's wellbeing. And it could cause a war that would tear Koroma apart."

"But-but—" I sputtered, unable to fathom those implications. "He is not violent! And I am the crown prince!" *Of what use is this rank otherwise... Of what use am I?*

"Naman," she said sternly, "the man has lied to the royal family's faces for *years*. Do you truly think there is some line he would not cross in order to keep his secrets?"

I had no answer. I had no idea what to say or do in this world that was much darker than anything I had ever thought it to be.

"He would kill you," she spat out, suddenly boiling with fury, "blame the insurgent, and mourn you publicly. I *will not* let that happen to you."

"But what about the woman?" I whispered, watching the whip cut open her back.

"Your interference will save her now," Riqeta answered, "only to take her life later, as punishment for drawing your attention. And you can do nothing for her or for anyone else if you are dead."

Her blunt, heated words impacted me like a blow to the belly —or a stab to the heart. But they were true.

"Please, Riqeta," I pleaded as I listened to the woman cry, "please help me save Koroma."

In response, she tilted my head toward her and kissed me.

Bittersweet as it was, tinged by the salt of my tears and the scald of her anger, that kiss told me that she was with me.

It did not matter if she loved me as long as she was with me in the struggles to come.

CHAPTER 6
DEATH FAR BEYOND THE BOUNDS OF WAR

Perspective: Princess Riqeta Shehenkorom, consort of the Heir to Koroma
Date: Eyyéala, the eighth day of the tenth moon, Thekharre, of the year 469, C.Q.

A rush of wind preceded the return of the scouts. Flying and sprinting at full speed, the Sholanar and Nasimih squads I had sent ahead to Mutanacere came toward the convoy across the broad expanse of plain ahead like a child running to hide behind her mother.

"Riqeta," Naman whispered, urging his horse closer to mine, as he watched their approach in far greater detail with his farsight, "they look spooked."

I frowned. "Spooked soldiers are an ominous sign." In all of my many military missions and engagements, I had never seen spooked soldiers...

The staff, straining to overhear our words, clustered nervously behind us. The soldiers maintained their composure, but their fear was palpable in the air. And I could not blame them, for Naman appeared absolutely terrified.

Even I, battle-hardened though I was, felt uneasy.

There was something about this land that, while ordinary in appearance, felt... tainted. Stained, sacrilegious, like blood spilling into the pool of an oasis and poisoning precious drinking water.

Much like the lies Naman had discovered.

Though more than a month had passed since his discovery and that afternoon in the Fliriene fields, the revelation of those lies haunted me. I had known the nobles were disrespectful, yes, but that glimpse of the extent of their treachery... and, in the time since, every further conclusion drawn by my husband and me and by our attendants, as well as every county of which we had caught sight on the journey south—all of it pointed to a more pervasive poison than anything we had ever imagined. And we still did not know the full extent of it.

It made all the pain of Zahacim and the horrors of war with Bhalasa seem like smaller concerns.

Hence why, though I had pushed my husband and our convoy to increase our pace, even I dreaded our arrival in Mutanacere.

There was something about this land that... that... that felt like the *source* of evil.

Which made little sense because Countess qia-Mutanecera had been such a person that even my suddenly suspicious husband refused to doubt her. Her dark coffee-colored face was known to sparkle with light and kindness, and her heir was surely not too much unlike her.

And yet...

Naman reached up and gripped the pauldron covering my right shoulder. "Riqeta," he whispered, actually shaking. "It feels... Koroma... she feels..."

I hesitated but quickly, before he could notice the pause, lifted a hand and covered his in a weak attempt at comfort.

Despite how I had made him cry, he somehow still seemed to want my touch. From the way he had asked me for a night together after those terrible discoveries, staying away from him had not been the correct choice. Despite the severity of our quarrel, he did not want space—he wanted *me*. Not only passion but also my affection. As awkward as I was with it.

So whatever time was left after our defense was arranged each day I gave to him. At the very least, I let him hug me while he slept, shared my meals with him, and rode by his side during the day.

It was torture, worse than anything the Bhalaseh had tried, my inadequacy all too apparent, but he needed to know that I was with him as he confronted the rot within his nation. My sister Serama's comfort, as rare as receiving it had been, considering how often I was on the battlefield, had been the primary reason for my survival in Zahacim. And now was my chance to honor that kindness by doing the same for Naman.

Perhaps *this* was why the Almighty had ensured our union, so that I would defend him amidst this evil.

I would *always* defend him. Always.

Remembering that promise, I asked, "How does she feel?" From what I recalled of Misleta's connection to Zahacim, the crown heir's bond was an unparalleled source of intelligence, exceeded only by the monarch's and, according to the lore, by the Quest's.

He gave me an anguished look. "Tormented!"

I pressed my lips together, reminding myself that he would probably want comfort. It was not easy to watch one's soldiers be tortured, even when one was already moving to rescue them—it could not be easy to feel one's own nation's pain, regardless of the actions one was taking to address it. So prompting myself, I linked my fingers with his and squeezed them.

The anguish on Naman's face eased.

Pleased, I halted the convoy.

Then the scouts reached us.

Panting, eyes wild, the Nasimih soldiers skidded to a stop and the Sholanar dove so quickly they almost fell to the ground, and all of them threw themselves at the feet of my horse.

"Your Highness!" Sergeant bia-Donacera cried. "It is gone!"

I frowned again, disturbed by this behavior. They were hardly looking at Naman... but not out of disrespect. Rather, like small children, they had run to their mother, to the person they believed would most be able to protect them.

For protectors like these soldiers, both by disposition and by loyalty, to feel this way... An even worse sign.

"Explain," I ordered.

Immediately the sergeant snapped to attention, prompted by my firm tone, and replied, "We traveled the remaining distance as you ordered last night, your Highness. The Sholanar concealed their passage by flying through clouds, and the Nasimih traveled in sprints, so that their feet would leave no marks. An hour before dawn, we arrived at the border of Mutanacere."

Sergeant bia-Donacera drew a deep breath, more rattled than I could have ever anticipated the calm, competent woman becoming. "Your Highness..." she whispered and bit her lower lip. "I do not have the words to explain what we saw. It was too horrible. I- I- we have never seen war, and this is- it is beyond us."

Normally I would never have accepted such a report. Experienced in war or no, a soldier was meant to uphold the duty of defense and manage the situations that came in the course of that duty with equanimity and courage. Experience did help, but a lack of it did not absolve a soldier of abandoning their orders.

But the fear I saw in the sergeant's eyes... sharp, desperate, *hopeless*... I had never seen its like before.

In one of my first missions, an ambush of Etheqore forces beyond Zahacim's western border, my platoon and I had been cornered with our backs to a sheer rock wall at the edge of a cliff. My soldiers glanced up and down and, from the terror in their gazes, I knew they wondered whether death by falling would be preferable to what awaited our trespass. The manner in which I had rallied them was what established my reputation as a fierce warrior (and demonstrated to my aunt the queen that she could send me carelessly into the worst circumstances and I would unquestioningly find a way to accomplish whatever she wanted).

This was not a similar circumstance. This was not a similar fear.

It was much worse.

For that reason—not only the growing compassion in Naman's expression—I did not reprimand them.

Instead all I said was, "Show us."

The soldiers shuddered but stood and offered proper salutes.

I acknowledged them with a nod and spurred my horse and the convoy into motion.

South, toward Mutanacere. Toward the evil.

The only sound of our passage was the thuds of hooves on grass. The Sholanar were too frightened to fly, the Nasimih too scared to run, and no one spoke, instead huddling in their saddles around Naman and me. Both the few who had scouted ahead and the many who had merely heard their words.

The stink of their fear was almost tangible.

Yet, though that same fear was apparent in Naman's eyes, it was less consuming somehow... Something within him, as within me, seemed to resist it. Something deeper than simply the determination to continue forward...

The sun rose to the height of noon overhead and started the western descent, shining bright in a blue sky undimmed by clouds.

That light felt increasingly distant, as though reaching dimly though a bleak fog, the closer we drew to Mutanacere.

"Riqeta..." Naman murmured, leaning close enough that only I would hear him. "I see nothing but darkness in my farsight."

I pressed my lips together, absorbing this critical piece of intelligence. *Because it is wish magic, only powerful spells can interfere with the cast of farsight. But I have never heard of a shield so absolute...*

Readying my most battle-worthy spells, I pressed onward.

The sun's light faded almost completely. In the approaching gloom, the wind wailed, the cries of the tormented echoing...

The horses abruptly stopped and refused to go any further. Eyes wild and white, foam gathering at their mouths, they bucked and struggled against the tugs on their reins. At my order, the scouts remained behind with them—to their relief—and the rest —to their chagrin—continued on foot with Naman and me.

The rolling plains darkened from the dry, life-leached yellow of autumn grass to taupe-brown swathes of scarred earth.

The unease within my heart sharpened, peaking so unbearably that it felt like a blade was trying to pierce the armor over my chest.

The taupe turned to soot. Then to pitch.

There was no village.

In the center of the three low hills that formed the boundary of Mutanacere was a... pit. A hole like the void. A black, yawning chasm intent on devouring me, from which there would be no escape if I fell. An abyss like a monster's eye.

It was looking at us.

Ripples of black shadow moved across the surface, a slow, lazy blink, meeting my gaze—

A putrid stench of rotting flesh and burning hair exploded into my nose, an odor more fetid than the reek of a battlefield—

Screams erupted against my ears, imploring, entreating, begging, *pleading* to be let go, for mercy, to be spared—

Blood flooded my mouth, not the faint tang of a bitten cheek or bruised lip but the overwhelming onslaught of my entire life's blood blasting up my throat—

The blade pierced my armor and drove into my heart.

I fell to my knees.

Almighty! Dalaanem! I shrieked, instinctively praying to the Divine and my Lady Queen and ancestor the first Quest Leader. *Almighty! Dalaanem! Help me!*

There was nothing. No response.

Almighty, Dalaanem!

Then...

The fear receded.

The agonizing assault on my senses dulled to twangs of pain I could handle.

And my ability to reason returned.

I pried open my eyes and looked around.

Naman, his hands clenched around the athar locket he always wore, looked back at me. His eyes were white all around his irises, the blue of which seemed a mere afterglow of its usual brilliance, his face was paler than snow, and his shoulders were shaking. But there was rationality in his gaze. He was not well, but he was sane.

Our attendants were writhing on the ground behind us, their screams mixing with those of the tormented emanating from the black chasm. Their fingers inflicted bruises and cuts on their own skin, and their convulsions left marks on their faces, but this real pain did nothing to remind them of reason. Their convulsions were slowly propelling their bodies toward the chasm...

Naman and I exchanged a desperate glance. We had to do *something* to protect them!

But how are we not as affected as they are? Clinging to whatever mental discipline that training and war had forced me to acquire, I rubbed a dagger and quickly recounted the last few minutes to myself. *I prayed... but surely at least some of them must have also—Naman's attendants are quite as pious as he is. Then why did mine have an effect? Well, there is the blessing of magical maturity, and thus the direct gaze of the Quest upon me, but how can I give* that *to them?* Leoma's cries peaked painfully, and actual blood spilled from her mouth. *Please, Dalaanem, help me save those you entrusted to me!*

"Riqeta," Naman spoke directly into my ear, "what about our circlets?"

"Our circlets?" I asked.

"The pain eased for me when I prayed," he explained, "and likely for you as well." At my nod, he continued, speaking to cohere our thoughts, "They possibly took effect because the fear did not blind us so thoroughly that it took away our faith. But one cannot force another to pray, not merely clearly but at all. Yet what we can do is offer them the closest recourse, the substance that *is* prayer. Athar. And as concentrated as the contents of my locket are, our circlets were touched by the first Quest themselves, so—

"—the effect should be greater," I finished, thinking through his argument myself.

Naman nodded. "Indeed."

He had hardly even acknowledged the existence of his circlet since the despair of his discovery—only much cajoling from his dearest friends among our retinue had persuaded him to retrieve it back from me, and only the reminder of royal responsibility from me convinced him to wear it today. Yet, today, in this moment, amid this darkness, his princely confidence appeared greater than ever.

In agreement with him and proud of his determination, I lifted my silver circlet from where it rested around my helm, the amethyst setting in the center lightly touching the plates of my forehead.

In tandem, Naman raised his gold circlet from his head and, without the slightest hesitation, turned, knelt, and slid the heir's sacred crown over Captain bi-Himacer's helm and down onto his brow.

The man shuddered, his wings unfurling, and his cries faded into silence.

Naman waited a moment before sliding off the jeweled band and placing it on Koroyi Iqrarie's head.

The chief of staff also stilled, finally calming, and the captain remained quiet, his agony not returning.

Almost laughing with relief, Naman pressed a ruler's kiss to both their foreheads and ran to the side of the next man.

Satisfied, I began the same process with the women staff and soldiers: slide my circlet onto her head, pause a second, slide off, kiss her forehead in the hope of offering comfort, and rush to the next woman. Staff or soldier—it did not matter.

Our circlets, mine thin and silver, with a single amethyst at the center, and Naman's thick and gold, with five radiant violet gems, worked the same wonder: at merely their touch, the agony of our people vanished.

The horror remained of the chasm and the screams and the stench, but it no longer felt poignant enough to destroy us.

I exhaled softly. *Gratitude, oh Almighty. Gratitude, oh Dalaanem.* My Lady Queen's reverential address brought peace to my heart. Enabling me to focus once more.

As my mind cleared, my gaze returned to the chasm.

Which seemed different now...

I blinked and tilted my head.

In the haze of fear, the blackness in the center of the three hills had seemed to be a rift in the earth. Now, though the light overhead remained weak, I saw the nature of that blackness more clearly: it was earth.

Blackened, like an infected wound so direly in need of treatment that the flesh was decaying, but still earth.

I narrowed my eyes, trying to examine it better...

Beside me, Naman gasped sharply.

A chill crept up my spine.

The blackened earth was... strewn... with bits of bone. Incé bone. The charred bone that remained behind when people were burnt alive.

I had only ever seen such a thing before as the result of an accident, but this... this did not have the feel of an accident. Unlike the blood filling my mouth and the dagger cutting into my chest, the screams in my ears and the stench in my nose were no fear-born illusion.

Death had been dealt here, death far beyond the bounds of war.

Just as the fear even now lingering in the air was beyond the bounds of war.

In war, as in many other areas of life, one feared death, and it was rational, sensible, the mark of a sane mind as only the reasoning sought to protect themselves from unnecessary pain.

But this fear was beyond that—it was not restrained, preserving, warning, but wild, heedless, devoid of caution. Fear itself.

Is it... but, no, such magic was destroyed... yet the description matches... My fingers clamped around the hilt of my sword. *I need more intelligence.* A question rising on my tongue, I turned to Naman.

He clutched his chest and screamed. Then dropped to his belly and writhed on the ground. Just like our attendants had minutes before.

"*Naman!*" I scrambled to his side. "Where does it hurt! Can you answer me?" Thrusting my hands into the blur of his movements, I simultaneously caught his shoulders and carefully used air to cushion his body and clothes, forcing him to still. Preventing him from brushing the sickened black earth.

As the convulsions eased, I flipped him onto his back and caught a glimpse of his eyes.

The blue was clear. Still sane, just in agony.

How horrible it was that any form at all of agony was something preferable!

But mere pain was certainly better than the wild fear.

Yet, if his prayers had saved him as they had me, why had it returned... "Naman," I said, trying to soften my tone so it would be more comforting, "what happened?"

Wheezing beneath my grip, he lifted both hands and clung to my wrists. "Riqeta," he whispered, beautiful eyes filling with tears, "I can feel their agony, the agony of the people who perished. Their memory is still here, maybe even *they* are still here, haunting this place..." He strained toward me, arms stretching for a hug.

I pulled him into my arms. Cradling him as I would a child (I still was not sure how a spouse was supposed to be held), I questioned, "Does the crown heir's bond indicate anything about who they are? About what happened here?" I pointed my chin toward the blackened earth in front of us.

Naman shook his head, before tucking it beneath my chin

and against the gorget covering my throat. "All I can understand from Koroma is agony and turmoil, and the same from whatever echo is left of the people here. But... but..."

He seemed unable to continue, so I spoke the words he surely wanted to say: "You think that these people are the citizens of Mutanacere."

"Yes," he replied.

I tapped the sheath of a dagger hidden along my forearm. "Do any of those sensations tell you about the fate of Mutanacere's nobles? About the countess, her husband, her heir, or her second son?"

He furrowed his brow in thought, so I took the opportunity to check on our staff and soldiers.

Some of them were stirring, but most remained unconscious.

I cannot move them all myself—even my strength is not enough to carry a hundred people, and Naman is kind enough to not expect it—but we cannot linger here. As soon as they are recovered, we must leave. The pressure of this place is building again...

Naman gasped softly, returning my attention to him. "The countess and her husband are here... but her sons are not." His hands tightened around my torso, and he curled further into me. "Riqeta..." He sounded ill. "Though this evil feels like it just happened... If the countess and her husband are part of these screaming- these screaming echoes, then whatever destruction occurred here happened a year and six months ago. Before her death. Maybe it was even the cause of her death."

My eyes widened. "And if her sons are not here..."

"They could be responsible," he finished, audibly choking on his own words.

I had witnessed much depravity—one of the issues about Zahacim's and Bhalasa's war this past decade, one which *both* crowns had suppressed from their fellow nations' notice, was the number of violations of the Quest's laws of military engagement —a number exceeding the one hundred mark instead of being confined to the single digits—but this- this was the worst crime to mar the face of Icilia in one-and-a-half centuries.

For a son to murder his mother... not just any son and any mother, but a countess and an heir, raised to believe, adhere to, and *breathe* every virtue... not just any murder but one perpetrated with such awful brutality... How could such a crime even be comprehended?

What has happened in Icilia that such evil has been reached?

"Naman," I whispered, "we need to find these men. We cannot allow them to do this to anyone else."

My husband shuddered but nodded against my armor. "But how can we prove that it is them? And what of the insurgent? You spoke much of not regarding that threat casually..." he gasped. "The insurgency was reported to be based near Mutanacere. What if these men *are* the insurgents?"

A deeper chill crept up my spine. "It is a possibility, Naman, which would mean the evil we are fearing is much greater than even what we thought in the last month."

My husband uttered a sob and wrapped his limbs around me.

"As for proof..." Berating myself for not having already done this, I invoked the magical catalyst in my blood and let it pool in my mind, then infused it with my will.

Strains of magic, black mixed with weak glimmers, flickered into view around us.

The fact that those strains were even still present, that they had not dissipated with the passing of the seasons, attested to the terrible strength of the spells used.

Recalling everything I knew of such examination, I carefully studied the residue.

Much of it, in the form of thick clouds of soot that drifted up from the blackened earth and flicked tendrils like whips over those under my protection, was unfamiliar to me. I dreaded knowing what that magic was.

Another unfamiliar residue inundated the sludge of the blackened earth. While mixed with a third.

That third was painfully familiar. And the spells made of it were clear enough to discern.

"Sorcery of the water," I stated, "specifically sorcery of the flood. The same type of magic as mine, but with a lilac Koromic glow, albeit a dirtied one. With this degree of strength and specific indicators..." I glanced down into Naman's tear-filled blue eyes. "It is unquestionably the magic of Mutanacere's heir."

"Not the younger son?" he queried.

"No, not him." I confirmed the words with another examination of the residue. "According to your archive of reports, his magic is sorcery of the water as well, but specifically the stream. It is a softer magic, and not easily distinguishable, except by one experienced in these forms. But as I do possess that experience, I can assuredly say he did not commit at least this part of the evil." I proceeded to describe all of my findings.

When I concluded, Naman's pale skin was tinged a sickly green hue. "He turned his own homeland into quicksand," he mumbled, sounding numb.

I checked behind me—most of our retinue were now awake, listening, and staring around in horror.

"Not merely quicksand," Naman continued, "but such a viscous and vicious substance that anyone who falls into it would never survive, dying of thirst and hunger as they lost their sanity under the attack of cruel magic..." A slim finger inched over the scarred soil toward the edge of the blackness.

I snatched his hand away. "Yes." I forced myself to put aside my horror. The magic still brightening my gaze showed the building masses of cruel residue overhead. Our prayers and our crowns had given us a reprieve, but another onslaught seemed imminent. "We need to leave."

Naman did not respond. Every bit of his beautiful face, from those sweet blue eyes to those kind pink lips to the lustrous red-blond locks of his hair and beard appeared... faded... as he stared at the remains of the once-vibrant county.

Terror gripped my heart. *What if both his natural empathy*

and the empathy of his crown heir's bond make him more vulnerable to the evil influence of this place? If he despairs... prayer loses all efficacy for the despairing.

Black cloud billowed toward me.

I clenched my teeth and swept Naman up into my arms.

He yelped, shocked out of numbness, and clung to my neck.

Holding him so that his head lay against one shoulder and his knees folded over the opposite arm, I adjusted my balance, stood, and turned. "Up."

That one word sent all the awake staff and the soldiers scrambling to their feet. The stronger and more resilient among them picked up the last few and hefted them into their arms as I had Naman.

Concentrating on the water vapor of our breaths, I released a spell that would shield us from magical attack. Against other magic it was nearly insuperable, but against this cruelty... well, at least it would cover our backs long enough for us to escape.

Again, an action I should have taken already, at least to protect Naman.

But, for once, I did not censure myself too much. This last hour brimmed with the horror of lifetimes.

With a deep exhale, I started the march back to where our scouts were hopefully still waiting.

Our attendants tripped over their feet to follow.

As I marched, Naman cuddled closer to me, compressing his taller form as much as he could. Adoration shone in his gaze, but so did a desperate question.

"We cannot address the matter of giving peace to this place, Naman," I answered, hating to tell him no yet again. "Not by ourselves. The crown heir's bond is one of knowledge, you and I do not have the right sort of magic, and lingering here renders us vulnerable. We would need a magician from the sacred athar orchards of Asfiya to attempt a chance at peace, and we would need the resources of Koroma's crown and the petition of your mother to ask such a thing of King Alafen aj-Shehasfiyi at this time."

From the shock on his face, my husband had quite forgotten those petty machinations amid these greater horrors.

I hated to remind him, so I said in consolation, "It is a mission to be undertaken, but not today. Today," a hard, brutal smile spread my lips, "today we seek justice even if it is by the blade."

Naman dipped his head in silent agreement.

Satisfied, I ascertained one more time that I would forget nothing of the murderer's magical signature.

And as I walked away, I looked back.

The chasm, the eye, the blackened earth blinked lazily back at me, lying in wait for its prey, sure of the power of its swallow, believing it was inescapable. We might leave intact for now, it indicated, but we would return, drawn against our will into its depths.

I raised a brow in a silent challenge.

Nothing would swallow Koroma while I still lived.

Nothing would harm Naman while I still breathed.

I would make sure of it.

CHAPTER 7
A MAN WREATHED IN SHADOWS

Perspective: Crown Prince Naman tej-Shehenkorom, Heir to Koroma
Date: Eyyéala, the twenty-ninth day of the tenth moon, Thekharre, of the year 469, C.Q.

Riqeta raised a hand.

The convoy stumbled to a halt behind her.

She swung herself down from her saddle and crouched in front of a seemingly ordinary patch of earth three feet ahead of her horse. In the bit of farsight I was never without now, her eyes narrowed in focus.

I held my breath. *Is this finally it? Oh, how I hope not! But we must find him...*

Tilting her head, Riqeta extended a gloved finger and touched the soil.

I bit back a cry of warning. She knew what she was doing, and my alarm would only distract her if true danger was to be found here. But it was not so easy to remember that.

The last three weeks had torn my nerves to shreds. The horror of Mutanacere lingered in my nightmares and leached warmth from my blood during the day, and every day brought a new understanding on what that evil really meant for my nation. A murderer, a *monster*, roamed my beloved homeland, had been doing so for over a year now, and I had had no idea. Nor did I have any idea of how to stop him now. A mere aftertaste of his evil was breaking me into pieces and destroying all my confidence and strength.

Yet, if I did nothing to confront him, my people would pay an even greater price.

Our staff and soldiers were already paying it.

Whatever nightmares and day-time delusions I faced were mere shadows of the horrors they experienced. Such horrific visions stalked them that most could not sleep at night or eat during the day. Both soldiers and staff members alike were losing weight and seemed paler, not as a result of natural color but as though the very blood was being siphoned from their veins.

Witnessing that deterioration, Riqeta and I had sent all of the staff members and over half of the soldiers back to Ináma. We could not ask them to stay, and they did not have the strength to refuse, despite their unwillingness to, as they said, abandon their lieges.

But even the few who seemed determined to remain and appeared well enough to do so were subdued, quiet, and prone to cowering behind Riqeta and me.

I understood the impulse all too well, for I, too, wanted to cower behind her. I wanted her to protect me, as she had when I had been blind, and I wanted to pretend none of this had happened. I wanted to believe in *all* of Koroma's nobles again. I wanted to return to the bright world of my childhood. I wanted to believe that the Quest's laws had never been violated.

There was no returning, no going back, no pretending ignorance now that I knew the truth.

The Quest's beloved land was starting to fall apart.

And it was my responsibility to act to save it.

Though I had no idea how.

Riqeta lifted a handful of clumped soil to the level of her chin. Then actually tasted a little.

Shocked out of my thoughts, I shuddered. *That* was why I could never excel as a soldier or a scholar of magic. I would eat whatever food was put before me, but putting anything that was *not* food in my mouth... I shuddered again. No matter how many times she did that, it always shocked me, though I understood the purpose.

Tapping the hilt of her sword, Riqeta sampled another portion. Then she dusted her hands and stood. "Naman," she called in a low voice, "his encampment is ahead."

All of my terror and unease crashed over me, like a storm-driven wave knocking a swimmer beneath the surface.

I felt like I was drowning, my heart pounding in my ears, my breath wheezing in my chest—

"Naman."

My name in my wife's voice was instantly calming.

Blinking back the effects of the panic, I looked to where she was remounting.

The light of her amber-brown eyes betrayed no fear.

Entirely steadying.

I exhaled deeply and offered her a smile. "What did you discover, my love?"

The forty-two soldiers behind me both recoiled and eagerly leaned in to hear her answer.

Riqeta gripped her mare's reins and brought her around to face our convoy. Raising her voice, she stated, "Prior to our departure from Samaha, a number of reports were received that indicated the insurgent was in the southern provinces, not far from his home county. Though we at first believed this meant he was based in that county, our observations of Mutanacere disproved that notion."

Like our attendants, I shivered at the distant reference to the monstrous eye-chasm and the delusions...

Not so affected herself, Riqeta continued in an even tone,

"Subsequently we determined that, for such reports to have been received, the insurgent must not have left the southern provinces since his crime. Because his exact position is still unknown to the crown, despite the intervening eighteen months, we further concluded that, for his base, he would choose the most defensible position possible that would also allow him to remain undetected. The southern provinces, with their low hills and flat plains, offer few options; the next nearest forms that allow concealment—the seas and the cliffs—are home to many caravans, aeries, towns, and villages, whose hunts and farms are more extensive that would be ideal for a strategic base. There are only two areas without much habitation: the eastern hills and a portion of the cliffs that are nearly absolutely sheer. The first has few resources for a large group, an army such as we estimated an insurgent would intend to gather. Thus, we decided upon the second."

Despite the grimness of the topic, I had to suppress a smile. All of these deductions had been determined by Riqeta herself as she examined a map only an hour after escaping Mutanacere. None of the rest of us had been coherent enough to help her, and yet she deigned to forgive our uselessness and speak the word 'we'.

The word itself brought a few drops of confidence to our soldiers' expressions.

A brief spark of satisfaction flashed in Riqeta's gaze. "We then rode hard toward these cliffs and, upon arriving here, began to search for any sign of his presence."

Again, the praise was all hers. She was incredibly generous to allow our soldiers and me any credit.

"By examining both the traces of magic drifting in the air and the impressions left in the soil, we have pinpointed the insurgent's base: at the northernmost and steepest point of these sheer cliffs." She paused a moment. "Brace yourselves."

That low-voiced exhortation—as much a plea as a command —brought the world into stark relief.

The insurgent is here, *and* this *is the moment.*

Such stark relief that there was no space amid the clarity for fear.

Apparently pleased with our reactions, Riqeta described her plan and issued her orders.

My heart seized at what she suggested, but I did not protest.

Only Riqeta could confront the monster. It was not my place to stop her just because I was afraid. It was not my place to limit her just because of my pride. To be a supportive husband, I needed to honor her abilities, and her abilities would shape the course of Icilia today. There was no more important moment than this one.

Onward we proceeded.

Closer and closer to the cliffs.

Unlike the eastern and southern portions of the Hafébunna cliffs, which were abrupt descents but still climbable, this section of that same line was completely vertical and flawlessly smooth. Slabs of hard, polished ebony stone as sharp as the flat of a blade formed the edge of the mountains, surrounded by lush trees at the top and the base but bleak themselves, beautiful but colder than winter ice. None could ascend the height without wings, and even the winged found the currents of strong wind flowing down the thousands of feet of lofty escarpment troublesome to navigate.

In previous travels, I had found the long, curving edge of stark black amid the lovely green earth to be a harsh but necessary reminder of the limits one must necessarily accept of mortal power. But, approaching it now... it looked like the hard smirk of a monster's mouth.

Almighty, Dalaanem, I chanted to myself, gripping my athar locket within the folds of my robes. *Almighty, Dalaanem...*

The cliffs loomed closer, the trees below too leafless to be called shelter, what leaves there were not bright but dull and rotting, and the trees above too far away to appear as more than twigs.

Neither above nor below was where my gaze was drawn —Riqeta had said that the monster's magic might have allowed him to carve into the rock of the sheer wall itself and that this was certainly the most defensible position.

Still closer...

Riqeta donned her circlet, letting the silver add a queenly air to her already regal posture, and I did the same. Our soldiers drew their swords and nocked arrows to their longbows.

Still closer...

The shadows falling over the trees surrounding us grew darker and the trees themselves more stunted.

Still closer...

The escarpment was a black maw that would consume the world.

Still closer...

A figure swooped down in a flash of metal from some unseen point high on the ridge.

Riqeta halted the convoy.

The figure smoothed out his flight with a flare of powerful wings, the metal resolving into armor, and landed lightly on his feet in front of us. Revealing himself to be a young man of the Sholanar, not much older than a boy, beardless, a faint mustache on his upper lip, yet with the bearing of a warrior.

His forest-green eyes flickered oddly between the extremes of reverence and hostility in his unexpectedly sweet face.

A face that was the older, less chubby version of one I had glimpsed as an adolescent.

"May the Almighty bless you, Koroyi Khonatir bi-Mutanacer," I greeted the murdered countess' younger son. "How is your health?"

The young man fluttered his large wings slightly, deep honey-gold scales lighting briefly with some emotion, but said nothing.

"I am Crown Prince Naman tej-Shehenkorom," I continued, "with me is my consort, Princess Riqeta Shehenkorom, and these are our attendants."

As Riqeta had planned, the mention of her famous name

caused the young man to startle—he nearly jumped back into the air before visibly controlling myself.

"We have come to meet with your brother," I stated the overt intention of our visit. "Would you take us to him?"

Khonatir fluttered his wings again, nervously I thought, but did not answer.

"Our mission is important, Koroyi," I said gently, trying to conceal my own nerves as I wondered where the monster himself was, "commanded by my father the king himself, so we really must speak with your brother. Do you know where he is?"

Khonatir opened his mouth for a moment but pressed his lips together. Then he glanced at Riqeta, sitting elegantly in her saddle by my side, and awe lit his gaze. The green of his eyes glowed, the honey of his scales shone against his chocolate skin, and all hostility fell away from the soft curves of his cheeks and beardless chin.

Maybe he can still be redeemed? I wondered, my heart warming at the obvious, chaste admiration of my wife. *Riqeta did say the signature of his magic was not present at Mutanacere...*

How dearly I hope he is innocent of his parents' and home's destruction! But I have no indisputable proof. Although...

I remembered the way I had known of the circumstances of his parents' deaths. *Perhaps the crown heir's bond can tell me something?*

Catalyzing a stream of my magic, which was now infused with the signature of the crown, I invoked my bond and extended my awareness toward Khonatir.

There was nothing there.

Nothing in neither my bond nor my farsight.

In the place where he stood amid the magic of Koroma, woven over all of her territory by the first Quest, there was nothing. No presence, no emotion, no heart... not even a corpse, for even the dead while unburied had a signature. No, it was as though Khonatir did not exist.

As though he were no longer a child of Koroma.

As though our Mother had disowned him.

As though he had been thrown from the ranks of Icilia's people and cast from the civilization of the Quests.

Such was the evil shrouding his form.

Reeling, I choked again and, unable to keep my composure, bent over in my saddle, trying frantically to swallow the bile rising in my throat.

"Naman." My name murmured in my wife's voice again calmed me.

Exhaling deeply, I looked up to try and salvage the meeting.

Genuine concern filled the gaze of that young man whose evil had torn him from most forgiving Koroma's arms.

I cannot understand it... Both sights fixated upon the noble boy I once knew, I absently urged my horse a step forward.

Then...

The world around us dimmed.

The light of the afternoon sun faded.

Hope itself vanished at the approach of fear...

Then abruptly returned.

And a voice called out, "Hail your Highnesses!"

Deep, smooth, rich, almost unctuous like the finest juices...

I turned.

Behind the huddle of Riqeta's and my attendants was a man.

A man wreathed in shadows.

Shadows of fear and screams and the agony of the dead.

Dead who had been stolen from life in the most brutal of ways.

Ways of which he was unrepentant.

His presence was not merely *missing* like his brother's but a void, a monster's baleful eye, a black chasm mirroring the hole left in the aftermath of his great crime...

His face and form were of the comeliest of men.

Well-shaped muscles and well-structured bones constituted an elegant build, of both broad shoulders and a tapered waist. Long legs and a long torso, all encased in fine metal armor, constructed the nearly seven feet of his regal figure. Strong lines and sweeping curves comprised his high forehead, his long, straight nose, his angular cheeks, his full, strangely mustacheless lips, and his pointed, oddly beardless chin. A helm of delicately worked iron covered his head. Thin, arched brows and thick, wavy locks of lustrous bronze accented the limitless, enchanting green of his hooded eyes... Shimmering with Mutharrim silver and alit with chips of soft red, the perfect symmetry and proportion of his countenance bestowed upon him such perfect charm, such pleasurable charisma, such consuming power that to look upon him was to become his.

Count Hisalir bi-Mutanacer.

The heir by blood to one of Koroma's most vibrant and virtuous counties.

As a child, I had adored him and eagerly ran after his every word like the tastiest sweet.

As an adolescent and young royal, I had thought him a valuable vassal of my brother's future crown.

As an adult and as crown prince in my own right... I wanted my wife to kill him.

I had never wanted the death of anyone at all before.

But for the man who had murdered his mother, his father, his people, the home he was born to protect...

Who could wreak that same destruction upon *my* family, *my* people, and *my* home... Upon Icilia...

Nothing else savored of justice.

Nothing else savored of *safety*.

Nothing less would serve the Quest.

Oh Almighty, I beg of You: may Riqeta's plan succeed! Oh Dalaanem, may your favor descend unto us as the drops of your blood flow in our veins and the devotion to your honor enlightens our souls...

That prayer bright in my heart, I dismounted and pressed my reins into the loose grip of a soldier.

His mouth was hanging open, the pupils of his eyes so huge that little color was visible around the edges.

Beside him, his wife stared, just as riveted, just as enraptured, not even moving to take reins from Riqeta, her hero and liege.

It was not just them.

All of our soldiers were so enthralled. So enthralled that they had forgotten not only their illnesses but also the reality that those illnesses had been inflicted by this man's hands. So enthralled that they had forgotten his crime. Even my old friends, Captain bi-Himacer and Lieutenant Gatiemt.

Such were the emotions in the bond.

Riqeta needed to make several gestures to catch their attention before they moved aside as previously planned and formed an aisle so that Hisalir could approach us. And even then their obedience seemed more for the shadowed man's sake than ours.

The corners of Hisalir's mouth curled, a dark amusement in his unrelenting gaze.

But, without a word, he walked between the columns of horses, his stride confident and proud. Without hesitation, he came before Riqeta and me.

And without a hint of reluctance, he bowed.

Deeply, smoothly, the movement so polished that his reverence appeared genuine.

A lie more vivid and shameless than anything the other nobles had ever done.

I forced a smile and made myself hold out my hand. "How the Almighty favors our meeting today, Count Hisalir bi-Mutanacer! My princess and I have been searching for you."

Those words, ominous in meaning though not in my delivery, caused the monster no pause. Nor did the act of cupping my fingers and kissing my knuckles in a show of allegiance. From his suave tongue spilled, accompanied by an alluring smile, "I am honored that you would deign to give even a moment of your time to this lowly vassal, your Highnesses."

I wanted to scrub my fingers of his touch and scour my ears of his voice. Even these few moments in his presence felt like live coals being rubbed over my skin. I loathed him more than I had ever hated anyone else.

But I needed to adhere to Riqeta's plan.

A monster could not be caught so easily.

So, stepping slightly in front of my silent wife, I replied, "I am pleased to hear this, Count bi-Mutanacer. For a few days, my princess and I worried about what report we would need to make to my father if we could not find you. The crown has waited for a visit from you these last eighteen months, as you know."

Hisalir himself did not react, his smile remaining in place, but Khonatir startled a little as he moved to join his brother.

So, the crown harboring such irritation and, as a result, giving such attention does not suit his plan... Pushing the point a bit further, I added, "Shall we discuss the details necessary for an upcoming visit, Count bi-Mutanacer?"

"Of course," Hisalir answered smoothly, with a note of affected concern. "I did not realize I had so trespassed upon the generosity of the crown, your Royal Highness. I assure you, I did not intend such." His eyes stayed on mine, but his brother was still glancing at Riqeta.

A little more deflection... They should not discover our intention until we are ready to reveal it... Bringing every moment of my royal training in intrigue and my upbringing in one of Icilia's most manipulative courts to bear, I responded, "To know your intentions is exactly why my princess and I have come." I offered a light, amiable smile, certainly complemented by my wearing robes and not armor. The sword tied to my belt was only custom. "I am certain a thoughtful discussion will clarify all matters."

Khonatir relaxed fully as Hisalir returned my smile. "I hope it will be so, your Highness," the shadowed man said, "and to that end, when I first heard of the possibility of your arrival yesterday, I took the chance to have a feast prepared in celebration. If it would please you, would you allow me to escort you to the meal?"

I nodded. "It does indeed please us, Count." *So this is his game as well. It is why he did not move his camp or attack. But surely he will not host us in his lair...?*

At my agreement, Hisalir swept another bow and began to walk deeper into the leafless trees, in parallel to the looming cliffside.

Ah, so not his lair. As Riqeta expected.

His brother, though almost the same height and more muscular, scurried in his wake.

There is something not quite right about their relationship... I should learn more, if I can...

At the raise of Riqeta's hand, I led my attendants in proceeding after him as well and flung my farsight ahead.

Concealed amid the forest at the very base of the escarpment was an enormous glade—one worthy of the Great Forest of Nademan—and within it was the feast the monster had mentioned upon a long wooden table and... an army.

Thronging together in the clearing were one hundred men and thirty women, mostly young but many of middling and elderly years as well, of all five kinds and possessing the accents and mannerisms of Koroma, Bhalasa, and Zahacim. From their bearings and characteristics, they came from different ranks and positions—some nobles, some citizens, some farmers, some soldiers, some artists. But what was common to them all was an almost feverish excitement in their eyes.

As well as the disdain and mockery that tinged their expressions upon Riqeta's and my entrance.

And... three among them were bleak voids like Khonatir.

Upon our appearance, all of them snapped to attention and rendered flawless bows.

Then hurried to seat my wife, all of our attendants, and me with obeisant whispers and servile gestures.

Riqeta and I were given matching thrones at the head of the table, Hisalir himself sat to our right in deference, Khonatir to his own right, and our soldiers were offered the rest of the table. Every one of the insurgent soldiers remained standing to serve.

It was all a farce of piety and loyalty.

Even the way they murmured in echo of my prayer at the beginning of the meal.

It was all a farce...

How long had such farces existed in Koroma? In Icilia?

Was there *more* evil of which I did not know?

My head spun and my stomach roiled and I felt I would vomit as I tried to maintain a steady stream of casual chatter over possibly poisoned food with a monster—

Beneath the table, a hand closed over mine. A calloused thumb brushed my knuckles and my fingertips, soothing away the ache left behind by the shadowed man's touch, calming me as little else could. Giving me confidence as little else could. Assuring me that she would defend my back even as all of our soldiers deserted me.

Perhaps we really would succeed...

Oh Almighty, oh Dalaanem...

Maintaining the lightness of my tone as the luncheon ended, I said, "I truly could not have hoped for a more joyous wedding, Count. It was a blessing, and even the sky was clear blue, despite the late spring rains, as though Icilia herself were celebrating as well, if I may be so bold as to say."

The monster chuckled. "Your joy warms my heart, your Highness." Though Riqeta was part of the conversation as well, he hardly looked at her—blatant disrespect because she was royal but more so simply because she was incé. The lack of acknowledgment far exceeded thinking she was not a threat—it was a sign that she did not *matter* to him.

Controlling a flare of anger, I let affection warm my smile in response. *I suppose, in this one circumstance, I am grateful to the Almighty for my poor reputation in intrigue. Otherwise, it would not be believable for a courtier to be tricked by that statement, that ploy of using expressions of interest in what another loves and cherishes to earn goodwill.* My other fist clenched in my lap. *It was one thing to chatter about the weather; it is quite another to drag the sacredness of my* wedding *into this! To let him disrespect Riqeta! How I want to be done with it!*

"Indeed," he continued, "when I heard of your blessings, I thought to myself that perhaps it was time I sought the same."

In my farsight, a number of his followers clapped their hands over their mouths, stifling laughter, and Khonatir discreetly rolled his eyes.

Another lie. How easily, how shamelessly he lies. The taste in my mouth only soured further. *And a quiet mockery as well.* "Well," I replied, "there is certainly no strict requirement to marry upon Koroma's nobles. The crown respects the freedom of your will."

More silent derision and contempt from his followers, and this time Riqeta's and my own attendants joined them.

Hisalir arched a brow and leaned back in his chair, a polished, challenging move. "Indeed? Is it not custom, at least, to expect nobles to marry for their bloodlines?"

At least an opening for another goal... I gave my most elegant shrug, to offset the intensity of my next words: "The crown certainly would like to see our nobles marry and expand our family—it brings us great joy—but there are ways to both respect your choices and ensure future stability. We do not coerce." To my chagrin, not a hint of even doubt appeared on his followers' faces. "But you, Count bi-Mutanacer, need have little concern." I gestured to Khonatir. "You may always ask your brother to seek to uphold this duty."

If my brother Raman and I had been confronted with such a statement, both before my coronation and after, we would have laughed, teased, and spoken of how blessed we were to have each other. And that such a choice was really our wives', Riqeta's and whomever Raman might eventually marry.

Heartwarming, loving, sweet—neither wanting to steal from the other. Despite any momentary flare of irrational emotion.

But these brothers...

"Hah!" the shadowed man exclaimed. "Khonatir could not uphold such duties." Though smiling, Hisalir speared with his brother with a speaking, sarcastic look, and the poor boy himself huddled in his seat, embarrassed, humiliated, yet holding such concern as he met his brother's gaze that I could not deny that he loved him.

It was too easy to see:

Khonatir loved his brother. Adored him, even worshipped him. It was why they were so attuned, why his reactions seemed suitable to indicate at least some of his brother's thoughts.

But Hisalir did not love him back...

I scrambled to remember all that I was observing. If, somehow, Riqeta was not successful—as Riqeta said, contingencies were too important to avoid making for the sake of sentiment—this would be valuable intelligence.

I wonder what this means about the possibility of Khonatir's redemption...

As a part of my mind began to ponder that question, the monster swung the conversation back toward me: "I must confess that a drop of your joy resounds in my own heart. For Koroma to be so honored by the valorous victor of the siege of Komásin..." He shook his head but still cast only the most cursory of nods in Riqeta's direction.

I bit back a frown. *Does that mean he does not believe Riqeta's reputation? Which... as upset as that makes me, would it not be a benefit to our plan? But surely he cannot be so foolish!*

My wife squeezed my hand, and the calmness of her composure did not change.

Gaining strength from her, I tilted my head and asked, curiosity not masking the delight evident in my voice, "Have you heard much of my princess' feats, Count?" Doing so burned, but I avoided looking at Riqeta myself. If he was intent on such disrespect, I would not correct him and draw attention to the spells she was likely casting. And, in the meanwhile, perhaps I could uncover some critical intelligence for her...

Hisalir uttered a laugh, a rich confection of sound dripping with sugar and charm. "Of course, your Highness! Who has not heard of the power and ferocity of the Sword of Prudence?" Finally he deigned to glance at my wife.

In that moment... with all of my understanding of intrigue and the thoughts and emotions of the people around me... I saw through the iron walls of his façade.

There was such darkness in his eyes.

A darkness I had never witnessed before but certainly seen described in the history of the Prince of Virtue.

And with the understanding given by those texts...

It was not that he underestimated Riqeta... it was that he wanted to *prey* upon her.

Not just kill but *violate*.

Anger and fear, blending hotly together, rose instinctively in my throat.

The monster's attention returned to me, and he smiled. So charismatically that, if I had been any less sure of his guilt, I would have doubted what I had seen.

But I did not doubt my perception.

My hand seized around my wife's.

And the urge built in my heart to run, to flee, to fly, to escape, to protect she whom I most loved—

My feet began to press against the ground, ready to push back my chair, acting almost against my own will—

My mouth began to open, ready to deliver whatever excuse required, speaking almost without my own choice—

Riqeta squeezed my hand.

Then against my palm she curled her fingers into a fist.

Our signal.

CHAPTER 8
BY THE POWER OF WILL

Perspective: Princess Riqeta Shehenkorom, consort of the Heir to Koroma
Date: Eyyéala, the twenty-ninth day of the tenth moon, Thekharre, of the year 469, C.Q.

There were thousands of things in which I was woefully inadequate. Some my cousins had scorned me with on too many occasions to count, and others my new life had taunted me with like an ambush in the middle of my greatest joys. I was a poor wife, a poor sister, and a poor child of Koroma.

What I was not was a poor warrior and scholar of magic.

My memory was excellent, and my application of it even sharper.

So, when confronted with magic I had never before witnessed in all of my extensive experience, I was able to draw upon my recollections of a book—a book that the third princess of Asfiya and I, as young girls, had snuck together into the most restricted sections of Asfiya's grand library to find and read—a book that detailed the spells that the Asfiyan Prince of Virtue had used to combat the blackest magic Icilia had ever known.

Conjury and its twin, alchemy.

Nearly two centuries ago, Asfiya's crown prince, in whom all three of the Quest of Light's bloodlines became one, led every nation of Icilia in a war against a group of invaders who wielded a magic that was the antithesis of the gifts the Shining Guide had left behind. That magic allowed those invaders to commit unspeakable evil: through fear, conjury overthrew the will of its victims.

It turned them into the slaves of its wielder.

And it fed upon fear, pain, anger, and the spill of blood. Upon sin. Upon evil.

With the same fuel, alchemy could transform a substance into any other substance. Twisting every law, defying every hint of nature and order, spreading the evil of which it was born. For most often it was used upon flesh.

To both sate their vicious desires and increase their power, the invaders violated women and men alike. Both their own and those they seized from among the people of Icilia.

For some months, Icilia seemed lost.

Until a woman born among the enemy defected. Though unable to speak either of Icilia's languages, she pledged her loyalty to all that the children of the Quest held sacred.

With her help, and eventually her love, the Prince of Virtue found a solution to the plague of conjury: only athar could truly withstand it.

Only athar.

Precious and rare and able to be wielded by only a few.

Which meant much of the burden of war fell upon the Mutharrim—those least affected by the invaders' ravages.

In a brilliant display of political and military acumen, the Prince of Virtue rallied his troops, gathered the seven nations, and managed to eradicate every last invader, save those who defected. And those who defected he ordered to swear to never use conjury again. All of these new citizens agreed and pledged their loyalty, and many married into the royal and noble families of the seven nations.

Though the danger was dispelled, the Prince of Virtue kept watch over every union, including his own, fearing the rediscovery of the evil magic in future generations. Only to find that, when conjury and alchemy were mixed with the magic of the Shining Guide's people, they formed something new: arms magic. Wizardry, sorcery, and the warrior magic. Control over the elements. Sacred magic in their own right.

The blessed discovery began a new age in Icilia, a new estimation of power and new disciplines of study, one without the fear of the evil, for conjury and alchemy had been forever bound, vanquished by the light.

But now they had returned.

For, with the tests described by the Prince and my own observations, I was certain: somehow, through some black crime, Hisalir had brought about in himself the unbinding of conjury and alchemy. All three types of magic, the evil two and the sorcery of the flood that was his from birth, perpetrated the atrocity at Mutanacere. Conjury was the source of the black clouds, and alchemy and sorcery were the makers of the quicksand that seemed like a chasm. My initial suspicions there were correct.

He was using all three here as well.

For I could see the spells drifting in the air, reshaping the cliffside, and... darkening Naman's eyes.

A tendril of black fog wove around his head, not repelled now by the crown heir's circlet because the monster had found an opening. A wisp of fear. A way past my brave husband's defenses.

He has held out for so long, I thought proudly, remembering the light conversation flowing around me as I inspected the monster's and his followers' magical signatures and inventoried his defensive enchantments. *He has shielded my spells and deflected beautifully all while engaging in what he most hates. But no longer. Now, it is my turn.* I set my jaw. *I will die before he overwhelms my husband.*

Naman's hand trembled against my fist as he registered our signal. But he seemed too far gone to fully understand.

I tapped my fist twice against his hand. Then, abandoning the idle calmness of my composure, I turned toward the monster and let my eyes narrow and the anger in them simmer.

The shadowed man's gaze, tinged by a cruel smugness, shifted from my husband to me. The darkness underlaying it was akin to that filling the eyes of the most corrupt soldiers whom I had executed for war crimes—but much *worse*.

I did not dare to ponder all that such a man would have done to his home. Not now when I needed to be fully without fear.

Meeting his gaze, I said, my voice low and even yet resounding, "Hisalir, we know what you did at Mutanacere."

Khonatir jolted in his seat, but Hisalir did not startle. Not even at the obvious slight of directly using his name.

Instead, a slow, dark smile curled his lips. "Is that so?"

With that, he let his façade fall.

His face grew colder, his body harder, and his eyes burned like twin black flames, the vibrancy of the green consumed by soot and pitch.

Everything about him was a lie. The charm of his appearance, the suavity of his voice, the display of his loyalty—he was untruth itself.

If anyone's soul could be fully black, his was.

And his magic was so potent that Naman still had not stirred.

Slipping my fist from his loose grasp, I slid the locket holding the strand of athar gifted by his grandmother from his robe pocket, where I had asked him to keep it for an emergency, onto his palm. I curled his fingers over it and prayed.

Naman jumped a little, shifting our touching hands. Then finally seemed to recollect himself. Bright blue eyes clearing, he met the shadowed man's gaze and declared, as planned, "We, the future monarchs of Koroma, have come to exact justice for your crime."

Silence.

No one moved, his brother and his followers as frozen as our soldiers.

Silence.

Then Hisalir barked out a laugh, loud, vicious, and scornful. "And how do you propose to do that?" He flicked his gaze to our soldiers, most of whom now betrayed reluctance at the execution of the plan to which they had agreed. "You have no army." Another flick to his followers. "And I do." They cheered. "Do you think that I will simply docilely attend a trial?"

"This is no matter for a trial," Naman proclaimed in return. Although his voice was not louder than the enemy's, it carried more power—the very land beneath us vibrated in tune with the rhythm of his words. "With your actions at Mutanacere, you have declared war upon the people of Koroma. So will you be treated."

"Again, with what army?" Hisalir asked, crossing his arms over his middle and leaning back in his chair, entirely uncaring of what was being said. A sneer lurked on his malicious mouth.

Naman glanced at me and nodded. Devastating anxiety filled his eyes, but so did trust.

Trust.

Trust that I would protect him, protect Koroma, protect all whom we loved.

Trust that I would not fail.

I would not fail.

Loosening my swords in their combined sheath, I lifted my hand away, kicked back my chair, stood, and again met the monster's gaze. "I challenge you to a duel, Hisalir. By my honor, by your pride, meet me alone on the battlefield, and may only the best prevail."

Hisalir laughed again, unconcerned, and stood as well, drawing himself up so that the nearly seven feet of his frame loom over the less than five feet of mine. "So shall it be, Riqeta."

Khonatir fell out of his seat, wings flapping frantically as he struggled to regain his balance. He cast his brother, then me, desperate looks, but neither his brother nor I gave him any heed.

I ignored his insult of directly using my name. "As the challenged, choose your arena."

Naman shook as he rose to his feet beside me. Though conjury no longer drifted around him, anxiety rather than triumph creased his handsome face. Despite the reality that there was no reason for him to worry now.

Hisalir glanced around the glade, large as a standard duel arena in Zahacim even with the many ranks of his followers present, and smirked. "This clearing suits." He flicked a glance at a scarred, broad-shouldered man of the Nasimih standing only a few feet behind him.

At the silent order, the Nasimih man, likely his captain, pivoted and began to shout orders in a growl of a voice.

Within minutes, the empty dishes, the table, and the chairs had disappeared. The monster's followers thronged around the edges of the clearing. Naman's and my soldiers hesitated for a moment, but then most of them followed the enemy. What few who remained (primarily the captain and the lieutenant) waited impatiently for me to dismiss them so that they might do the same.

Abandoning their lieges.

Naman and I were all alone.

All alone amid those who would kill us if only it were convenient.

The circlets on our heads, the power of the too-distant crown, and my sword and magic were our only protection.

They would be enough. I would see to it.

Hisalir met my gaze again. "What are your terms, Riqeta?"

"Death," I stated simply. "If I triumph, I may end your life without retribution. If you triumph, you may do the same."

A squeak left Naman's lips. Though he had known what challenge I would give. Without it, there was no way to effect the monster's execution.

Hisalir grinned, a cruel pleasure stretching his mouth over his bared teeth. "I accept those terms."

Khonatir whimpered, sweet face contorting with fear, then promptly hushed at a glare from his brother. Despite the protest in his kind green eyes, he spread his wings and glided over to the circle of spectators.

Naman started to walk in that direction as well, but I raised a hand. "Until there is a chair placed for his Royal Highness the crown prince to sit, the duel cannot begin." The demand could have been made earlier, when the chairs were being moved, but I intended to make a point.

"You have already established that I am not one of your citizens," Hisalir replied, crossing his arms and smirking. "Why should I make such an accommodation?"

I raised a brow. "So do the laws of military engagement as legislated by our Rulers the Quest of Light dictate. This duel will be by those laws of engagement, so they must be followed in all matters."

There was no chance in this life or the hereafter that the shadowed man would follow those sacred laws. But *I* would, and I wanted my adherence known.

Despite all the pressures placed both by my aunt and sisters and by the enemy in wars with Etheqa and Bhalasa, I had never once broken the laws of engagement. Nor I would do so today. I would not let such a breach taint the justice rendered by the monster's death.

Hisalir sneered and rolled his eyes but did not object as Khonatir hurried to place a chair near the edge of the clearing.

As protocol required, I walked with Naman to the chair and waited, casting a pair of protective enchantments, until he was seated. Then I bowed, kissed his hand, and, still holding it, asked formally, "Your Highness, would you deign to pray to the Almighty and the Quest for my victory in your name?"

Naman glanced from my hands folded beneath his to my face. His beautiful eyes blazed, like twin blue stars, full of such light that I could only believe that the Almighty surely listened to his pleas. There was terror in those jewels, unquestionably, but also confidence... "You can win, Riqeta, my love," he whispered. "Do not let him force you to forget."

I nodded, not quite sure what he was doing. On the one occasion I had fought such a duel for Zahacim, Misleta had muttered a brief prayer before tersely sending me off to battle, and these reassurances, unlike our touching hands before, were not part of the plan. Even if they were causing that odd swell of warmth in my chest.

Naman suddenly pulled me forward by my hands and pressed a hard kiss to my mouth. "May the Almighty bless you, Riqeta, and, please, please, keep you safe!"

I blinked, stunned, warm everywhere, my plates vibrating strongly enough to emit a buzz. The monster and most of his followers were laughing, but I did not pay them any attention. For a single moment, the only person in the world was Naman.

"*Please* be safe," he whispered, looking anxiously into my eyes. "I love you. You must return to me, my princess."

Not sure what to say, I just nodded. I would not lose, and he knew it, so I did not understand why he was fretting.

"Please, Riqeta," he pleaded again before letting me go. Then, returning to protocol, he finally said, "May the Almighty grant you victory."

Quickly composing myself, I saluted, pivoted, and marched to the center of the field. My lips tingled with his kiss, and I caught the memory and held it inside me. Then, from one step to the next, I performed a mental check of my armor.

A full shirt of the light chainmail I most preferred protected my torso and middle, with extra plate reinforcing my chest, while pauldrons, vambraces, greaves, and cuisses guarded my limbs. A gorget shielded my neck, metal-backed gloves designed for a firm grip covered my hands, and similar boots preserved my feet. My helm defended my head, and my long hair was bound tightly into a flat bun at the base of my skull (every daughter of Zahacim knew that unsecured hair could be yanked). The circlet hanging at the top of my brow was a familiar weight and was designed to bear the stresses of battle. The chain carrying my wedding ring was too deeply buried beneath my armor to be caught and twisted. A dozen blades were hidden on my person, and the little shield I sometimes used was fitted neatly over my lower spine. The attire was familiar, and I was comfortable.

This was key.

Next, I evaluated my magical and physical strength. The seventeen spells I had already cast this day meant my strength was not at its maximum, and my monthly cycle throbbed in my middle, but I could control the intense discomfort, I had slept well yesterday, in Naman's arms, and my belly was sated and my throat moist. Magical catalyst pooled beneath the plane of my concentration, making every bit of magic visible, and my spells were ready. The hymn required for casting sorcery, *In obeying the Almighty's laws there is salvation*, echoed effortlessly in my thoughts.

This was almost ideal.

Finally, I considered my mind and my heart. There was not the faintest hint of doubt or fear to be found. I *knew* I would win. My faith in the Almighty and in the first Quest was complete. My triumph here would serve the Divine, and I believed that the Divine wanted me to triumph.

This was perfect.

I was ready.

Unsheathing my swords and holding a hilt in each hand, I halted in front of my opponent.

In Naman's name, I will teach him the wisdom of reverence for the Light.

That resolve stated, I cleared my mind of all save what I needed to duel.

His height is not what is challenging about him. I have fought equally large and tall warriors before, in the war against Bhalasa, and they were able to fly. The greater challenge is his black magic...

Hisalir bared his teeth in another feral grin. "Are we done with all your acting, little princess?"

My composure, the calm of my face and body, did not so much as twitch. Coolly I replied, "Draw your sword, Hisalir."

The shadowed man uttered a jeer of a laugh before drawing forth from the sheath buckled to his belt a long, thin sword with dual serrated edges.

Not the large greatswords men of his height usually use. Only three feet. Rather similar to mine, actually—except my blades are not fully serrated on both sides. Interesting. Most do not have the daring to use serration. Perhaps the drills from my fourteenth year...

"May the best win, Hisalir," I said per ritual, raising my swords.

"May the best win, Riqeta," he returned, smirking again, doing the same.

Stillness.

I watched him, and he watched me.

Stillness.

Not a whisper of sound. Even the forest was quiet, not an animal daring to make a noise.

Stillness.

Then...

I struck.

One hand swiped overhead in a diagonal blow aimed at his upper chest, while the other swept in the opposite direction below at his left knee.

Hisalir dodged the first and parried the second. Then twisting his arm, trapped the second, locking the serrated edges against each other, and threw a punch at my exposed chest.

I ducked the punch, tilted my second blade to break the lock, letting the serrated slide off the flat, and brought the first down in an overhead chop.

Hisalir leapt back, dodging again, and pulled his sword loose in a clang of metal.

Then immediately swung his sword up and cut sideways. Dirty purple shadows, a tainted version of mauve, wreathed the blade. The addition of enough charge to render the iron as heavy as a boulder. If it hit me, the pain would give his conjury a path.

Releasing my own spells, I charged my swords—giving them an amber glow—and tipped my body backward. Trapped his blade between mine, the serrated edges holding each other locked, the vibrations of the particles reversing each other out, while both my feet pushed off the ground and collided with his belly. At the last moment, I charged my boots, adding force to the kick.

Hisalir reeled backwards, uttering a low cry.

Tilting my swords again, I let his blade slide away and contracted my stomach (ignoring the heightened cramps), tucking in my legs, spinning, somersaulting myself up and over until I landed back on my feet, facing him.

He steadied himself out of a reel and wheezed, trying to catch his breath. The flames in his eyes flared, and his gaze seared lasciviously down my form. Lingering on my chest and the place below my waist.

I brought forth the memory of my husband's kiss, his sweet, wonder-filled gaze, his gentle, caressing touch, and did not flinch. Did not *fear*.

Anger sparked in the monster's gaze, but his demeanor remained calm. A spell brewed around him in flashes of black...

Murmuring a spell, I gathered moisture and condensed it as vapor around my swords, then charged both the gas and the metal, holding all the trace elements of the air in the water, and struck. Leaping up and forward, slashed down diagonally inward, hitting both of his shoulders. At the precise moment of impact, released a burst of energy.

Delivering an electric shock.

And the seed of another spell into the liquid of his bloodstream.

Hisalir stumbled back, the sound of his gasps filling the clearing, and fell to his knees. Now anger twisted his face.

I crouched back, casting another spell. *Not the right moment for a winning blow—he is nowhere near defeat—and he has still yet to show his greatest advantages...*

He removed a hand from his hilt and slammed it into the ground.

A fine mist flew up around him, one marked with tainted mauve, swirling into such a frenzy that I could not see anything.

One of the complex enchantments I had cast earlier pinged. Indicating the presence of alchemy, though I could not see its approach amid the eerie shadows.

I ignited a more precise version of the same spell. It alerted me to the slimy feeling creeping through the earth. Rather like the curse left behind at Mutanacere.

Closing my eyes, I crouched, blades at the ready, and leapt upward in the emblematic move of Zahacim's warrior princesses. I tucked in my legs, released another spell for guiding moisture to support my movements, and *listened*. For one quiet moment above the solid earth.

The heavy breaths of a big, angry man, audible despite the muffling quality of the mist.

I somersaulted over his head, swiping a pair of heavy, back-handed blows that threw him forward and broke his armor. As well as delivered more seeds for a coming spell.

Hisalir shrieked with pain and frustration.

Another somersault, and then I landed behind him, back to him, and pivoted as the mist cleared.

Hisalir turned, green eyes now fully blackened by anger. Shadows drifted over his cheeks in place of the usual silver blushes of the Mutharrim. His gaze fixated on the red blood coating the tips of my swords.

The draw of blood was a small victory, but my breath was catching softly in my chest, my pulse quicker than ideal. So many spells were draining my well of physical energy and magical catalyst, and I estimated I was halfway depleted.

I needed a defense. A few moments to recover.

Hisalir raised his blade, crouched, and charged.

I parried, dodged, and ducked. Avoiding blocks and blows. Moving backward, losing space, but letting myself recover.

Amid the shower of blows, my warning spell for alchemy pinged again.

Viscous shadows coated the monster's blade. As he raised it for a swing such that I would have to block, need both blades to block, his longer reach making it impossible for me to move away in time to avoid his blow.

Reacting in seconds, I released a spell and charged the air immediately around me such that it began to glow. Coating myself with light.

Just in time.

A savage war cry ringing in his smooth voice, Hisalir struck downward, colliding with the double barrier of my twin swords.

The serrated edges locked.

And the alchemy spread over my swords... then floundered, like oil spreading in a thick film over water, unable to penetrate.

Gratitude to the Almighty for the Prince of Virtue's wise advice. Now...

Calling forth all my strength, I shoved up my swords.

Hisalir's eyes flashed, mauve shadows burst from his hands, and the air lost its charge.

The alchemy struck.

The steel of both my swords crumbled in a shower of dust. All that remained were the leather-wrapped wood hilts.

"*Riqeta!*" Naman screamed.

Dropping the useless hilts, I threw myself backward, fell to the ground, dodged Hisalir's blows with a roll, and sprung to my feet with two serrated daggers drawn from my greaves.

The monster lunged after me, and I easily switched to the shorter reach of my daggers, dodging and ducking more than parrying and blocking.

As I led him around in a circle, I dared to cast glances at Naman. *I hope no one has tried to take advantage of his fear...*

My husband was not in his seat. Instead, he was standing, pacing back and forth, biting the tips of his fingers, pulling his hair, tearing at his beard—his lovely eyes wild with terror.

Besides Serama, no one has ever actually been afraid for me before. No one has ever cared whether I returned from battle.

How different it was to the way my aunt and my cousins had simply used me! Sent me to kill, believed I would win, untroubled by my death and irritated by my life. They were my family, my blood and my heart, but I had been merely a tool to earn victory for them. Even to my aunt, my adoptive mother, the only mother I had ever known.

She had never feared for me. Never acted as though the loss of me would destroy her. Never felt as though harm to me was a heavy cost to bear. Never once treated me as though I were the center of her world, as her other daughters were. Never asked me to return. Never wanted me to live more than her to triumph.

But Naman... I was winning, and still he was afraid. As though he would prefer *my* return and *my* life over his own triumph, my earning a victory in his name. As though *I* were all that mattered. As though he *loved* me.

How desperately I wanted to believe that!

How desperate I was to protect him from this evil. But to do that, I needed to win...

I ducked beneath Hisalir's guard and thrust a charged dagger in the thin slit of space between the greave and the cuisse on his left leg. Delivering a final seed.

The monster roared. Lifting his other foot, he kicked my middle. And as I flew back, he grabbed the blade of my other dagger, reducing it to dust as well.

I let the momentum carry me to the ground, into a roll, and then back to my feet. Agony burned through my middle, mixing with the pain of my monthly cycle, but I controlled both, minimizing them and distancing myself from them so he could not use them against me.

Hisalir ripped my blade from the gap in his armor and snarled, more a beast than a man. He crumbled the dagger into dust as well and then threw aside his helm.

I blinked, startled. *I have never seen anyone actually toss aside their helm like that in the middle of a battle. Unless...* I called forth an image of the monster's face. *I have never met a man who does not obsessively maintain his mustache and beard, much less one who removes them entirely—mustaches and beards are an emblem of love for our civilization, like a woman braiding or pinning her hair. And caps and covers for our heads have the same meaning. To do the opposite is hatred... which explains why his brother and all of his followers have shaven chins or loose hair and uncovered heads. So...* My eyes narrowed. *He is indeed going to use it.*

The shadowed man raised both hands, from waist to shoulders, curling them into fists.

Black wisps of magic formed around them.

Then he met my gaze, smiled cruelly, and shoved his fists forward.

The unseen magic exploded into visible black clouds.

Clouds that slithered toward me like the approach of a viper, coiling to strike.

Conjury.

If it struck, it would overthrow my mind. It would turn me against Naman.

And there was no way to avoid it. No way to run fast enough or far enough to evade its grasp.

In the corner of my vision, my dear husband clutched his heart, the Almighty's name rising from his lips in hoarse gasps.

Hisalir tossed his head back and laughed.

There was no escape.

I must protect Naman! He is mine *to protect!*

I closed my eyes and centered myself on the Almighty's name, the name of the Shining Guide, and the names of the first Quest. I chanted them first in the sacred language of Alimàzahre and then in the common tongue of Siléalaah, again and again.

E'Qahre, e'Zahràdalle, e'Dalaanem, e'Fidaanem, e'Ajaanem...

The black clouds wound around me and crept toward my feet. Snaking around my ankles, spiraling up my legs, swirling about my waist, feeding on the spasms in my middle and strengthening, reaching higher...

My esteemed ancestor the Prince of Virtue had stated that only athar could repel conjury.

Only athar.

Light might offer some defense against alchemy. But, against a direct assault by the coils of conjury, there was no such remedy.

The smoke threaded around my chest, wrapped around my throat, and spread over my head. Suffocating my air and stifling my hope...

"*Riqeta!*" came Naman's distant scream.

Almighty, Shining Guide, my Lady Queen, my Graced Queen, my Honored King...

The black fume seeped inside my nose. Boiling my blood.

Two more names came to my tongue, unbidden: *Lucian. Malika.* Beneficence and Fulfillment.

I had neither athar nor the magic to set it alight.

But I was a servant of the Rulers of Light.

And that was *enough.*

My esteemed ancestor the Prince of Virtue had stated that only athar could repel conjury.

But there was another way, a way of which he had not written but a way I could achieve.

By the power of will, to become one with the Light, permitting no space for fear.

The smog assaulted my heart. But I did not fear, my faith absolute. I allowed the darkness no anchor.

E'Qahre, e'Zahràdalle, e'Dalaanem, e'Fidaanem, e'Ajaanem... Lucian... Malika...

Light coalesced at the very core of my being.

With every recitation of the sacred names, it pulsed outwards.

Breath by breath, vein by vein, inch by inch, repelling the black magic.

Excruciatingly slowly, leaving ample time for the molten smoke to char my flesh...

My will remained strong. My courage did not falter. There was no fear within me. My pain was far away, and my blood held no horror for me. My anger was only for the Quest's sake. I desired only to serve the Almighty, to nurture Koroma, and to protect Naman. I chose the Light without reservation.

The shadowed man's conjury wielded no power over me.

The black magic could wound neither my soul nor my body.

It retreated.

Falling to the ground and fading like ordinary mist.

I opened my eyes to Naman's tearful joy and the monster's shock.

Drawing a pair of straight-edged lightweight swords, I leapt forward, pushing off the ground, swung my legs up, and kicked Hisalir's chest. At the same moment, I ignited the spell I had seeded into his blood.

Hisalir fell, energy draining from his body in like water from a sieve.

As his back hit the earth, I pushed off his chest and twisted midair, landing in a crouch behind his head.

With my blades at his throat.

Another spell locked his armor, hardening and fusing the metal such that he could not move.

Unable to move, gasping for breath, bleeding, darkened green eyes wide, the monster stared up into my face, looming upside over his.

I tensed my swords and cut into the skin of his throat. Blood erupted in pulses of red.

"Wait!" Hisalir cried. "I yield!"

I froze.

"I yield, Riqeta! I surrender!" Hisalir pleaded, his unctuous voice rising so many pitches that it resembled the shrillness of a child. "Let me go! Please, Riqeta!"

I glanced down into his gaze.

"Don't kill me, Riqeta!" Hisalir begged.

There was no arrogance, no falsehood, in his eyes. Black

flames still burned, but desperation rendered them nothing but the faintest of embers.

I glanced up.

His followers and our soldiers seemed frozen where they stood, and Khonatir's honey scales swung wildly between gold and umber.

My dear husband stood gripping the arms of his chair. The desperation lining his eyes and spreading his lips melted to a look of pure and utter trust. A sign that this was my choice to make.

I glanced back down, brow furrowing as I stared at my fallen enemy.

In my ten years of military service to Zahacim, beginning when I was eleven and ending shortly before my twenty-first birthday and my wedding, I had slain many opponents. In the desert, in the mountains, on the plains, in villages, in castles and palaces—hundreds upon hundreds had met their ends at my hand.

In all of those battles and executions, by myself and as part of an army, I had never once broken the laws of engagement. Never once caused damage that would last beyond the end of the attack, neither to bodies nor to structures nor to spirits. Never tortured, never pillaged, never raped. Never once murdered an innocent, never once killed one who yielded. Despite great pressure to do so.

That, the combination of my prowess with complete discipline, was why I was reputed so highly. Why Naman had even considered marrying me. Why, despite all the torments burdening my spirit, I had never doubted that I was an adequate servant of the first Quest.

But this moment was a temptation unlike any ever before.

Hisalir deserved death more than anyone I had ever fought. His crime was unrivaled in Icilia's history for its evil, and so was his potential to wreak greater harm.

If I do not kill him... he will kill so many more. He will destroy Icilia!

Yet I had vowed to never break the laws of engagement...

My hands twitched uneasily on the hilts of my swords, drawing my gaze to the gleaming blades of my favorite pair. Naman had forged them for me with his own hands as a courtship gift. They marked the first time I had understood that he truly did want to marry me.

They reminded me of what I was supposed to be at his side.

If I do kill him... I will destroy Icilia.

Bile rose up my throat as my choices unfurled before me.

Should I accomplish what I most desire and become worthy of Naman's love, I will be his queen and the lieutenant monarch of Koroma. Because of that future position, all of my words and actions from our wedding onward now reflect upon him and upon Koroma's crown. And with my prior reputation of discipline, I will set an example for all of Icilia.

So... if I break the laws of engagement today, I will ruin not only my reputation but also Naman's... If the monarchs of one of Icilia's nations are directly *known to have violated the laws of engagement, then who in Icilia will then ever adhere to them?*

The darkness and chaos of Zahacim's war with Bhalasa will spread...

For nothing will remain forbidden.

The seven nations are so fond of war that their battles will wreak destruction beyond anything even I, who have seen so much, can imagine.

Beyond anything Hisalir could do.

For Hisalir will harm and savage and kill many—but the people of Icilia has the strength to recover, as we did after the conjurors' cruelty. We can return from the darkness with the right example—we will believe that Guide when she does come. But if I do this, if I violate the laws in this way, then the seven nations will themselves cause the same harm as Hisalir , while his followers continue fighting in his name, and no one will believe the Guide—for they will say that, if those known for their virtue like Naman and me do not follow the laws, then why should they?

The laws, the very soul, of Icilia will be destroyed...

And there will never be any recovery.

My hands clenched on the hilts of my swords.

"Please, your Highness," the monster begged.

I refuse to accomplish Icilia's destruction for *him.*

I uncrossed my blades and pulled them back. Then, rising, I walked to Naman's side.

May the Almighty bless Icilia with the Quest, for nothing less will remedy what I could not prevent.

CHAPTER 9
SPARKLING WITH SOMETHING AS BRIGHT AS SUNLIGHT

*Perspective: Crown Prince Naman tej-Shehenkorom, Heir to
Koroma
Date: Eyyéala, the twenty-ninth day of the tenth moon, Thekharre,
of the year 469, C.Q.*

Riqeta uncrossed her blades and pulled them back to her
sides. Then, the stern focus of her expression
unchanged, she rose and walked toward me.

Hisalir stared up at the sky, eyes wide, heaving sighs of relief as
he struggled weakly to break the melted edges that locked his
armor together.

His brother, Khonatir, had collapsed to his knees, hands
clasped over his heart, his lips moving faintly, as he cast looks of
utter gratitude in Riqeta's direction.

Both Hisalir's followers and our soldiers simply gaped,
mouths hanging open, at my wife.

My wife, my beloved Riqeta, whose gaze was only upon me.

My pulse was still pounding wildly in my ears from the duel
and those endless moments of her choice, yet I curved my lips up
in a smile. I had no idea what she needed after such a battle, but I

wanted to be present for her, and perhaps a smile was a good way to begin.

There was no answering smile as she reached me and offered a formal bow, as she had at the start of the battle. "Your Highness," she intoned, "in service to the Almighty and the Quest, are you pleased with my victory in your name?"

Everyone in the clearing, both foe and those not quite, seemed to hold their breaths.

For what she was really asking was whether I was pleased with her decision to spare Hisalir.

And I... I *was*.

I had wanted my wife to kill him.

His death would be safety and justice and service to the Quest.

Yet... after he yielded... sparing him was all of those blessed intentions and *more*.

Riqeta had saved the honor of Koroma's crown and of the Quest's monarchs by keeping the laws of engagement inviolate. She had retained for us the Almighty's blessing. Because of that, recovery from whatever crime the monster next committed would be possible.

It was a greater victory than his death alone would have achieved.

A choice reminiscent of the blessedness and brightness of sunlight.

And it was all hers.

Saying that it was in my name and attributing it to me was in accordance with etiquette and properly reverential to her future monarch, but really it was all hers. The Almighty's, the Quest's, and *hers*.

These were the things I needed to say, but my foolish, frantic tongue could not seem to find its eloquence.

So, instead, I grasped her elbows, tugged her toward me, bent down, cupped her face, and kissed her.

A full kiss, gently caressing, savoring her taste, enjoying the reality that she *lived*. That she had *survived* the blackest, most utterly terrifying evil I had ever seen.

For a few moments, I did not care that our enemies were watching or that these things were supposed to be private. I did not mind the bloody swords in her hands. All that mattered was Riqeta's choice—and, though she did not return the kiss, she did seem to welcome it, angling her face and her lips to allow me better access.

Until at last she drew away. Her expression immediately hardened.

Before I could wonder whether I had made a mistake, she grabbed the hilts of both swords in one fist, seized my hand off her right cheek with the other, and pulled me behind her.

My heart warmed—she was protecting me.

In front of the silent, staring throng, Riqeta declared, her amber-brown eyes luminous gold in the sunlight, "The best has prevailed on the battlefield! Though death was not dealt, the result is clear: I have achieved victory over Hisalir bi-Mutanacer."

No one dared to move. Even Hisalir ceased his struggles—though he could not turn his head to see us, from his expression of intense focus in my farsight, I did not doubt he was listening. Fear still flooded his blackened eyes.

"By the terms of the duel," Riqeta continued, "there can be no retribution." Her fiery amber eyes (so perfect a description despite her water sorcery) swept over the followers and the soldiers. "In the stead of death, on my own honor, I offer you one chance for redemption."

The offer was within her right, as the victor of the duel, yet, regardless, I would have agreed. How badly I wanted to help redeem the monster's followers! Even if they were on the path to monstrosity themselves.

Khonatir fluttered his wings, looking longingly at Riqeta, but did not move. The monster's followers exchanged glances but did not move either. Some of our soldiers stirred and left the enemy's ranks, Captain bi-Himacer and Lieutenant Gatiemt among them, and assembled behind Riqeta and me, but most, including Sergeant bia-Donacera, did not move.

Even in defeat, Hisalir was too enthralling.

Riqeta nodded sharply, pivoted, pulling me behind her, and marched toward where our former attendants had picketed our horses across the glade. The few soldiers remaining with us, only twelve in number, rushed after her.

I glanced back.

Hisalir, still trapped where Riqeta had felled him, was beginning to seethe, the black embers flaring to flames in his eyes.

Khonatir was gliding toward him, even as his gaze flickered wistfully to Riqeta and me.

How different they are... I watched the two brothers with both my physical and magical sights. *One evil and one so inherently good.* Sympathy washed over me. *How blind Khonatir is to his brother's falsity. Far more than I was to the lies of the nobles. May the Almighty bless him with redemption! Riqeta and I could not achieve it, but, perhaps, someday, someone will...*

Although I do wonder: he adores Riqeta even though she defeated and—as the monster likely thinks—humiliated his brother. But would he have adored her if she had killed Hisalir? Particularly after he yielded? To Khonatir, it would be his hero killing his beloved brother... I shuddered. *Perhaps it is best for Icilia that we do not know what such betrayed adoration and broken love would have unleashed...*

We reached the picket line, and Riqeta proceeded to examine my saddle, before indicating with a quiet word that I should mount.

As I did so, a shine of silver caught my gaze.

The hilts of Riqeta's destroyed swords and daggers were still lying in the dead grass.

How horrifying it had been to watch them crumble in her hands! Even though she had not been left unarmed...

Though my heart was skipping beats at the memory, I opened

my mouth to call Riqeta's attention to the remains of her precious blades.

But, before I could, Riqeta uttered a terse order, and the remains of our convoy lurched into motion. Within minutes, we were riding away through the bare-branched forest.

Behind us, Khonatir was rubbing his hands over the melted metal of his brother's armor, painstakingly undoing Riqeta's powerful spells, his sweet face creased with concentration and the enormity of the task. Even as he worked, his brother fumed, his skin graying (instead of silvering, like others of the Mutharrim) with the raging intensity of his fury, but remained silent.

Those hilts were abandoned.

I attempted to call her attention once more. Surely we could retrieve them before we entirely left!

Perhaps—I have not yet had an occasion to observe this—she does not feel sentimental about her weapons...?

Then, even as we rode, Riqeta pulled out a handkerchief, wetted it with a spell, and began to carefully, almost *lovingly*, clean blood from the edges of the swords she had held to the monster's throat.

The lightweight swords *I* had given her in our courtship, I realized, glimpsing the plainness of the barely functional design and the placement of a single brown quartz jewel in each hilt. While the others she had lost, far more elegant and adorned with silver as befitting a royal, were ones she had brought with her from Zahacim.

Ones with which she had fought more battles than I knew— and gifts from her beloved family.

And yet she had abandoned their remains.

My heart swelled to think she so valued my crude gifts, though she did not love me. Even as I wondered why she would abandon those her family had given her...

It was an easier topic upon which to dwell than the consequences of that duel for Koroma's future and for Icilia's as a whole (though no less dear), so I let it consume my attention as the miles passed.

Questions formed in my mind, flashes of observation gaining substance from reflection, so much so that my need for answers burned as acutely as a dehydrated throat.

I had known of her plan to defeat the monster, yes, but, now that I had witnessed how difficult its execution actually was, I was in awe of how strong her will was. And I wondered, as I had once before, just what she had needed to withstand in war to sharpen her determination to such degree.

Her iron will, her unbreakable discipline, was not born of her descent from the Prince of Virtue and the first Quest. I shared that ancestry, though from a different direction, and I, too, was royal, educated, and magically powerful. Yet, as I knew unerringly in my heart, I was not capable of the same feat. I was faithful, devoted, pious—but *her* faith, *her* devotion, and *her* piety were hardened like steel from trials and tests unlike anything I had ever experienced. Indeed, in comparison, I was an untested child, while she bore the seal of having proved the depth of her conviction.

Far from shaming me, these thoughts suffused me with pride. Riqeta was glorious, and I was *proud* of her and *honored* that she had accepted my hand.

Yet I could not help but wonder what those trials had been. And whether they still plagued her.

If she needed a confidant, then I wanted to be hers. If she was willing.

Oh Almighty, oh Dalaanem...

Thus consumed with concerns and questions, by the time we reached a suitable campsite, atop a defensible hill in a region to which the monster would not be able to track us (as Riqeta said), I had mustered enough daring to speak.

As soon as our tent was standing and we were alone, I blurted, "Riqeta, my love, I must speak with you!"

She looked up from removing her greaves and cuisses and the knives beneath. "About what, Naman?" Her fingers continued to efficiently open straps and ties, but there seemed to be a wary glint to her eyes.

I did not want her to be wary of me! "We do not have to speak if it does not please you!"

The wariness faded somewhat. "There is much of which we must speak." She straightened and began to unbuckle her belt, vambraces, and pauldrons.

I unbuckled my sword-belt and shrugged off my robe overcoat and tunic, then wondered whether she would let me help her for once.

Riqeta slid her gloves from her fingers and neatly placed them atop the stack she was making of her armor and weapons, near our boots on the rug laid out over the ground. Then she plucked a series of smaller knives from within her chainmail.

I should not ask, I thought, mouth dry. Though I had been too frantic and afraid for her to think so at the time, today I had finally received the awesome chance to witness her fight a duel worthy of her talent. She had been so beautiful to behold...

Riqeta slipped out of her chainmail shirt. Then, without hesitation, began to change from the light but sturdy leathers she wore under her armor to a nightdress. Her wedding ring gleamed silver on its chain...

I spun around, hiding my flushed cheeks, and switched to a nightshirt and trousers. Both her nightclothes and mine were covering, thick, and long-sleeved, suitable for the autumn nights, but the sight of her... *Come, Naman, this is not the moment! Her health matters more than my desires.*

"Naman," Riqeta called, "would you require water for washing?"

Startled, I glanced at the basin by our bedrolls—Colan usually filled it every night as we set up Riqeta's and my tent. But... he was not here. Riqeta and I had sent him back to Ináma two weeks ago.

If he was here... Perhaps he, too, would have betrayed us. I swallowed, tears welling in my eyes. *How could they abandon us! All the years of love and loyalty between my soldiers and me, and they abandoned me for a monster? The evil of whom they were already aware? And there is no guarantee that the ones who did return will stay, nor that those who were sent back would have remained loyal. The change was no act—the bond confirmed it. How could they...* A sob spilled from my lips as the true horror of it all crashed upon me in a tidal wave of anguish. *How could they...*

A pair of muscular arms turned me and wrapped around my waist, and a strong hand patted my back.

"It is too much," I whispered, clinging to her and pressing my face into her neck, desperate for comfort. "It is too much, Riqeta!"

She only continued to pat my back and did not answer—but I did not expect it. We both knew that, with his survival, the threat posed by Hisalir was far from resolution. And the nobles' lies had not even begun to be addressed yet.

The world was growing dark...

"I suppose I can finally see something of the meaning of my birth prophecy." A pained smile spread my lips. "The clouds of his conjury... they were black shadows on the blue sky. And if the sky's patterns are a reference to understanding what is to come, then such has been the true purpose of this entire journey. Discerning the way it will all become."

Riqeta patted my back once more and then drew me to arm's length. Gazing up into my eyes, hers a fervent liquid gold, she stated, "We are together in this war, Naman."

Those words washed over me like a wave of warm, soothing water, dispelling my anxiety and pain. As always, she knew exactly what I most needed, even when I did not.

My gratitude, oh Almighty, oh Dalaanem...

Smiling contentedly now, I dipped my head and lightly kissed her lips. Then, wanting to return what she had given me, I asked gently, "Riqeta, why did you leave the hilts of your swords and daggers behind?"

My wife froze in my embrace. Her expression shuttered. Her eyes cooled. But she did not pull away.

"Please, my love," I carefully entreated, "please let me be present for you as you are for me. The battle could not have been easy, my princess."

Riqeta pressed her lips together and lowered her gaze—something I had never seen her do. Except in front of her aunt and her eldest sister.

The tinge of fear to that reaction—after she had shown today how truly impenetrable she could be to fear—wrenched my heart.

Tightening my embrace, I sank down onto our bedrolls, extending my legs, and tugged her sideways onto my lap, cradling her the way she usually cradled me. Pressing my lips to the rough plates of her cheek, I murmured, "I love you, Riqeta. There is no need for fear with me."

That fear spread over her face until it crumpled her expression.

My heart crumpled in concert. "Riqeta," I whispered, deciding to try one more time, "there is nothing you could say that would turn my heart away from you. We are together forever, my princess."

She tilted her head back and looked deep into my eyes.

I held steady, trying to be courageous like her, though my pulse was roaring with the fear that she might find me unworthy of her confidence—

Riqeta broke the connection of our gazes and looked away.

I suppressed a sigh. So not today, if ever—

She threw her arms around my neck and leaned into me. "Those hilts remind me of terrible things, Naman."

I blinked, uncertain whether I had really heard that confidence, then quickly catalyzed so I could watch her expressions with my farsight. Pulling her closer, enjoying her warmth, stroking her soft, loose hair, I replied, "My love, you do not need to tell me, but... what terrible things?"

Her arms squeezed me slightly. "Their cruelty."

"Whose?" I asked, my heart again beating faster at the thought of someone being *cruel* to her.

"My family's," Riqeta whispered. And in my farsight... suddenly she seemed lost, her features dim with pain, like a small child unable to find her home.

"Ohh, Riqeta," I murmured, recognizing that agony, having witnessed it on the faces of too many children in Ináma, though I did not understand why. Zahacim's royal family was known for their devotion to their daughters. But perhaps that was not true for Riqeta... Rocking back and forth, I softly urged, "Tell me, Riqeta, my love."

And she did. As tears of the deepest anguish fell down her cheeks, she spoke of the terrible unkindness of her family.

After her father's death, his eldest sister the queen became her guardian under the laws of Zahacim. But when Riqeta, only a little girl, attempted to seek comfort from her beloved aunt, the queen spurned her, slapping her instead of embracing her. Within days of her father's funeral, the queen stole Riqeta's keepsakes of her parents, the prestigious rooms she had shared with them, and most of her rights as an heir to the throne. Despite Riqeta's secondborn status, the queen made it clear that she was less than all of her cousins, especially the queen's own daughters.

Those daughters followed their mother's lead. Abandoning any previous affection, the princesses taunted and mistreated Riqeta, their abuse reaching beyond words to punches, kicks, uncaring swipes of their swords, and the stealing of food, bandages, and other essentials. Their mockery often resulted in the spill of her blood. And though the daughters of the queen's sisters were also not too well treated, they joined in the abuse.

It should not have mattered whose daughter she was—for she was their sister regardless—but they had forgotten such truth.

Only one cousin was different: Serama, the youngest. From how Riqeta's eyes glowed as she spoke of her, Serama was her only true sister, in the way Zahacit princesses were supposed to be. She was the reason Riqeta's stride had never faltered, her world, her heart as the best of siblings were.

My own heart eased a little to think that, amid all the pain, Riqeta had always had one person who truly loved her.

Then, in Riqeta's twelfth year, insurgents challenged the crown, an assassin struck at the queen, and Riqeta proved herself more adept than her cousins in battle. Of all of them, she was the only one to detect the assassin's movements, and her quick response saved the queen's life.

In recompense, angered that a mere niece showed herself to be more talented than her own daughters, the queen sent Riqeta to combat the insurgents. At only eleven years of age, denied the counseling required by Zahacit law for her first kill.

Riqeta proved herself there as well, a valuable warrior under the command of the elder princesses, her aunts and great-aunts, and so, once the insurgents were defeated, the queen ordered her to lead an attack on Etheqa in response to a resource dispute. At the age of fourteen.

Zahacit law mandated that the minimum age for a soldier, whether princess, noble, or citizen, was fifteen.

At fifteen, having performed admirably in fulfilling the queen's every order, no matter how difficult to execute, Riqeta was a legion commander in Zahacim's war against Etheqa and led the decisive battle that won her nation the war.

In the year following, when Zahacim and Bhalasa declared war upon each other, she was made the commander of half of Zahacim's army, alongside the crown princess, and the direct head of the nation's special forces.

She was given rank but no honor. No respect. No love.

With every passing year, the queen's orders became increasingly more dangerous—and more illegal.

In the war with Bhalasa, her special operations squads were asked to do so many things that tore the laws of engagement to pieces. Thefts, assassinations, murders of innocents—twisted actions that were, while not as concentrated an evil as Hisalir's, still *evil*.

Actions ordered directly by the queen and her heir.

Actions reciprocated by the Bhalaseh king and *his* heir.

Crimes that Riqeta did everything to avoid committing, while still not failing her aunt, and that she did everything to discover and prosecute.

For, because of the iniquity allowed by their rulers, more than a few of the soldiers, on *both* sides, used the war as an occasion to indulge their very *worst* passions. Men and women, Areteen, Sholanar, Ezulal, Nasimih, those who possessed magic and those who did not. Citizens *and* nobles. Allowed such license by orders from the royals themselves.

It was war untamed by the laws of the Quest.

Beneath the cover of battle, Riqeta, with Serama at her side, hunted down and executed every such violator she could find. But she could not touch the royals, and so the violence did not stop.

Until my father interceded. Unknowing of the horrors, only thinking that the war had gone on for too long and believing he had a solution.

The summit where Riqeta and I had met was the first time she had had a chance to actually *rest* in a full decade.

Not just *any* decade but the decade in which she transformed from a girl to a woman.

Thus was she shaped, and thus was the true reality of the reputation of eastern and southern Icilia's most fearsome warrior.

"I am worried, Naman," Riqeta whispered into my shoulder, "that Hisalir will find a way to seize advantage of this madness. That he will harness the evil brewing in Zahacim, Bhalasa, and Koroma and spread it until the seven nations drown in it, and the laws and the rules are all dead beneath the weight of his crimes." She exhaled a shuddering breath. "I chose the correct path. Killing him would have done all of these things and much more. But this path will not be much easier to bear..." She rested her head on my shoulder and quietened. Stiffening slightly.

Exhaling a sigh myself, I drew her away from my chest.

She let me, but her expression blanked.

I smiled as warmly as I could and, pulling my sleeve up over my hand, began to gently wipe away her tears. Each drop, like each of her words, was such a source of pain for me, and I could only hope that, in entrusting both to me, she had found some hint of relief. I could only pray that drying the one would help ease the weight of the other from her heart. I did not want her to regret granting me her confidence.

Again, Riqeta let me, but now her expression filled with confusion.

How many years has it been since she possessed the security to cry? How many years has it been since anyone besides Serama dried her tears?

My heart welled with a desire to shower her with affection, to show her that she deserved so much more than even this, to soothe away every hurt and grief until her heart was radiant with every joy.

With that prayer in my heart, I managed to find my eloquence enough to say, "Thank you, my love, for your trust. I promise that I will not break it. You are safe with me." Returning my hand to her waist, I pressed a kiss to her lips, sealing the vow.

She accepted the kiss only for a moment before pulling away. Tilting her head back, she looked into my eyes, her own desperate and her lips pursed into a small pucker, sharpening the angles of her face. Her lips parted slightly, but then her forehead creased, and she seemed to struggle with what to say.

I waited patiently, ignoring the tears still spilling down my face. I suspected I would be weeping for some time to come. Her suffering felt like gashes on my own soul.

Riqeta hesitated a moment more, then used the sleeve of her nightdress to clean my face. In brusque strokes, yet sweet nevertheless.

I leaned into her touch, kissing her hand whenever it passed my lips, my tears finally ceasing.

Once the last drop was gone, she said, seeming to push herself to meet my gaze, "I am sorry for not telling you, Naman. You are hurt, and that was not my intention. You have been so open with me, and I am sorry for giving you only silence in return."

It was as though her words granted permission for the hurt beneath my shared anguish to rise. While she had been speaking, I had refused to consider anything else, unwilling to let pity for myself distract me from being present for her. But now... I could not help the hurt likely crumpling my expression.

Riqeta winced—something I had never seen her do before.

I sighed and made my lips curve upward. "From all my journeys to Ináma, I have understood that such abuse does not leave many resources for trust. It is not easy to confide such things... And how could I expect you to trust a strange man who seemed unreasonably infatuated with you?" I forced a chuckle, but it did not sound quite right. Then the words I had not intended to say fell out of my foolish mouth: "Did you not marry me just to escape?"

Riqeta recoiled, violently, nearly falling from my lap before she steadied herself with my help, and stared at me, mouth falling open. Her beautiful amber-brown eyes filled again with tears, and, in a manner entirely unguarded unlike ever before, she whispered, "Is that what you think, Naman?"

I could not hold her gaze or bear the pain within it. My eyes fell to the embroidery hemming her sleeve. "I do not know what else to think." I sniffled, trying to hold back more tears. "Apologies for my idiocy, but I-I-I *need* to hear the words— they matter so much to me— and—"

A strong hand gripped my chin, curling into my beard, and pushed my face up so that my eyes met hers.

Her glorious amber-brown eyes were sparkling with something as bright as sunlight...

"I love you, Naman," Riqeta declared. "I have since I realized that you are actually a good and just man, one who has honored the Quest's laws with every breath." She actually beamed, her dimples deep dips above each corner of her lips. "My aunt and my cousins could not poison me against you, and nothing else will either." Then her smile faded. "I swear upon my faith: I only married you because I love you, and I only defected to Koroma because I did not want my family to hurt you as well. I did not want to tell you, either of my history or of my heart, because I was afraid my taint would repulse you." Her eyes fell. "I cannot lose you, Naman. You and Serama and Princess Diyana sej-Shehasfiyi are all I have in the world."

As she spoke, my heart filled and swelled and burst with light and love, a ray of the sun shining in my chest, and, laughing happily, I kissed her, enjoying her response, deeply caressing her lips until it felt like my breath became hers. Then, still laughing, dizzy with joy, I threw myself back on our bedroll and pulled her down atop me, enjoying how her hair spilled onto my face. Wrapping my arms around her, I held her to my chest and announced, "I am the happiest man in Icilia!"

How grateful I am to you, oh Almighty, oh Dalaanem! Thank you for fulfilling my prayers in the most beautiful way!

Riqeta chuckled, sounding a little overwhelmed. "I did not think you would be so happy."

"I *am* so happy!" I kissed her head, loudly smacking my lips, and began to curl my fingers through her hair. Then I teased, "You have not told me anything about Asfiya's third princess! I expect to hear why she ranks so highly in your heart in the morning. And how your rival for the title of Icilia's fiercest warrior became so dear a friend!"

Though her lips curved into a smile in my farsight, Riqeta responded seriously, "I assure you that I will, Naman. I have no other secrets, and I will never keep another secret from you."

"Whatever pleases you," I said, grinning. "As always, I rely upon your judgment." I spoke lightly, but utter sincerity welled in my voice.

In response, silence... Then she said, a note of wonder in her tone, "How in Icilia did the Almighty find me worthy enough to bless me with you?"

Alit by the same wonder, I laughed and repeated those words, meaning them as she did.

She breathed a chuckle and relaxed atop me.

The proximity of her presence... the perfume of her natural scent... the passion of her words of love... the thoughts of her beauty built within me until I could not help but ask, "Would you like to spend tonight together, my love?"

Riqeta lifted her head and cast me a wry look. "We were already going to do that."

A flush heated my face, neck, and ears. "Well, I mean—"

She laughed suddenly, her expression more open than I had ever seen it. "I do know what you mean. And yes. Although..."

I tensed, sudden fears of her being hurt worse by the duel than I had known filling my mind—

"Naman," she said, her plates buzzing, "I am on my monthly cycle."

Her cycle? But that means... Wait, was she bleeding... But the duel! My mouth fell open once again this day. "He kicked you right there! And-and-and you were in pain! *Oh, Riqeta!*" I tugged her against me, a sob tearing from my throat as I thought of how difficult the duel must have been for her—and how brave she had needed to be, with the attempts he had likely made to take advantage of both her blood and her pain.

I could not imagine any of it, nor was it my place to demand to know of her cycle, and certainly she would not have allowed the duel to take place if she believed herself to be truly disadvantaged, but... I wished I had known. If only to offer her comfort...

How even more glorious did I now know her victory to be!

"Oh Dalaanem," Riqeta breathed. "No one besides Serama has ever cared, and my family and half of my soldiers were women who understood the pain." She raised her face from my neck and kissed my nose. "You are amazing, Naman, and I love you. And do not worry—I protected myself, and I am well."

I sighed and smiled softly, the peak of my terror ebbing in the wake of all of those wonderful words. I would never tire of hearing them...

"I still would like to spend the night with you," she said, "but in a limited manner, as appropriate."

"Of course," I agreed, once again awash with joy, my smile turning besotted.

Riqeta raised her head again, her arms winding tightly around me, and our lips met in the most passionate kiss...

The most terrible day of our lives was followed by the best night.

CHAPTER 10
BLESSED TO EVEN BE ABLE TO SEE THIS EVIL APPROACH

Perspective: Princess Riqeta Shehenkorom, consort of the Heir to Koroma
Date: Eyyéthar, the twenty-second day of the eleventh moon, Mirkharre, of the year 469, C.Q.

A change in the air, fainter than a flicker, caught my attention.

A smile tugged at the corners of my lips—only one person could move so quietly...

In the next moment, my husband disappeared from my side.

A gasp, a thud, like a body crashing against stone, and I spun to see Naman pinned to the wall of a nearby house, his back flat against the stone, and a dagger glinting silver at his throat. Shock and fright began to twist his expression.

She is here. Delight started to blossom in my heart. Naman's expression hurt, but I thought, or rather prayed, that he would see this moment as I did...

His attacker, a short, hooded armored figure who held him against the wall with an arm across his chest, seemed to loom over him as she snarled, "Have you been treating my sister well?"

The smile pulling at my mouth spread fully.

How I loved that she cared so much about my well-being!

So many months had passed since I had seen her at my wedding in the Zahacit capital of Rushada.

How I loved that she was *here*, in Ináma, thousands of miles from her post in northern Zahacim!

Even as I wondered why...

Naman exhaled a laugh and relaxed against the wall. "Princess Serama-zahak, that is a question for your sister, as only she can judge whether she is well-treated. Although I do hope she would say yes." He grinned down at her, even as he remained careful of her blade. "The Almighty's blessings, Sister."

I beamed, my heart glowing like a sun-warmed jewel at the proof of my faith in him.

Serama scowled up at him, her fingers tightening on the hilt of her dagger. Then a reluctant smile quirked her lips. "You are not so bad, your Highness." She stepped back, removing her arm from his chest and her blade from his neck. "Though it is always wise to verify one's assessments."

Naman blinked. "Verify?" He did not even raise a hand to check whether she had left a nick.

I could not help but laugh a little. "Serama is the one who advised me that I was choosing well in accepting your hand, Naman."

My husband gasped, then beamed, as bright as a star, and threw his arms around my little sister. Loosely, lightly, still quite proper, but with such genuine enthusiasm that Serama only smiled and returned it, patting his back with her open hand.

How strange a sight it was, my husband in his soft lilac robes embracing my sister, whose plate and chain mail gleamed silver under the midday sun. Her mahogany hair, several shades redder than mine, the bun barely visible beneath a warrior's helm, clashed strongly with his red-blond curls, neatly combed under his cap and circlet as they were, as did her firm stance and weapon-laden belt with his gentle demeanor. And yet they were in harmony together, two of the three people I loved most united in their love for me.

Gratitude to the Almighty, I thought. *And especially because, without the both of them, I would never have understood how blessed I am.*

Serama waited until Naman withdrew, beaming, then turned and threw herself at me with all the force of a charging warrior. "Hanny!" she cried, the Zahacit word for beloved sister sweet on her lips and in her alto voice. "Hanny, I miss you!"

Grinning, I caught her, easily absorbing the momentum of her leap, and held her to my chest, as I had since she was a child. "Serama," I whispered, tears suddenly welling in my eyes. "Hanny, how much I have missed you."

In response, she snuggled into me, wrapping her arms around my waist and pressing her face into the curve of my neck. And, for a moment, though she was eighteen, only an inch shorter, and had fought for two years at my side, it was as though I embraced the little girl I had helped raise. Indeed, for one eternal moment, we were returned to the days of our childhood, my desperate need for solace and her equally fervent need for love untainted by expectation. She had been my best student and I her first teacher, she my advisor and I her confidante, the two of us united together in our love for the Quest and for Icilia.

From the devotion I glimpsed in her gold-amber eyes, the devotion that matched my own, our bond was immortal. Beyond the reach of time or distance or even the allegiance of nations. Together forever, gifted to each other by the Almighty.

Just as Naman had described our own bond.

At that wondrous thought, I kissed her head. "I love you, Serama."

She giggled softly, a sound she only allowed in my presence, and tipped her head back to kiss my cheek. "I love you, too, Riqeta." Then that softness flowed into her usual animation as she drew back and declared, "Now tell me everything I have missed!" A playfully dark glance at her brother by marriage. "How is life with that one?"

Naman—who had been watching us with such utter joy that his blue eyes glowed like the unshadowed sky—laughed again. Even as eagerness rose in his expression for my answer.

I offered him a smile, before looking back at my sister. "I am happy." If these last three weeks in Naman's arms on the journey north were any indication, I would never be short of happiness again.

My husband actually squeaked, such was his excitement.

Serama dropped her gaze, her lips curving wider as she squeezed my hands. "I am glad for you. It has been long in coming."

I squeezed hers in return, acknowledging the unspoken memories of the dark side of our childhood. Then I frowned and asked, "Are you cold, Hanny?"

Though she was a powerful sorcerer of the inferno and so naturally was warmer than most, Serama had always despised the chill, whether in the desert or in the mountains. The aversion went deeper than fear for health, as she was one of the freeze-resistant Areteen and furthermore trained to withstand low temperatures. So surely she was cold here, where snow fell in great gusts beyond the shelter of the city and the temperature even within was not too far above the freezing point!

Serama giggled and briefly flung her arms around me again. "The heat spells you taught me to craft work wonders! I can even wear armor now without any fleeces! The outposts are so much more pleasant now!"

Some of my tension drained. She was adjusting to the reality of my departure. That was excellent, because I knew both that I would never return to Zahacim and that she would never leave our birth-nation.

Perhaps understanding the direction of my thoughts, my sister dipped her head, a silent, solemn acknowledgment. Then smirked. "No need to wonder whether *you* are cold—you regard the cold as little as one of the Sholanar does." She twisted to look at Naman. "Have you realized yet that she uses only the faintest spell for warming and some padding, Hally? Is that not so perfect for the renowned Sword of Prudence?"

Naman seemed overcome by the address, the Zahacit word for precious brother, but managed to compose himself enough to awkwardly say, "No, Hanny, though I had wondered. I am glad she is not cold, and indeed, it is."

Serama grinned again, equally delighted by his address in response, not minding the awkwardness. Then she said, switching abruptly back to solemnity, "Please, Hanny, we have much to discuss."

Though joy filled my heart at watching my sister and my husband bond, I nodded, steeling myself for the conversation that would come. I did not need to look at Naman to know his agreement, but I still met his gaze and asked, "If you would allow?"

The conversation to be had would involve sensitive Koromic matters, and, though I trusted Serama with my soul and my duty, she was a foreign princess. The crown heir needed to approve.

His smile fading, Naman sighed and answered, "Of course." He gestured to a nearby little public garden, currently empty amid the cold and snow, tucked into the side of the royal residence. "If you would cast a spell to prevent anyone from hearing us, this would be the best place to talk. We have a little time before the appointment with Duke Theriett."

Serama and I nodded and began to cast, in tandem as we had long done, spells for warding our speech, as well as ones for warmth. By the time we sat down on the iron chairs arranged in the center of the dormant flowerbeds and tiny shrubs, the garden was more protected than many of the palace's meeting rooms, and perhaps warmer as well. The warming spells Serama and I were using had both melted the snow in moments and evaporated the water left behind.

Naman folded his robes around him, a motion of unconscious elegance, and looked up at me. Asking his lieutenant to speak for him.

I can hardly comprehend how many of my rights Naman has restored, I remembered, my lips tilting up at the corners again.

At my side, Serama beamed, and, for both of us, the hurt of her eldest sister casting me, her rightful lieutenant, aside finally began to heal.

That delight quickly vanished as I began to speak. In concise terms, I described the reason for Naman's and my mission in the south, what we had pieced together regarding the lies of Koroma's nobles, and our discovery of the true nature of the insurgent. Then the duel. And the desertion of most of the Koromic soldiers present.

None of them had come after us, and the ones who had remained loyal to us seemed to regret their decision at least a little. There was magic, conjury, that had clung to them for a time, but it did not account for the full breadth of the change.

Naman and I suspected that the monster's soldiers had whispered something to them. Something they refused to now admit to us. Something that exploited the vulnerabilities that lingered even in the hearts of the honorable. Something they could still whisper to others.

It was why I no longer used the soldiers' assistance in guarding Naman.

If Koroma's honorable soldiers were so easily recruited, would not the tainted armies of Zahacim and Bhalasa eagerly pursue the monster's banner?

"I cannot help but think," I concluded, "that this is the beginning of an age of evil. When conjury first appeared, the Prince of Virtue quelled it within a few years because all of Icilia united behind him. That is not possible today."

Naman sighed. "I would wish it were not true, but even I am not so naïve to deny our disunity. And, now that we have looked into the eye of that evil, it would be blindness entire to deny that this darkness is coming."

Serama scowled at her hands. Then she glanced up at both of us with an approving smile. "Riqeta, you chose best in sparing him when he begged for his life. The laws of engagement are clear that yielding is a superseding law; adherence to it is greater than the terms of dueling to death. Hisalir was dishonorable to even ask, but your response was a decision worthy of your honor and your prudence, and I am proud of you. We will find a way to bear whatever consequences come of it."

I exhaled, elated, despite the horror, at her approval. I had known she would, with even greater certainty than I had known Naman would, and I did not doubt myself, but the words were still a draught of utter reassurance.

Her smile turned bleak. "But the situation is worse than you know. Zahacim may have sworn to the alliance last year, but already she grows discontented, and her heart is beginning to turn against Koroma." She hesitated, wetting her lips. "Riqeta, Misleta wants to challenge you and your loyalty to Koroma in war."

Naman gasped and exclaimed something, but I could only stare.

Does Misleta truly hate me so much that she would risk her soldiers' lives in war?

Horror seized me, as black as conjury, that Koroma's soldiers would die needlessly and so *brutally* because of *me*... That what happened with Bhalasa would be repeated with Koroma...

All while Hisalir himself continued to wreak evil upon our land and our people...

A matching pain in her own gaze, Serama placed a hand on the pauldron covering my left shoulder. "Her anger has only begun to blaze, but it is coming, Riqeta. Not in what remains of this year, nor next year, nor perhaps the year after—but it is coming. I would not be surprised if Zahacim soon began to renege on the trade agreement."

Naman reached over and grasped my hand, kissing it and threading his fingers through mine. Exhaling softly, he lowered his head for a moment. Then he glanced at me and said, smiling wanly, "We will find a way to bear this consequence as well, my princess." He squeezed my fingers. "It is not your fault, Riqeta."

I pressed my lips together and sighed. "It is difficult to believe that."

"But it is true," Serama replied, dropping her hand from my shoulder to her sword-hilt. Her expression set into hard lines. "Misleta's darkness, like Mother's, is her own fault. They used you, Sister—do not spare them a single thought of guilt."

I did not raise a dispute, seeing the wisdom in their words. As Naman said and as I had learnt through the harsh crucible of war, I could only be responsible for my own actions. The rest needed to be trusted to the Almighty's blessing.

My husband and my sister offered me smiles, seeming pleased by my acceptance.

Then Naman asked anxiously, "So, then, with this possibility of war on two fronts, is there any alliance we might make?"

I rubbed the hilt of a lightweight sword. Only one name came to my mind: "We could attempt to speak with Princess Diyana." As was custom for Asfiyan royals, I did not refer to her without her title, though she had always been below me in rank.

Naman nodded. "Your dearest friend and first cousin would listen, would she not?"

"She would," Serama said, "and her husband, Prince Beres, is the sort of magician you need to heal Mutanacere. He is a compassionate and honorable man, so I can easily see him agree to do it, even if the cost is high." She tapped the hilt of a dagger strapped to her belt. "But the question is whether her father and her eldest sister would listen to her."

"Indeed," I said. "Princess Diyana has wonderful sisters and loving parents. But King Alafen-asfiyi and Crown Princess Rajana-asfiyi are not easy to persuade once they have chosen a course. Now they have designated Koroma as their rival, they will not bend easily."

Naman sighed, shoulders slumping, and covered his face with the hand not holding mine. "I cannot see the path forward." He smoothed his mustache, before grimacing. "In four months, my world has gone from mostly bright to mostly dark. And, with every revelation, we seem further and further lost in the depths of an abyss we cannot escape. As though that eye has already swallowed us!"

It was my turn now to squeeze his hand. "Naman, we must trust in the Almighty and in the first Quest. The first Quest brought our ancestors out of the darkness; surely they will not ignore the pleas of their children."

"And, indeed," Serama added, "we are blessed to even be able to see this evil approach."

"That is true." Naman sighed and then offered Serama a faint smile. "Thank you for traveling all these miles to tell us this, Hanny."

I opened my mouth to express my gratitude as well.

Serama switched back to her usual boisterous demeanor. "Please, Hally! It is a *pleasure* to get away from our old aunts!" She turned to me and placed a hand on her heart. "They actually banned magic from the sparring arena! And they will not let us soldiers read anything beside the oldest of tomes!"

My lips twitched at the corners. "Serama, those are *your* recommendations." Before my wedding, Serama and I had presented a list of ideas to the elder princesses for helping the army recover from the war.

"So!" She widened her eyes, perfectly imitating the fussiest elder princess, and tucked a fist at her hip. "It is all simply preposterous!"

Naman, who was already giggling, burst into an open laugh, tossing his head back and covering his mouth.

Serama promptly did the same, laughing so hard that tears spilled down her cheeks.

I allowed a brief chuckle and waited until their levity cooled. Then I said, standing, "We should begin the walk to Duke Theriett's office."

Their faces aglow with lingering amusement, Naman and

Serama rose. Both of them, but especially Naman, seemed lighter, lines of tension disappearing, the laughter having drained the stress of our discussion and endowed courage to withstand the approaching darkness as only joy and love could do.

That lightness came just in time, for, moments after we left the garden and started up to the third level, a group of small children jumped on Naman and me. Laughing, giggling, shrieking questions, they insisted on demanding all of our attention as we walked—and, the moment they realized another princess was with us, all of Serama's as well.

As we explained the difference between daggers and knives, Serama and I exchanged a glance full of reminiscence. It was custom in Zahacim for the princesses to teach the ten-year-old children of each village on the use of weapons every spring. Those days had been some of Serama's and my favorite memories, until Misleta removed me from the roster of teachers. Even that delight Naman was now returning to me.

Amid the children's high-pitched questions and laughter, the walk to the duke's office passed almost too quickly.

At the door of the large, low horizontal building, Naman gently bid the children farewell, promising another visit to the orphanage before we left.

Since we had arrived in Ináma the day before yesterday, Naman and I had spent every morning with the children and every evening with the patients at the hospitals. Neither group seemed any less eager yet for the next visit.

Once the children had scampered off, I turned to Serama and said, "Would you wait at the royal residence for us? Or here, if you are comfortable?" As a foreign princess, she could not come with us to a meeting with a Koromic noble. Though I wanted to spend every moment I could with her before she left...

Serama saluted—exactly as she had when I was her commander—and began to settle into a guarding stance by the door.

"Oh, Hanny, why do you not join us?" Naman exclaimed. "I am sure your analysis would be valuable."

My sister and I stared at him.

That was a huge demonstration of trust—the sort that would receive negative remark from the whole of the Koromic court—the sort no crown heir should allow, *especially* after he learned Serama's nation prepared to attack his.

And yet he took this risk. Because he truly did trust her. All because I did.

My plates vibrated so hard I wondered distantly if they might crack.

Naman smiled, his eyes crinkling at the corners, and went inside without ceremony.

Serama flashed me a delighted smile, her plates abuzz, and gestured for me to enter first.

Exhaling and inhaling, I did so, putting aside the wonder of the moment and concentrating on what needed to be discussed.

The little entry hall beyond the door opened onto a grand library, circular, towering two stories high, its ceiling merged with the base of the tier above. Hundreds of books, painstakingly written and copied by Koromic, Asfiyan, and Etheqore scholars, filled the pine and spruce shelves lining the walls all the way to the top. In the center of that delightful array of shelves were sets of low, plush chairs organized around sturdy oak tables perfect for bearing the weight of dozens of tomes. Each set was placed upon a jewel-colored, circular rug, and the rugs covered the floor like miniature circles neatly spaced within a larger one. Large, enchanted slabs of white quartz inset into the walls bathed the chamber in shades of warm yellow, and under those lights a few scholars strolled and read, enthralled by the volumes around them.

It was the sort of cozy room Princess Diyana (a bigger devotee to books than Naman, Serama, or me) would declare she wanted to spend a season exploring.

How I hoped that, one day, she might be able to visit me! A

dream I only dared to have because Naman seemed so very happy to welcome my friends.

But that thought was not relevant here.

Amid those shelves, across from the entryway and on the right and the left, were doors that led deeper into the building.

Composing myself, I waited until all of three of us had removed our boots and then led the way through that wonderful library into the hallway on the far side.

At the end of the hallway, in front of his office's door, waited Duke Theriett, the governor of Ináma.

Unlike all the nobles Naman and I had met over the last few months, the duke was standing at attention, and, the moment that he glimpsed our faces, he rushed in our direction. Bowing deeply, the elderly man raised his hands to hold ours.

"Your Highnesses!" he exclaimed. "Have I told you yet how terrified I was when your attendants returned and you did not!"

Naman beamed, Serama grinned, and even I could not help but smile.

After so many weeks of nobles who thought themselves above the crown, Governor Theriett was our reminder that the Quest's favor yet remained in Koroma.

So, chuckling, Naman and I let him kiss the knuckles of our right hands—for the third time this stay—and then tugged him to his feet.

"May the Almighty bless you, Duke Theriett," Naman murmured, folding him into an embrace. "How glad we are that you care for us so."

The white-bearded man clutched Naman to his chest, as a father holding his son. "I feared we had lost you, your Highness!" he cried. "Do not expect me to quickly recover from that shock!"

"No," Naman said, looking up into the duke's pale gray eyes, his own reflecting the memories of this journey, "I would expect no such thing."

The trace of anguish in Naman's voice—which cut at my heart like a serrated knife—seemed to draw the duke's attention, for the old noble frowned. "If it pleases your Highness, my ears are open to listen to your troubles." He dipped his head to me. "You as well, your Highness." As was so sweetly characteristic of the man—and befitting for the governor of the City of Healing—he focused more on our health than whether our mission was fulfilled—and he did not even flinch at Serama's presence. Indeed, his gaze included her alongside me.

Naman glanced at me and, at my nod, said, "Duke Theriett, we have much to discuss."

The duke nodded, still frowning, and ushered to his office.

His office, I noted upon entrance, was a spacious room approximately twenty-five feet square. The only furnishings were a large oak desk, carved on the legs and edges to resemble stone textures, a matching cushioned, ornate chair behind it, two plainer padded chairs in front, a sturdy stepstool, and bookcases along each wall that were filled with the bland spines of record books. Light came from several pieces of quartz hanging like lanterns from the ceiling. Doors led out of the study on both the left and the right—possibly to a bathroom and to the duke's private chambers.

Duke Theriett urged Naman around the desk and onto his own ornate seat.

Serama and I exchanged a look. Within seconds, before Naman was fully seated, our wards, for detection and muffling our voices, were cast on each door.

With more bows, the duke invited Serama and me to sit in the padded chairs (which were high enough that, sitting upon them, we could see over the desk) and, waving off any concern for his age, took the stool. He shifted it so he was facing all of us, near the desk's right edge. Then, clenching his hands together in his lap, he said, "Please, your Highnesses, tell me of your troubles."

With a nod between us, Naman and I told him everything. The revelations about the nobles, the truth about the insurgent, the possibility of war, and particularly the determinations we had made about the orphanage and hospital staff's concerns.

After greeting the duke upon our return two days ago, Naman and I had spent many hours poring over the records of the orphanage and the hospital with both institutions' heads and key staff members (though the originals had already reached the capital per my earlier directive, the staff had still kept copies). Together, we had sorted out unnecessary expenses from necessary ones and produced many possible ideas for further economies.

For the nobles' lies meant their situation was not likely to improve.

And soon the crown might not have the funds to remedy their deficits.

So, though the discussion was painful, our only recourse was to aid as many as possible, while retaining the existing staff, on the minimum amount of currency. Many wonderful things, from tailored uniforms to sweet desserts, would have to be cut. Only the essentials for food, healing, and education could be kept.

As we told him all of these conclusions, the duke's face lost more and more gloss, until his Nasimih brown skin more resembled scratched tree bark than smooth glass. Horror and agony dimmed his gray eyes and twisted his features as his spine seemed to lose all steel, leaving him slumped forward on his stool like the frail old man he had never before appeared to be.

Confirmation, though bitterly learned, that he was innocent of all blame in these matters.

When the last word faded, he slowly shook his head, as though the motion would undo all the evil of which we had spoken. "This cannot be," he muttered.

Naman, Serama, and I said nothing.

"*This cannot be!*" the duke spoke louder. Then, leaping to his feet, shrieked the words. Stone circlet askew, gray eyes ablaze, magical fire sparking around his fists, he yelled wordlessly, the deep notes of his voice slicing into a piercing scream, and ran back and forth, his steps chaotic and disordered. A lifetime of all composure, discipline, and decorum fell away like the tears spilling down his cheeks.

Naman, Serama, and I did not react. Though I doubted that any of us were too easily withstanding the sight of his pain...

"How could he do such a thing!" Duke Theriett thundered. "How could he hurt his mother when she gave him all the respect and riches a young man could ever want? No matter the demands on her time! How could he hurt his father when he gave him all the love a son could want? No matter that blood did not connect them!" He angrily swiped tears from his face. "How could my peers do such things to their people! How could they cheat the wretched when they wax eloquent about compassion! How could they cheat *me* this way?" His features crumpled further as he halted in the far left corner of the room. "Is there any truth at all left in Koroma?"

The question seemed to break his heart, such was the misery darkening his gaze. Such was the lament in his voice as he cried out, "Dalaanem!"

That sacred name brought a flicker of light.

Turning, hurrying a few steps, he threw himself at Naman's feet. "How has it come to this?" he begged. "How could this have happened, your Highness?" The creases linking the corners of his nose to his lips and marking his cheeks and forehead sharpened so much that there seemed to be nothing left of his face save wrinkles. Yet, at the same time, he looked up at Naman with all the terrified desperation of a child.

Pushing back his chair, Naman slid to the ground and hugged the elderly noble.

I thought he would not answer, for what answer was there to give?

Yet then my husband whispered, "Prosperity does not last, or the Shining Guide would not have promised us the Quests."

I startled at the words. *That is true wisdom!* Amazed, I glanced at Serama and saw the same thought in her wide eyes.

Duke Theriett relaxed a little, but then he asked desperately, "So what can we *do*?"

"Other than pray the Quest will save us?" A mournful smile

curved Naman's lips. "Ensure that our own loyalty does not waver the slightest bit. In the prayer that the Quest might someday deign to come to save us."

"May the Almighty grant so," Serama and I whispered. "May Dalaaneman favor us so." The address for the Quest Leader, 'our Leader' in the sacred tongue, rose from our lips in anguished prayer.

The duke sighed. "May the Almighty give us strength. May Dalaaneman be pleased with us." He clutched Naman tighter for a moment, now the son holding his father. Then, wearing an embarrassed smile, he withdrew and shuffled back on his knees. "My apologies, your Highness."

Naman chuckled softly. "Of course, Uncle." His cheeks flushed a sweet pink. "I am always happy to be your solace as you have always been mine."

The duke's smile brightened a little, the embarrassment fading, gloss touching his features, before he helped Naman and himself stand. He ushered Naman back to his seat and returned to his own. Then, clasping his hands again, he said calmly, "My apologies for my outburst." He looked to me. "Your Highness, is there any action I might assist you in taking?"

I suppressed a sigh. *Is that not the real question? But to answer... What can I say but the truth? And in front of a man who kneels at my husband's feet, surely I can speak it without fear of revealing weakness.* Allowing a wry smile to quirk my lips, I replied, "Crown Prince Naman-korom and I are still discussing what action we might take. Princess Serama has already been of great aid to us—" I nodded to my sister— "but we have not yet managed to ascertain a course of action."

As I had expected, the duke's expression brimmed with understanding. "It is not an easy situation to answer, your Highness."

"Indeed, no," I said, "for, if all the nobles, save you and Princess qia-Kafalira, have committed to pursuing these various forms of treason, then the answer to these evils cannot be so easy as an accusation or an investigation." I chuckled wryly. "It is not as though we can imprison all of them."

"Nor would it solve our troubles." Naman sighed. "The crown relies upon the nobles to rule Koroma; we do not have enough officials and attendants to do much at all without them. We would be defenseless in war."

"And war is coming," I said grimly. "Not only with Zahacim —with Hisalir bi-Mutanacer."

The duke closed his eyes, exhaling deeply.

"So," Serama spoke for the first time, "we can move neither forward nor backward. Stamping out the evil is beyond our capability, but nor can we simply not act." She scowled, her fists clenching in her lap, then blew out a breath and turned to me. "It is the worst situation, Sister, and I will do anything you ask of me."

My plates vibrating at the show of support, I opened my mouth to answer. Then paused.

The ward I had placed on the door to the right was rippling...

I leapt to my feet, a lightweight sword drawn.

The door burst open.

A man shot through with a dagger in his hand, straight for Duke Theriett.

Pushing off against the ground, I jumped onto the desk, jumped again, and slammed feet first into the man, throwing him onto the ground. Immediately I leaned forward into a roll, then spun, and leapt again to my feet.

The man was already up, dagger still gripped, charging toward the duke. Too close to the noble to kick now.

Slipping around, I raised my sword and blocked his downward strike. My eyes widened as I finally caught a glimpse of the attacker's face.

Duke Theriett's grandson, Charan.

His eyes were bulging, murderous fury gleaming black within them.

"Charan!" the duke gasped. "What are you doing!"

"Charan, stop!" Naman cried.

The young noble smirked coldly. "Your time is over, old man." Casting his gaze down at me, he sneered, "Move out of my way, you little Areteen traitor! Short little stone-struck!" The last word was a particularly vile kindist slur.

I did not react, save to push him back a few steps. The strength in my arms overpowered his, despite his height of six feet.

Charan spat at me.

The saliva evaporated in the air—surely Serama's interference. I risked a glance back to confirm that she remained in her seat. As a foreign princess, she could *not* attack a Koromic noble, even such a monstrous one, without provoking war—an opening Misleta would seize. There was a possibility I myself, as a newly defected royal, would face censure for this, but she certainly could not help.

Despite the frightening glare on her face, she was still seated.

As were Naman and the duke. Though perhaps more out of shock.

Excellent, I thought. *All the better to protect them.* I pushed further. *For Dalaanem and Koroma!* The cry resounded in my mind, though it did not leave my lips.

Charan growled and broke away. Slashing wildly at me, he darted around and charged again toward his grandfather.

I blocked him again, this time nicking into his arm, an encouragement to desist.

Still he tried.

Another block, another nick.

Another attempt.

Block, nick.

Attempt.

I grabbed his shoulder and spun him forcefully away, the motion twisting his wrist so that he dropped his weapon, and slammed the pommel of my sword into the back of his neck.

He crumpled to the floor, his limbs thudding against the harsh stone.

Crouching, I pressed my fingers to his neck, checking that he still lived, and glanced up.

The duke was just staring, his skin so coarse that it seemed ready to flake away. All remnant of strength, of pride, of *hope*, was gone from his face. His breath was so shallow and his hands and knees so badly shaking that I worried his heart would fail.

For he seemed like a man whose heart had been torn, beating, from his chest.

Naman was already wrapping his arms around the old noble's shoulders. "Duke Theriett, let us go to your room," he was murmuring as he urged the man to rise. "A glass of water and a nap will do you well."

"But- but- my grandson!" the duke babbled, though he did not resist Naman's gentle tugs. "He is all I have, save you! His father- his mother- my wife- they are all gone! He cannot be gone, too!"

"Oh, Uncle Falahan," Naman said, the duke's name lined with a sigh, "my princess will take care of everything for us." Turning his head to the side, he gave me a nod before opening the door on the left and disappearing with the duke into the stairwell beyond.

I wrapped a ward tighter around him, protection against any other threats until I returned to his side. Then, bending down again, placing my sword aside, I pulled thin but strong braided silk rope from a pouch on my belt and proceeded to straighten Charan's limbs before tying them together.

Silence.

Then Serama said, calmly, as though an attack that shattered Icilia's laws had not taken place immediately before us, "I notice that you no longer use the swords and daggers my mother let you have when she promoted you to the rank of commander."

I glanced up at her as I pulled Charan's hands to the small of his back. "As Naman mentioned earlier, Hisalir destroyed them." No anxiety troubled me—I knew how she felt about those weapons.

"You did not return for the hilts, correct?" she asked. Her hands and feet twitched, and her plates vibrated, but she did not stand to try to help me restrain the noble—again, something a foreign princess really should not do.

"I did not." I looped the rope around Charan's wrists.

"Excellent." She offered a somber sort of grin. "Good riddance to those reminders, Riqeta."

I nodded as I tied a knot, keeping the rope loose enough that it would not injure the man's limbs—consideration he perhaps did not deserve but which the laws of engagement required.

"So the swords you use now..." Serama squinted, eyeing the weapon beside me. "That is one of Naman's gifts, is it not?"

I glanced at the narrow, straight-edged sword. Sticky spots of blood coated the last third of the blade to the tip—a tip which was now permanently red, as Hisalir's blood could not be washed off, despite all of my attempts at scrubbing it clean. Yet the marks of battle did not dim the weapon's shine.

Unlike those weapons Hisalir had broken, this sword was made with love. And love alone would it serve, though with gruesome deeds.

As I would.

"Yes, it is," I replied to my sister.

"Excellent," Serama said. "Because you will need its service, Hanny." A bitter smile spread on her lips as she gestured at the study. "Riqeta, as your prophecy states, the truth is always revealed through your hand: there is more evil in our world than we realized. First in the war with Bhalasa, then with the monster Hisalir, and now with this Charan. And I doubt this is the last time your hand will reveal evil and we will be forced to accept the consequences of such a revelation." She uttered a shout of mirthless laughter. "Blessed to even be able to see this evil approach, yet unable to stop it. May the Almighty save us!"

Observing the rage twisting Charan's features even in unconsciousness, I could not help but agree with her words.

To seek wealth over all else, betray one's lieges, and abuse one's people were already great evils. But to murder one's parent, the grandfather who had raised one and made one his heir... Charan's assault proved that not only Hisalir pursued such monstrosity.

So what other evils lurked in the shadows?

Dread brewed within my belly that Naman, Serama, Diyana, and I would soon be forced to know them all by name.

Even as I longed to ensure the truth was known.

CHAPTER 11
THE ONLY SOLIDARITY TO BE HAD

Perspective: Crown Prince Naman tej-Shehenkorom, Heir to Koroma
Date: Eyyélab, the seventh day of the twelfth moon, Alshatte, of the year 469, C.Q.

T he moment my stallion reached the top of the icy hill, I glanced up.

There, on the snow-covered horizon, was the sight I was most anxious to see, the view my farsight had already beheld: the towers of the capital of Samaha, soaring from their bases at the foot of Rifom's largest mountain, over the grand white walls, to a height of nearly five hundred feet, tipped with conical roofs each a different shade of purple.

Home.

After nearly four months and a lifetime's worth of evil news.

Finally.

"Do you see?" I eagerly asked. "Do you see Samaha now, my love?"

In my farsight, Riqeta nodded, the corners of her lips twitching in the way they did whenever she was attempting to not laugh at me. "I do, Naman."

"Is she not beautiful, my love!" I exclaimed. "How the purples glow under the midday sun! How vibrantly the snow reflects the glow!"

That twitch of amusement broke loose into half a smile. "Indeed, Naman." And to my delight, her manner eased just a touch.

I beamed and, urging my horse a few steps to the right, caught her hand and kissed the gloved fingers.

That smile became full, warming me as thoroughly as the rays of light above.

Much had changed between us since that night after the duel. With her most dreaded secrets known to me, Riqeta relaxed around me, a stiff tension vanishing from her shoulders that had before seemed part of her personality. She still remained grave and unwilling to laugh often as we traveled north, but I now understood it was more a part of her battle-ready discipline than any disdain for me (a conversation with Serama late the evening before her departure had also helped clarify these matters). Though now, at night, she stayed with me, allowing me all the cuddles and kisses I wanted.

I had before believed I had tasted happiness. But this last month, despite all the evil, had taught me that there was so much more to savor. For Riqeta, already the love of my life, was, now that she confided in me, the woman of my most cherished dreams...

Grinning, I kissed her fingertips again, enjoying the feel of the sun-warmed metal-backed leather. The earthy, metallic scent, once a dislike, was now as sweet as perfume to me...

"Naman," Riqeta said, jolting my attention back to her face, "I have a question I would like to ask you." There was a note of something in her voice—it was not quite wariness, not quite caution, but it did seem a sign that whatever she was about to ask was important to her.

My lips spread wider, and I turned so she would be able to see

my face. "Please ask!" I was always eager to know what was important to her.

Riqeta glanced at me, then away, before pressing her lips
together. A deep breath. A clench and unclench of the hand gripping her mare's reins. Then, hesitantly, the question: "Naman,
would you want children?"

My hand jerked on my reins, causing my stallion to prance
uneasily before I settled back into my saddle.

Riqeta stiffened, her expression blanking.

I forced myself to smile despite my shock. "Riqeta, whether to
have children and how many is your choice and the Almighty's,
not mine." *I do not want her to feel as though she must have a child
just so I can have an heir!*

She pressed her lips together again and looked away.

That is not the answer she wants... "Although," I said and
waited until she turned back to me before continuing, "I confess
that I have always dreamed of having children of my own, my love."
Grinning sheepishly, I gestured south. "I have spent so many years
in Ináma that I dreamed of children before I dreamed of a wife."

Riqeta stared at me for a moment. Then, like the sun shining
above, she grinned, fully, broader than she ever had before. White
teeth framed by rose lips, vibrating plates, and deep dimples in a
beautiful smile, she laughed, shaking her head slightly.

Dazzled, I could not help the blush heating my cheeks or the
foolish edge to the wide grin spreading my lips in response.

Still beaming, Riqeta kicked her booted feet out of her
stirrups.

I blinked, wondering what she was doing—

She crouched on her saddle before jumping to my horse.

"Riqeta!" I belatedly shrieked, my heart leaping up my throat.
"What are you doing!"

She laughed again and, with more casualness than she had
ever shown before, easily sat—despite her armor—on the other
side of my saddle's pommel, at the base of my horse's neck (my

stallion did not even twitch). Then she wrapped her metal-encased arms around my neck, nudged me forward, and, her vibrating plates tickling my mustache and beard, kissed me.

I was so startled, so *dazzled*, that I could not even respond to her passion.

It did not seem to bother Riqeta, for she laughed a third time and rested her hands on my shoulders. "Thank you, Naman," my wife whispered. "May the Almighty bless you."

Still too overwhelmed, all I could do was stare at her.

Peace brimming in her expression, Riqeta leaned in closer and pressed her head to my shoulder, her plates buzzing against the cloth. Then abruptly she tilted her head back. "Would you want daughters, Naman?"

I blinked rapidly, trying to unstick my tongue so that I could answer.

She waited patiently, this time not showing the slightest stiffness or disappointment with my slow reply.

I inhaled, exhaled, slowly managing to calm my rapidly beating heart. Then I smiled and tipped my forehead against hers, beneath the curve of her helm. "I love you, Riqeta. Any child you bring into this world will be beautiful. Though, if the Almighty were to allow me a preference, I would pray for a daughter. One who is shaped by your legacy of prudence and mine of wisdom into so much more than either of us." I kissed her, gently, sweetly. "To raise a child with you is what I most want from this life, my princess."

Riqeta's lips spread again, her smile small but as dazzling as her grin. She lowered her gaze to my mouth, and we kissed again.

A prayer and a promise, a plea for a child to the Almighty and a vow to wait as long as necessary, given in words that transcended the use of voice.

The mark of a love that had already changed Icilia's balance and would transform her future—for the better, as surely a child of Riqeta would do.

When we drew apart, my stallion was placidly continuing

onward, his mate and Riqeta's mare by his side, and our staff and our soldiers were averting their eyes. All of them were exchanging happy smiles, even the ones who had nearly betrayed us, and for a moment the absence of those who had did not seem so stark.

For a moment, with our attendants, everything felt as it had before.

How I wanted that to be true as my farsight lingered upon the faces of Captain bi-Himacer and Lieutenant Gatiemt, both riding ten paces ahead of us.

But there was no returning to what had been.

And though great happiness lay ahead, so did great evil.

The pain at that reality that filled my heart echoed in Riqeta's eyes as she returned to her horse. It tinged my sights of Samaha as the city grew closer through the mountains, and it underlay Riqeta's motions as she organized the staff and the soldiers and sent some ahead to the capital. That pain pervaded all the feeling of homecoming, rendering it bittersweet.

An hour before the early winter sunset, our convoy climbed up the steep road (which the ministry of trade had thankfully cleared on time of snow and ice after last week's blizzard) crossing the final set of foothills to the great gates.

Sculpted from large slabs of silvery purple stone and strengthened with steel, the great gates were the primary entrance through the white walls that encircled the city.

Those walls, thirty feet thick and two hundred high, had been built by the second monarch of Koroma to withstand sieges from all of the five kinds, featured small stone shelters every fifty feet, and were so veined with magic that many of the soldiers who patrolled them swore they had a sentience of their own.

Beyond the walls lay a city equally rumored to possess sentience. For the great towers and the smaller turrets in between never seemed to crumble, creak, or suffer the slightest blemish. No matter that centuries had passed since the first monarchs, nobles, and citizens built them with their own hands.

As our convoy approached, the great gates—usually closed

during the winter to prevent snow and wind from swirling inside —swung open. Beyond them waited a full company of soldiers, as well as what appeared to be almost every citizen who lived in Samaha. Almost every single one of my friends, my acquaintances, and dozens more who I knew from greetings on the street. Best of all, their happiness and love flooded my crown heir's bond.

I could not help a grin. As when I had returned with Riqeta as my new bride from Zahacim, the message that the royal convoy was arriving had so quickly spread that the city herself seemed to have come to greet us.

The same memory gleamed in Riqeta's eyes as she donned a regal smile alongside her circlet, briefly dispelling the bitter-sweetness.

I considered doing the same but discarded the thought. The circlet I was settling around my cap was enough regality, my people needed to know how happy I was to see them, and Riqeta never seemed to mind me being true to myself in public. She never stifled my reactions, as others did, and, I knew beyond question now that I could trust her to defend me if I needed it. So I smiled widely, letting my eyes crinkle at the corners and my cheeks flush pink—which drew responding smiles from the citizens.

How the Almighty has blessed me with them!

The moment Riqeta and I passed through the gate, the soldiers executed a perfect salute, and both they and the citizens cried, "Long live the crown prince! Long live the Sword of Prudence!"

Our attendants quickly took up the cry as well.

So great was their enthusiasm that the sound of my title and her epithet reverberated throughout the snow-blanketed city, echoing off the walls, the towers, and the turrets, carrying us all the way to the doors of the palace itself.

At those doors, at the top of a grand flight of stairs and the base of the highest-built structure in the city, waited the royal household, all wearing the restrained smile that I knew to be the mark of barely controlled delight.

Father, Mother, Raman, Aunt Basima, Uncle Falan, even Aunt Bolana, about two dozen more distant cousins... all of the staff and the remainder of the soldiers stationed in Samaha... but none of the nobles.

I had not expected them to be present—after my coronation, they would have all returned home for the harvest and would likely not return until after spring planting—but still their absence felt like a poor omen.

Though perhaps their absence would make the discussion Riqeta and I needed to have about them easier...

Even as those thoughts filled my mind, happiness filled my heart. Nearly four months had passed since I had last seen my family, and these evil days strengthened the devotion I held for them.

How much I had missed them... how much I had missed my home...

But mine was right here, happy to see me, and Riqeta's was not, nor would they ever be happy to see her. Save one person...

As Riqeta and I dismounted before the stairs, I whispered, quietly enough that our voices would not echo against the stone, "I am sorry Serama could not remain with us, my love." I lifted my right elbow for her.

Riqeta's lips curled briefly into a wider smile. "Thank you, Naman." She wrapped her gloved hand around the offered elbow (to the cheers of half the city). "I know she could not be away from her post any longer without attracting Auntie's and Misleta's attention. Nor would it have been prudent for her to come here and risk news of a royal welcome reaching their ears. It was wise that she leftInáma sooner than we did." She gave a nod to our staff and our soldiers, dismissal and permission for them to take leave for a few days.

"Still, I am sorry you are away from home," I murmured, threading my fingers through those of her other hand and squeezing them, hoping to express how dearly I wished Serama could have stayed with us... But, without risking war, she could not defect, even should I convince my father to offer, and neither Riqeta nor Serama were willing to take that risk. So their parting seemed without end.

Riqeta flashed another bright smile up at me. "Naman," she said as we began to climb the steps, our boots crunching on the snow, one hand on my elbow and the other holding mine in front of us, "how can I miss home when I am with you?" And, upon the heels of dispelling the last of my worries for our marriage, she paused, rose up on her toes, and kissed my lips.

The entire city actually screamed with excitement.

Even after seven months, the wonder of the Sword of Prudence choosing Koroma for her allegiance had not faded.

I grinned into the kiss, my heart full of gratitude to the Almighty and joy at both her love for me and our people's for her. "I am happy you feel at home here."

"At home with *you*," she corrected. Then, with those beautiful words, she led the way up the steps, her hands keeping me steady.

The surety of her grip was what sustained me as, the moment our family and our staff finished greeting us, my father declared, "My Son, my Daughter, come! Wash away the dust of the road, and then join us to present your report."

I inhaled deeply. *That means almost immediately. Which is what we expected, as we have not sent a single report back since the moon of Alkharre...* I swallowed as I bowed again to my parents. *They do not show it, skilled as they are in manipulating emotion, and my crown heir's bond will not reveal their emotions, but, beneath their delight, they must be so angry...*

None of my alarm was present in Riqeta's expression. Her regal smile warming just slightly, she bowed a second time. "At your orders, Father."

The slight iciness in Father's eyes melted at that, and he chuckled and tugged her again into his embrace, not minding the dust rubbing from her armor onto his tailored lilac robes. "I am always happy to see you, Daughter," he whispered. "May the Almighty bless you."

The citizens cheered again—which was likely at least part of his reason for that hug.

Riqeta did not seem bothered by it as she linked her arms around his waist and leaned into him. For a moment, wistfulness tinged her gaze...

Despite all of my trepidation, how I hoped the moment meant that, someday, she would be able to regard my parents as her own. None could replace her beloved birth parents, but mine perhaps might come to be dear enough to alleviate some of her long-held grief...

Riqeta stepped back and gave a third bow. "We will see you in thirty minutes, Father, Mother." She took hold of my hand, and both of us waved to the citizens—prompting yet another cheer—before climbing the last few steps and crossing the marble threshold of the open palace doors.

The second we were past them and our boots in the hands of a waiting staff member, Riqeta pulled me forward, quickening her pace as she angled across the grand entry hall to the staircases that would lead us to our apartments.

The purple-veined marble, the lush carpets, the rich tapestries, the stained glass, and the chandeliers of luminescent quartz of the public areas flashed in front of my eyes, rapidly transitioning into the sparser private wings in a blur of coarser lilac stone and frosted windows, until Riqeta unlocked the door of our marriage suite and nudged me inside.

The rooms—airy, spacious, the carpeted floor covered with minimal furniture and the cream walls filled with Riqeta's personal armory and the many dozens of gifts we had received over our travels and at our wedding—were my refuge, though I had only had them since Riqeta and I married—but I had hardly a second to appreciate the sense of homecoming. With a speed possibly born of the rigors of her own court, Riqeta quickly retrieved sets of fresh robes, urged me to wash and change, and pulled me out the door as soon as I rolled up my socks.

"Why are we hurrying so much?" I wheezed as we dashed, hand in hand, through the corridors. "It is a private family meeting! Even though we are wearing our circlets! Surely we can attend with a little leisure!"

"Our reports are late, Naman," Riqeta said grimly, not at all out of breath, "and we are about to present something Mother and Father will find difficult to accept. Punctuality in this at least will help alleviate their anger. It will help them believe us."

A very Koromic consideration... one I should not have forgotten. Swallowing any other protest, I lengthened my stride to keep apace with her. Though she was a foot shorter, she was so much faster—I could tell she was purposefully checking her speed to not leave me behind.

I dearly appreciated it, for the closer we came, the more I dreaded my parents' reactions...

We turned the final corner—only to nearly slam into a figure standing there.

A figure in lilac robes and the silver circlet, adorned with a single pale amethyst, that I had worn before my coronation.

"Raman!" I exclaimed as Riqeta pulled me to a halt beside her. "Why are you standing here! I almost hurt you!"

My brother, his beloved face grim, turned and stepped closer to both of us, coming so close that his front brushed ours. "Riqeta, Naman," he said quietly, "you need to be careful. Mother is not happy, but Father—he is furious. You do not know what we thought when your attendants returned to Ináma with no word from you... That, and the lack of reports was an embarrassment."

I winced. "Yes, Raman, but—"

"With respect, Brother," he interrupted, jewel-bright hazel eyes graver than I had ever seen them, "I do not and will not ever question your judgment. Neither yours nor my Sister's." He dipped his head to Riqeta, who responded with a smile. "Your words need to be said to our parents." He pressed his lips together. "You have not had a minute to ask yet, but—Naman, they were upset enough that they recalled me from my post on the northern border. A border we *need* to guard, with Crown Prince Nirio-nadem's particular ire about last year's trade agreement..." He suddenly took my open hand in his. "Please be careful, Sister, Brother."

I beamed, my heart warmed by his concern. "Thank you, Brother." I squeezed his hand. "I treasure your support. Please, always remain with me."

"Of course, Naman." Raman wrapped his other arm around my back in a brief hug. Then he stepped back and bowed, donning his usual playful smirk. "After you, your Highnesses."

Riqeta and I chuckled, both of us, by the glance we exchanged, appreciating his humor, meant solely to relax our tension.

But no amount of humor can change these tidings.

Sighing, I nodded to my brother. Then I looked to Riqeta.

My wife, standing straight and confident, appeared as regal and commanding in her robes and cap as she did in her armor and helm. The wedding ring she now openly wore on her right hand shone in the last hints of red sunlight streaming in through the windows lining the corridor. Her amber eyes gleamed with power, and the focused purse of her rose lips held the courage that had defeated Hisalir himself.

Surely, together, we could do this.

Surely we could convince the monarchs who loved us both so much of what we had seen.

Surely believing the best of my parents was not blindness.

Clinging tightly to Riqeta's fingers, praying to the first Quest Leader for strength, I walked forward, through the open door of the meeting room, two minutes prior to the appointed time.

Decorated in unembellished streamers of pale lavenders and rich blue-violets, the chamber was cheerful, bright in the glow of lanterns made with yellow quartz, and the round oak table with its eight cushioned armchairs reminded me of countless conferences held by my long-passed grandparents while Raman and I played underneath. In some places, the rugs still bore faint stains from our more mischievous games, as well as those of the generations of young royals before us. Despite my mother's dislike of blemishes and messes, no one ever truly moved to erase those marks—this chamber was a symbol of what it meant to be the royal family, living and ruling as one, surrounded by protocol yet with love between us as tightly woven as silk.

How I prayed that love would prove strong today.

As I entered, Riqeta and Raman on my heels, I found that Father, Mother, Aunt Basima, Uncle Falan, and Aunt Bolana were already waiting for us. Their expressions were calm, composed, regal beneath their various circlets, but some strange energy crackled in the air...

"Please, my children, take your seats," Father said, waving at the open chairs on the opposite side of the circular table from him.

The three of us bowed and obeyed. Beneath the cover of the table, Riqeta again took my hand.

Father threaded his fingers together, before folding them down and tightening his grip. Then, lifting his gaze to mine, he said simply, "What happened, Naman, Riqeta?"

I squeezed Riqeta's fingers. Then, as evenly and as eloquently as I could, I described our journey, from the day we sent our last report, the day Riqeta and I had seen Count Flirien's land, to the day of our return. I described all the abuses we saw, the horror of Mutanacere, the confrontation with Hisalir and Riqeta's duel, the treason of most of my soldiers, the return to Ináma, Serama's news, Charan Theriett's assassination attempt on his grandfather... Every description, as Riqeta and I had discussed on the road home, but no conclusions.

And as we had discussed, I spoke alone. Though I doubted my parents would ever be upset with her, I did not nudge Riqeta to contribute, as she had asked.

My parents, my brother, my aunts, and my uncle displayed no emotion as we spoke. Except for lifts of eyebrows and my brother's horrified gasps when I narrated Riqeta's duel.

When I reached the end of my report, I dipped my head. "Abbi, if you would allow, I would request leave to offer Riqeta's and my conclusions." I purposefully used the less formal address children used for their parents, in the hope that it would lessen his anger.

Father nodded. "Do so."

Again with as much eloquence as I could muster, I explained our conclusions, from the lies of Koroma's nobles to the evil magic Hisalir wielded. As well as the way we worried his influence would spread.

No emotion at all.

When I was done, Father asked, simply again, "Why could none of this be sent in the form of regular written reports?"

I suppressed a wince. "These are delicate matters, Abbi, and troubled times. We did not want to risk our couriers being intercepted, particularly once we realized the insurgency is a far greater threat than previously supposed."

"This insurgency..." Father tapped his thumbs against each other. "Did you see its effects in counties other than Mutanacere?"

I hesitated, racking my mind for details of the confrontation. "No... but the followers with Hisalir bi-Mutanacer were more varied in clothing and speech than if they had all come from one county."

"Hmmm." Father pressed his lips together. "But you do not have conclusive proof than the insurgency affected more than one county?"

Raman kicked my leg beneath the table, but I did not need the warning as my fingers tightened on Riqeta's. "No, Father."

"A lack of proof troubles me in another area as well..." Mother furrowed her brow. "What proof do we have that Countess qia-Mutanacera's son wielded conjury? Actual *conjury?*" She glanced at Father. "The Prince of Virtue eradicated that magic, and the scholars are clear that it cannot reappear."

Father nodded in thought.

"Ammi," I protested my mother's statement, trying to keep my tone even, "we *faced* it! We experienced its effects. The feel of fear overriding all rational thought..." I shivered. "It cannot be mistook for something else."

"Truly, though?" Mother questioned. "If it really was conjury, you should not have been able to resist it. Either of you." A gentle smile. "Not that I desire evil to befall you, my dearest Son and Daughter, and I am glad you have returned in good health to us. But the Prince of Virtue allowed no exceptions in his writings: conjury could not be defeated by anything beside athar magic."

"She is right," Father agreed. "If it was conjury... well," he shuddered, "we would preparing for your funerals rather than your future as monarchs."

I stared at them, shocked by this denial.

Squeezing my hand—saving me as always—Riqeta spoke then, "With respect, Father, Mother, it was unmistakably conjury. I conducted every test that the Prince of Virtue prescribed, and I can attest most thoroughly to its effects."

"Still," Mother shook her head, "how could you resist it then?"

"Through prayer and faith," Riqeta replied, posture straight and regal as she met Mother's gaze, "and so much force of will that only the Almighty could grant it."

Mother shook her head again but did not reply.

"Is that not a sufficient answer—" Raman began.

"I find myself concerned," Aunt Bolana said, ignoring him, from the often-disused chair on my father's left, "by your claim that Countess qia-Mutanacera's son is himself the insurgent." She drummed her fingers on the tabletop, shaking her head. "I know I am rarely at court, but I well remember the countess. She was a paragon of virtue. It is difficult to believe her son would ever stray from the Quest's path or hurt his mother."

"Hisalir bi-Mutanacer is a wonderful young man," Uncle Falan agreed, "and very well-liked at court, both among currently seated nobles and their heirs. Forging a friendship with him would have been an excellent move, Naman."

My mouth fell open at this praise of the monster *himself*. At this advice about the great evil of our age! At this impugning of my judgment... From the very uncle who had enthusiastically championed me since the very day I was born...

"Uncle Falan," Riqeta interceded, "he demonstrated great disrespect for the crown."

Uncle Falan shook his head. "You accused him and challenged him to a duel, Niece. Not once did I hear any mention of an attempt to negotiate. Naman's entire conversation was only a diversion for your spells. Indeed, you both had already decided his guilt before meeting him. How could you expect him to react with anything beside disrespect when that was how *you* treated him?"

"Uncle," Riqeta said, "it was not a situation for negotiation—"

"You were too quick to declare war, Riqeta," Aunt Bolana said, kindly as though chastising a beloved but easily confused child. Not with the respect owed a warrior, royal, and future queen. Not with the respect owed a fellow woman. "I suppose that is the best we could have expected, but it was not right for Koroma."

Riqeta's fingers tightened on mine to the point of pain. Though I could sense only her presence and not her emotions in my bond, I knew how deeply she hurt... so I lightly kicked my brother's foot, hoping they would listen if he spoke.

"With respect, Aunt Bolana," Raman started, his tone suave, bumping my heel with his in acknowledgment, "Riqeta's judgment is renowned for—"

"Moreover," Father said, interrupting his firstborn son, with a nod to his sister, "if he truly is as evil as you claim, you should not have let him go, Riqeta."

"Despite his surrender?" Riqeta asked, tilting her head, the hurt masked beneath the earnest sincerity of her question.

"What does his surrender matter?" Father waved a hand. "If you truly judged him an enemy of Koroma, you should have slain him on the spot."

Dalaanem! Praying desperately, I gave my wife a frantic glance. "But, Abbi, the laws of engagement—"

"And if he truly was so powerful," Mother added, speaking over me, "you should not have been able to defeat him."

"His followers would have retaliated at least," Uncle Falan agreed, "if his hold over them was as you say."

"Indeed," Father said, not a hint of compassion in his words though his own bond, the monarch's bond, likely did tell him of her hurt. "I am not satisfied with this outcome, Riqeta. If he were a threat, you should have destroyed him. If he were not, you should have convinced him to rejoin us. As it is, I can only conclude that he is not truly a concern based on your actions."

Riqeta stiffened slightly, pain glimmering deep in her eyes.

Desperately trying to rally my words, I opened my mouth to defend her. "Abbi—"

"Additionally," Father said, ignoring me, "I find this report of your attacking Charan particularly disturbing." He flattened his hands on the table. "Without respect for the nobles, our government ceases to function, Daughter, and this was a true lack."

"Abbi," I rallied my voice, "Charan attacked Duke Theriett! Uncle Falahan! The only worthy option was to defend Uncle! Charan wanted to kill him, and he would not stop!" *Dalaanem, please, may he believe me...*

Father raised an eyebrow. "Under the shadow of all of these other items, from not slaying this so-described monster to not sending reports, I am afraid that I cannot trust your judgment in this matter, Naman." His lips curved in a benevolent smile. "You have so much to learn about ruling, my Son. A few mistakes, even big ones, are to be expected."

Raman grabbed my left hand.

"As you have much to learn about Koroma, my Daughter," Mother said compassionately, the indulgent smile I had loved as a child spreading her lips. Riqeta, Raman, and I simply stared at them, hands clenched together in the only solidarity to be had. How had it all gone so wrong...

"Indeed," Aunt Basima finally spoke, and I turned to my favorite aunt, desperate for at least some support. "Not least of them, Naman, are these allegations against the nobles." She arched a brow, just like her brother. "Can you substantiate them?"

"Auntie," I pleaded, hoping at least she would listen, "the reports—"

"Comparing reports is *not* proof," she stated. "You need witnesses, documents, others not of your family and household to corroborate your testimony—do you have any of that? For at least Count Flirien's lands?"

"No, but—" I began.

"Then do not say something as weighty as this claim that they are all lying," she said. "They are the supports of your reign, Naman."

"But, Auntie, it is *true*—" I tried.

She actually scoffed. "Naman, your parents, your aunts, and your uncle have known Koroma's nobles for all the years of our lives. We have played together, worked together, ruled together—from births to weddings to deaths, we are together. As are you, Naman."

"These same women and men you are accusing," Mother built on her point, "rocked you in their arms when you were an infant, helped us clean your scrapes and your vomit, clothed and fed you, and gave of their own wealth to all the projects you desired. They unified behind you for both your wedding and your coronation, Naman. How can you slander them this way?"

Father shook his head. "Do not make this error, my Son. The

nobles are loyal and truthful; do not see monsters where there are none."

"Or you will turn them *into* monsters," Aunt Basima stated, her usually kind hazel eyes grave with warning. "The desertion of your soldiers—which is another source of concern, really, about the result of this mission—that is a strong indicator: when you disrespect the nobles, the citizens also do not stay with you. They do not then trust your profession of respect toward them."

"Your response was too harsh," Mother declared. "Your soldiers would not have abandoned us otherwise. Indeed, as I perceive, your actions have imperiled the crown by eroding the compassion of our reputation."

"But, Abbi, Ammi, Aunts, Uncle," I exclaimed, desperate to come to an accord with them, "you yourselves agreed that the crown needed to give a strong response! *You* were the ones who worried that the nobles would not accept my accession as easily as they would Raman's!" My brother tightened his grip on my hand —another warning. But, clinging to the first Quest Leader's name, I could not abandon this last attempt. "Do you not remember the care you took to allay or deflect each of their concerns at the court session in which you gave us this mission? We acted as you prescribed—as strongly and decisively as we could!"

Father raised both brows now. "Naman," he spoke slowly, with terrifying finality, "a strong response is not the same as using the blade alone. We trusted you to balance speech and force, to be eloquent in both your words and the swing of your sword, as a ruler of Koroma should, and you were not." From the cast of his gaze toward Riqeta, it was clear that he blamed her for this. Then returning his eyes to me, he concluded, "You did not even complete your basic duty of reporting to your monarch. This was a failure, Naman, Riqeta, and that is the end of it."

All Riqeta, Raman, and I could do was stare.

Father, Mother, Aunt Basima, Uncle Falan, and Aunt Bolana gazed at us a moment more, their lips curving into the beneficent smiles that were the mark of Koroma's royal family, urging us to see the wisdom of their words.

Then Father nodded. "There is much to ponder. Let us reconvene for the evening meal. I am certain the head chef is preparing your favorites, Naman, Riqeta, and I myself have a few surprises planned." He winked, as though he had not just declared us entirely incompetent, and rose to his feet, prompting everyone else to stand as well. He nodded again to Riqeta and me, offered his arm to Mother—who smiled lovingly at us—and swept out of the room with her by his side. Aunt Basima, Uncle Falan, and Aunt Bolana trailed after them, laughing softly and casting us affectionate smiles as well.

Only Riqeta, Raman, and I were left.

We glanced at each other, the same shock and horror I felt reflected in Riqeta's and Raman's eyes as well.

I fell back into my seat, my chest heaving, my breath quickening, until I thought I would faint—

"Naman," whispered a voice, my favorite voice, as two hands gripped my shoulders. "Naman, please, look at me."

Realizing I had closed my eyes, I blinked them open and glanced up at her.

Her lips were drawn tightly together into a pinched circle, and her expression showed nothing but focus. Yet even as I watched, a single tear slid from her eye into the stilled plates of her bronze cheek.

My own lips trembling, I threw my arms around her waist and pulled her close to me, burying my head into her neck. "Riqeta..." I whispered, tears spilling down my face. "How could they do that to us?"

She wrapped her arms around my back and rubbed it but did not answer. Not this time.

I held her as tightly as I could, then tugged her onto my lap so that I could cradle her and tuck her head beneath my chin. Despite the hard edge of her circlet, she felt soft now, fragile in my arms, as though the armor shielding her from harm was gone, and

I despised it. If only reassembling that protection would be as easy as donning plate and chainmail! But I was destined to fail her in that just as surely as I had today...

"I am sorry, Riqeta," I whispered. "I am sorry that they treated you this way." I kissed her rough cheek. "I trust your judgment above all others', and I wish my trust were enough, my love. You are exactly the lieutenant monarch Koroma needs."

She withdrew slightly, leaning back so she could meet my gaze. "As you are the monarch Koroma needs." Despite the tears now coating her plates and the channels between them, her amber eyes burned an intense gold. "Even if no one sees it beside me."

I gave her a shaky smile. "Thank you, my princess."

A thud startled me (though not her, of course), and the two of us turned to see Raman on his knees by my chair. The misery of his expression entirely unmasked, hazel eyes bleak, he whispered, "Naman, my future king, I see it, too. Riqeta, my future queen, I know your wisdom is beyond any of ours. I trust your judgment far beyond my own, my monarchs." He leaned forward and pressed his forehead to the side of my knee, careful to avoid touching Riqeta's foot. "Please, my king, my queen, forgive me for not defending you. For not warning you!" His shoulders shook as he began to cry.

"Oh, Raman," I murmured, not liking his need to show such obeisance, the ache in my heart inflamed by his tears, "it is not your fault." At Riqeta's nod, I shifted a hand from her waist to grasp my brother's shoulder and gently drew him back. "Brother, please, it is not your fault."

Riqeta removed a handkerchief from her pocket and began to wipe his tears, her usual brisk discipline returning to her motions. "Indeed, no," she said, "and truly I would say even our family is not entirely at fault."

"Why do you say so?" I asked, surprised. She certainly had not professed any such lenience toward the royals of Zahacim!

"Indeed, why?" Raman asked, leaning into Riqeta's touch.

He gazed up at her like a lost child, much as Duke Theriett had looked at me.

"Because," Riqeta said, patting my brother's face dry before turning to mine, "Father and Mother are only defending the prosperity they have labored day and night to build. When Father acceded to the throne, Koroma was ravaged by war, first with Bhalasa and then with Nademan. He poured his tears, his sweat, and his blood into resolving those conflicts and forging peace and then in earning a name as Icilia's peacemaker. It was what earned him Mother's hand, and together they built or revitalized all the institutions we now treasure, from the orphanage to the system of reports. Aunt Basima, Uncle Falan, and Aunt Bolana rallied the court, the military, and the citizens behind them as part of those efforts."

She smiled sadly as she put her handkerchief away and tilted her face so I could dry her cheeks. "Our report shows that all of their endeavors are ultimately hollow, that Koroma's prosperity was false or flaking away even while they still thought it was secure, and this they cannot accept. As you yourself wondered, Naman, our report for them means that they have not served the Quest. But while you have given ten years to your service, they have given forty to theirs. How could we have expected them to accept our conclusions so easily?

"Thus, I do not think we can blame them. At least not yet—for, soon enough, they will need to confront these evils if the crown does intend to protect Koroma. But not yet."

I stared at her in amazement, my hand frozen on the slant of her cheek. "How compassionate are your words..."

Her plates buzzed beneath my fingers.

"That is more properly Koromic than anything Aunt Bolana or any of them said," Raman wryly commented. "After they had the daring to imply that you do not understand Koroma." He sighed and then smiled up at us. "Brother, Sister, let no doubt trouble your heart: if you say something is a particular way, it is. I believe you. I will do anything for you. I will be your ally even if no one else is."

I beamed, my face flushing, warmed by his words for the second time that day.

But, before I could thank him, Riqeta shrewdly questioned, "Even though you already offered your throne to him?"

He steadily met her gaze. "Even so. Indeed, as we can now see, such was the Almighty's will. Naman is Koroma's rightful king, as you are her rightful queen. The only king and queen who have the prudence to rule in these evil times and the wisdom to recover from them, for you discern the shadows and reveal the truth."

The words resounded in the chamber with the weight of a royal declaration.

How I prayed they would hold true of our reign.

EPILOGUE: THE PRUDENCE TO RULE IN THESE EVIL TIMES

Perspective: Queen Riqeta naj-Shehenkorom, lieutenant of the Monarch to Koroma
Date: Eyyédal, the twenty-third day of the fourth moon, Likberre, of the year 477, C.Q.

My baby beamed up at me, her sparkling blue eyes so bright that they gleamed like pieces of sky beneath her pale gold lashes, striking against her glowing cream skin. Little coos flowed from her red rosebud lips, as though she were speaking to me in a language I could not understand.

I stared back, unable to look away, still aware of my surroundings because of the extensive training of my early youth. And because such fiery instinct now burned in my chest, such burning urge to protect, that I thought I might crush anyone who dared to merely glance at my child askance.

She was precious, perfect, my peace, and all the years I had waited for her seemed to melt beneath the cast of her blue gaze.

My baby's little lips parted and curved, revealing her toothless gums, as though she could hear my thoughts. Her eyes gleamed with an understanding so much beyond what an infant could possess, much less a three-day-old newborn. Indeed, her every behavior was that of a much older child.

More than precocious, I thought, unable to restrain a grin so wide it pulled at my cheeks. *She has the Almighty's blessing.* Sighing, I pressed a kiss to her mouth. "Thank you, my Daughter." Gently I began to rock her back and forth, lightly shaking the pillow on which I held her swaddled form. *All my gratitude to You, oh Almighty... Thank you, Dalaanem...*

More sweet coos poured into my ears—now my favorite sound in all the world. I treasured each and every one of them...

"Riqeta!" my other favorite voice called, before Naman entered the antechamber. His blue eyes, so like our daughter's, brightened at the sight of us, and he came and knelt by our armchair. "Blessings, my princesses!" he exclaimed. "How do my darlings fare?"

Our baby made soft kissing sounds, her blue eyes affixed to the ones that were a less vibrant mirror of hers. Indeed, save for the shape of her eyes and her lips, she already deeply resembled my husband, beyond merely inheriting his kind—a proof of our love, and how I adored it.

I smiled softly. "We are patiently waiting for the ceremony to start, my love."

Grinning, Naman wrapped one arm around my back and placed another beneath our baby's pillow. "Do you know, my heart," he said, looking into our baby's attentive eyes, "that today you will receive your name?"

She cooed, as though answering yes.

We chuckled softly, and I continued, "The throne hall is full of people who have come to celebrate you, my heart. Our guests include nobles and citizens from all over Koroma and royals from most of the seven nations." My voice almost broke as I remembered who was not here, but I tried to not let my smile falter—this day was too special for her to let misery taint it. "Abbi and I invited them when we realized you were really coming, my heart, and they arrived just before you were born."

For a moment, the memory of learning I was finally, actually with child, after seven years of doomed attempts, two lost pregnancies, and painful, irregular cycles, and that, too, at the fifth month, overwhelmed me. I was clinging to hope with the last of my strength, as was Naman, and suddenly we had realized my belly was swelling in the way only the presence of a child could cause. A peace washed over us, a blessed knowledge that beyond doubt we would see this baby born. So we had immediately decided to invite all of the royals, nobles, and citizens we could for the naming ceremony (it was our right to invite or no, and we had chosen to call them, with the prayer of offering hope to Koroma). But Serama and Princess Diyana, both auxiliary heirs and so allowed to travel only at the pleasure of their monarchs, had been unable to come.

I had not seen them in more than seven years—Princess Diyana since my wedding to Naman and Serama since her visit that autumn. I had not even met their firstborn children, Serama's lovely Henata and Princess Diyana's darling Darian, nor had I ever met Serama's husband, Atres. Though Naman and I had exerted all the prestige we had as Koroma's monarchs, even going so far as to send personal invitations, despite Zahacim's traitorous alliance with Hisalir, they were not here. How dearly I missed them on this sacred day...

His own smile wavering slightly, Naman kissed my cheek before resuming our explanation, "Ammi and I were even able to request the presence of the Guardian of Names. He does not travel much now in his elderly age, and we have heard that he declined to personally attend several recent ceremonies and sent letters instead, but he agreed to come for yours! Is that not exciting, my heart? The Almighty is surely happy with us!"

Our baby uttered a high sound quite like a giggle.

"Yes," I said, my heart so soothed by that sound that words returned to my tongue, "his presence is quite an honor, my heart." I remembered that I needed to teach her who this person was—it still felt so strange to explain all I knew to a new mind.

"The Guardian of Names is an almost divine figure, born anew every generation, who is below only the Quest and who is our link to the Almighty when the Quests rule through name alone. Indeed, names, for the Guardian, although not a figure of political authority, reinforces the Quests' laws by giving the people our names—as well as, usually only for royals, prophecies. Like for Abbi and me." I glanced up at Naman, who smiled, and then I recited both of our prophecies.

Prophecies that had come to be more true than we could have ever imagined.

And today, for the first time since our own naming ceremonies as infants, we would meet the one who had given them. The same Guardian.

I wondered what the Guardian would prophesy for my baby...

I dreaded that whatever he would say would foreshadow a far darker future than anything Naman and I could yet see.

But, still, that was not a thought that should mar this sacred day.

My lips curving, I concluded, "Abbi and I chose today because it is the first Eyyédal after your birth—the day of the week that honors the Shining Guide—and giving your name today will, in essence, dedicate your life to the Shining Guide and his Master the Almighty. It is our prayer that the Quest of Light will look with favor upon you, our heart."

Our baby grinned again, an expression that, despite its lack of teeth, seemed reminiscent of the sun.

"Ohhh," Naman sighed, sounding as charmed as I felt, and kissed her forehead. Then he stood. "I should see whether everyone is in place. Raman promised that all would be ready at exactly mid-day, and my farsight tells me it is that time now."

I nodded, knowing what he really meant: he wanted to check with his own eyes that no conjuror had managed to enter the palace, for farsight, as we had learned from Khonatir bi-Mutanacer, could not detect the presence of a conjuror.

Ohhh, Khonatir... Three and a half years ago, he had sought out Naman and me, his heart beaten and broken, with the prayer of leaving his monstrous brother behind. After much conferring, we had sent him to Asfiya, hoping that the sacred land would heal his heart, and it had, and he had received the blessing of a spouse —but soon after King Alafen aj-Shehasfiyi had exiled him, as had the rest of Icilia's monarchs, including Naman's parents. All we knew of him was what Princess Diyana had confided in a letter: he and his new wife, an Asfiyan noble named Elima Izzetís, had vanished into the wild northern mountains of Bhalasa. How much Naman and I prayed that they still remained safe and free! Though we had not been able to help them...

The same anguish echoing in his eyes, Naman nodded back and strode to the door that led from the antechamber onto the throne hall's dais. Opening it slightly, he watched the movements in the hall.

Suppressing a sigh, I turned back to our smiling baby. As much as I wanted to perform such checks myself—whether seven years or seventy, my desire to protect Naman would always burn strong—I knew I was still not fully recovered from the birth. Though it had been a short, easy birth (far easier and far shorter than a birth should be for a woman having her first child after her thirtieth birthday), my body was still sore, uncomfortable, and a little hollow. More than three days needed to pass before I could expect to begin to return to my full strength.

But, even if I lost that strength as the healers fretted, the sacrifice would be worthy, for I had my baby now.

Smiling, I tucked in the lilac swaddling cloth, woven of athar thread and trimmed in gold, more tightly around her tiny form, clothed in palest lilac, and adjusted the little cap, cream and gold, shaped much like the low cone of an adult's cap, atop her little bald head. Tapping her little nose in the hope of another giggle (which she gave), I resettled her atop her violet pillow in my arms, ensuring that my elbow properly supported her head. Then I glanced up as Naman returned.

"They are waiting for us," he said, his smile forced. And for a moment, the threads of white hairs gleaming within his red-blond mustache and beard, matched by the white now appearing in my walnut hair, despite our not yet having reached our thirty-fifth birthdays, seemed all the starker... The gold of his crown, a circlet around his cap formed of eleven three-peaked crown symbols tipped with amethysts, only enhanced that contrast—just as the amethyst-inlaid gold lieutenant's circlet (much resembling the crown heir's) I wore around my cap seemed to highlight these marks of my worries.

Exhaling deeply, I carefully stood, swaying to my feet, easily balancing our baby's slight weight. Then, ignoring the aches that rippled out from my middle, I went to the door, my lilac and gold athar robes (a match for both Naman's and our baby's clothes) flowing around my warrior's stride much as they had before my pregnancy.

Naman joined me, pushing the door open before resting his right hand on my waist. "Dalaaneman," he whispered, for courage, as we now often did in these evil times.

"Dalaaneman," I agreed.

Our baby cooed, adding her own response, her voice a greater source of courage than even speaking this name.

Together, we walked out onto the dais.

The raised platform was an island of calm amid a sea of reluctant bows and curtsies. Dressed in their most elegant finery, dozens of royals, nobles, citizens, and soldiers watched us, standing only with relatives or close friends, gaps of the plum and lavender floor tiles visible where their groups maintained distance among one other. Some still wore their boots, violating the sanctity of the hall's floor.

Though they had all chosen to travel here, and all were carrying baskets of pale lilac flower petals as was customary, most watched me warily, and smiles adorned only a few expressions— those of Duke Theriett and several young nobles, Naman's and my only noble allies, and of perhaps half of the crown officials, soldiers, and citizens present.

Save a few, the nobles of Koroma were loyal now only in name to their monarchs, but the citizens, especially of the capital, remained ours. For now.

For now, their loyalty kept Koroma from drowning in the gushing tide of Zahacim's betrayal and Hisalir's influence.

Oh Dalaanem, may the sight of Koroma's future give hope to her present...

I shifted my gaze to the two figures waiting for Naman and me in front of our thrones.

The one standing in front of the other and wearing lilac robes trimmed in silver was Raman, Naman's older brother and in many ways the last of our family.

For, despite all of our prayers and hopes, Naman's parents, with his aunts' and his uncle's support, had steadily opposed every attempt we had made to prepare Koroma for the coming evil since our return from Mutanacere in the winter of 469 C.Q. until their deaths nearly two years ago. They had even declared Charan to be Ináma's heir, despite Duke Theriett's objections and our discovery of his open admiration for Hisalir. To such degree had their opposition been that, despite Naman's and my accession to the throne, we did not possess the loyalty of Koroma's nobles, unlike all of our predecessors for more than two hundred and fifty years. Indeed, we had needed to remove Aunt Basima, Uncle Falan, and Aunt Bolana, along with their spouses, from court in order to gain even a modicum of control. Only Raman was fully with us.

The moment he saw us, he tipped forward into a deep bow, his lips spread wide in a grin. "May the blessings of the Almighty be upon you, your Majesties, your Royal Highness!" He remained bent until Naman and I rounded the thrones and reached his side in front of them. Then, with a flourish, he gestured to the other figure. "In the name of our Rulers the Quest of Light, I present your Majesties and your Royal Highness to his Excellence, the Guardian of Names." He took a step to the left, revealing the other figure.

The Guardian of Names.

A tall, elderly man of the Sholanar, his long beard, mustache, brows, and lashes stark as snow against his deep brown, nearly black, skin, his silver-scaled wings folded neatly against his back. Robed in silver athar trimmed in gold and intricately embroidered with swirls of white, red, blue, green, purple, and brown in various shades. Crowned with a simple white athar helm bearing script in the sacred tongue of Alimàzahre. Bearing an aura of such immense power, such wisdom, such virtue, that Naman and I bowed without hesitation, our hearts knowing he deserved our reverence.

Our baby, secure in my arms, cooed a greeting.

The Guardian's eyes, the same pale silver as his wings and robes, focused on the face of our baby.

Then he himself offered a bow. "May the blessings of the Almighty be upon you, Wisdom and Prudence both."

Naman and I stared, shocked.

Behind us, the hall erupted in hastily stifled murmurs (despite their reluctance in offering reverence, the gathering still did not dare to chatter in his presence), while Raman's regal smile disappeared into open-mouthed astonishment.

The Guardian of Names was almost a divine figure!

So why is he bowing to us... With the names he gave us in our prophecies...

Our baby shifted in my arms and, somehow, despite all the tight swaddling, raised a tiny, dimpled arm. "Aaaah!" she cried.

The Guardian chuckled and, stepping closer, extended his arms.

I carefully placed my baby, along with her pillow, into his hold —trusting that he was one of the few people in this evil time who would carry her safely.

Silver eyes sparkling, the Guardian expertly began to rock her, gazing down into her blue eyes.

As custom dictated, Naman and I knelt in preparation for the blessing. Beneath the cover of our long sleeves, Naman threaded his fingers through mine, squeezing anxiously, his monarch's signet ring with its little silver wedding circle, which matched my own, pressing familiarly into my fingers.

I squeezed back—the Guardian was smiling, so surely this at least would go well for us.

The Guardian suddenly spun on his heel, toward the throne, silver wings flaring out, shielding him and our baby from everyone's view.

Naman's palm turned slick with sweat in mine, and I quashed the urge to reach for a knife.

A deep laugh rumbled from the Guardian's form, before the murmur of words, so quiet only Naman, Raman, and I likely heard them: "Oh Dalaaneman... How much the Almighty has blessed me to serve you in this way as well..." Then, even lower, a word that sounded very much like "grace."

Pivoting back, the Guardian beamed down at Naman and me, our baby held securely in his arms, her little hand resting on his chest, over his heart.

Her cream, gold, and lilac clothes, swaddling, and pillow gleamed against his silver robes.

Then the Guardian of Names began to speak in the sacred tongue, and the rest of the world faded, all the light there was emanating from the two of them, from *her*, as though she was the very source of Light.

"In the name of the Almighty and the Shining Guide sent unto us," the Guardian proclaimed, "I am the Guardian of Names, humble servant of the Quest of Light, and, by the blessing for which I am forever grateful, I proffer this name to you: Malika."

Malika... I gasped. *Malika... That is the name I heard during the duel seven years ago... The name that saved me! Alongside Dalaanem's!*

Beside me, Naman, who I had later told of those light-filled moments, seemed similarly struck, shock filling the intertwined strands of our monarchs' bonds.

Neither of us missed that the Guardian was speaking with deference, even differing from the usual ritual through the use of proffer instead of bestow.

"Malika," the Guardian said again, bending his head so his lips hovered over our baby's right ear, "Malika... Malika... Malika..." The repetition faded as he recited musical words, ones in a language no one in Icilia knew save him, so quietly that only she could hear them. Aloud he then declared in sacred Alimàzahre, reciting blessings that again differed from the usual ritual, "May the Almighty bless you, Malika, and be pleased with all that you are. May the Almighty grant you wisdom and prudence, freedom itself, through you bestowing happiness to us all. Praised be the Almighty."

Malika beamed, cooing softly up at him, waving both arms, as though in acceptance of her name and the blessings.

The Guardian kissed her forehead. "Malika," he breathed, "graced by the Almighty." Then he intoned in the common tongue of Siléalaah,

"Graced by the Almighty, Daughter of the Light,
  Wisdom and Prudence will flow in your wake,
  Freedom served by you, bestowed for your sake,
  Given to the people of Icilia within your sight."

Utter silence, save for Malika's sweet coos.

No royal, noble, or citizen ever received more than two lines for their birth-prophecy—Naman and I had only received two lines each! Yet our daughter was receiving *four*...

The Guardian kissed her forehead again. He cuddled her to his chest. Then, with a bright smile, bending at his waist, he offered her back to me.

Raising both hands, I placed them beneath her pillow and carefully, delicately, accepted her form. Bringing her to my chest, I gazed down upon her, Naman leaning in so that his head rested against mine.

If your name is Malika, my heart, I wondered as I thought of her by name for the first time, *then whose is the other... Who is Lucian?* Like Malika's, the name felt holy in my mind.

Malika giggled, red lips spread over toothless gums, vivid blue eyes shining like stars in her little cream face. Two tiny hands reached up for us, excitedly waving, beckoning us to come closer.

Naman and I lowered our heads.

Those two tiny hands touched our lips, soft as clouds and as gentle as the life-giving rain.

Instinctively we puckered our lips in kisses.

Malika laughed brightly with delight. Then, with astonishing contentment, fell asleep in my arms.

Naman and I stared, too enthralled to look away...

A whispered, "your Majesties," from the Guardian of Names was what reminded us that the ceremony still had one portion left.

Rising from where we knelt, Naman's hand wrapping around my elbow, we turned to face our guests.

They stared in silence. Disdain not fully masked by wariness glinted in most of their eyes.

Only Raman, a handful of nobles, and some of the citizens and the soldiers were chanting the ritual blessing of "Be blessed by the Almighty! Be favored by the Quest!" Only they were smiling, awed, delighted, filled with hope by the honors given to the child who would one day be their queen. Only they were tossing handfuls of their lilac petals toward the dais in celebration of their future monarch.

Among those few faces were a pair... a pair who seemed as enraptured as Naman and I felt. Their beige Nasimih faces glowed with enthusiasm greater than even Malika's uncle's... Meriel and Nikos Dinasiette, I remembered, soldiers from Khuduren, both possessing wish magic, who had brought their young daughter, Zabraka, with them as part of their nation's delegation—though

Naman and I had cautiously limited our interactions with our guests, we had invited the Dinasiette family to dine with us, for Meriel was my second cousin. Both were descended from the Quest of Light as Naman and I were.

Their grins and enthusiastic tosses of petals soothed me, reminding me that we were not without family, not without allies.

I glanced back at Raman, up at my husband's already care-worn face, and then down again at Malika's serene expression.

Nor would we ever be.

Since the Almighty favored her so, we would never be alone. There would always be hope.

Though I did not dare to pray for our baby's happiness. She would beyond question be blessed with the prudence to rule in these evil times. But these times were still evil, still so full of pain and loss. So what I prayed then, what I begged the Almighty to grant in the name of the first Quest Leader, as the Guardian of Names stood behind us at this sacred ceremony, was that Malika would somehow find fulfillment in her life.

Fulfillment, as her name itself revealed.

EPILOGUE: THE WISDOM TO RECOVER FROM THESE EVIL TIMES

Perspective: King Naman aj-Shehenkorom, Monarch to Koroma
Date: Eyyésal, the eighteenth day of the fourth moon, Likberre, of the year 483, C.Q.

With Malika's giggles brightening the walls, the throne hall warmed, as though absorbing the sound of her voice. Rays of sunlight streamed through the windows, bouncing off the dulled tapestries and the thrones, glittering in time with the sound of her voice. Under its influence, the pallor that darkened this once-sacred space vanished...

Though smiles rarely came to my lips now, I could not help but grin, soaking in the sight of Malika eagerly waving her little sword as her mother instructed.

When Riqeta raised her blade, Malika copied the maneuver. When Riqeta thrust forward, Malika did the same. When Riqeta sliced, so did Malika.

The sunlight gleamed on Riqeta's polished armor as it did on Malika's silver robes, on Riqeta's polished helm and bun as on Malika's silver cap and bun, their expressions full of the same deep focus. Though Malika was not yet old enough for a circlet of any sort, a halo of light hovered around her brow when I squinted just so, a halo matched by the shine of Riqeta's lieutenant crown, fitted around her helm.

It was like watching two mirroring figures, mother and daughter, training together, a glimpse of the power they would someday jointly wield.

The difference in kind, Riqeta's Areteen plated bronze forehead, cheeks, and chin in comparison to Malika's translucent pale Ezulal face, somehow only deepened that impression.

How I loved the sight.

A gasp brought my eyes back to the warm little bundle I held against my chest, the four-month-old baby within the swaddling beginning to cry. Pale blue eyes spilled little heartbreaking tears down a chubby white face.

"Arafan," I crooned, rocking back and forth, "Arafan, my Son, my heart, my darling, I am with you, Arafan, Arafan, I love you, Arafan…"

The loving words seemed to soothe him, calming him enough that he settled back against me. His weight in turn relaxed me as well, lessening the anxiety that burdened my shoulders.

I inhaled deeply and leaned back into the soft cushions of my throne.

When I was a child, I had sat on my father's lap upon this very seat, as Malika and Arafan did now, sometimes even leaping atop it as Raman and I chased each other through the hall. My parents had often joined those chases, laughing alongside us, the promise of tickles the direst threat they ever uttered.

Though nearly eight years had passed since their deaths, the anguish of their betrayal still had not faded. Nor did I think it ever would, for the seeds they had sown in the court, suspicions about Riqeta's and my judgment and concerns about our loyalty to Koroma, sprouted more and more poisoned fruit with every year that passed.

In the last six years, all of Riqeta's and my allies, noble and citizen alike, had disappeared. Some had passed into the Almighty's reward, like Duke Theriett succumbing to a venom stirred into his afternoon tea or Captain bi-Himacer and Lieutenant Gatiemt falling in a skirmish with Hisalir's followers on the western front, but most had abandoned us, swayed either by the other nobles' lies or by Hisalir's deceptive whisperings. The only people left to Riqeta and me in the world were Raman and our personal maid and valet, Leoma and Colan (who had finally married soon after Malika's first birthday).

Oh, it was beyond question that Serama, Atres, Princess Diyana, Beres, Elima, Khonatir, Meriel, and Nikos returned our loyalty, as devoted servants of the Quests as we were, but all four couples were now beyond our reach. No one knew whether Elima and Khonatir yet lived, Serama and Atres were trapped within the quagmire of Zahacim's betrayal, Meriel's and Nikos' letters no longer reached us—only Princess Diyana and Beres had managed to convey a message, and that had been to a request to send our daughter and heir to their court.

Riqeta and I appreciated the message, filled with concern over our daughter's safety, but we doubted that Asfiya's court was in any better health than our own. Nor did we believe a convoy bringing Malika to that nation would ever survive the journey. And, indeed, for as long as Riqeta still lived, she would protect her better than anyone else could, her mother's heart rendering her warrior's spirit far more fearsome than it had been even in her early youth.

Asfiya was not safer than Koroma, Hisalir's evil designs surely set against both.

No place in Icilia was now truly safe.

With the nobles and the citizens now outright welcoming Hisalir's influence, Koroma was drowning. The crown, deprived of income from our own farms and trades, surviving only on the dregs of our coffers, was failing. Compassion, losing its bastion in the penniless orphanages and hospitals, was dying. Shadows swarmed all around us, besieging what remained of our nation's heart. What hope we had was now gone.

I did not know what the next year would bring.

I could not offer my precious daughter a feast for her birthday. I could not promise the full set of armor and weapons she would soon be skilled enough to wield. I could not vow her crown would survive for her to someday wear.

We only dared to remain in the palace because it was now entirely empty at night save for us, Raman, Leoma, and Colan and because Riqeta had spent over a decade building its layers of wards.

I did not know what the next month would bring.

Though our decision had seemed right at the time, how we now wished that no one had ever known Malika was born!

For Riqeta and I could not prevent the evil from spreading—

Another whimper drew my gaze to Arafan, who was squirming again in his sleep.

Sighing, I pushed the bleak thoughts from my mind, not wanting them to affect our baby when fretting would not solve our troubles. Pressing my lips to his little capped head, I rocked him until he settled. Then, activating my farsight for my hourly examination of the capital and her surrounds, I looked up again at his mother and his elder sister.

Riqeta corrected Malika's grip on the hilt of her blade. "Be careful, my heart," she was saying, "for, if your hand slips, the edge will cut your own hand."

"But Abbi made this one without an edge!" Malika chirped, clear little voice bright as a note of sunlight. Her vivid jewel-blue eyes, so much brighter than my own, turned toward me, accompanied by a sweet smile, before she looked back up at her mother.

I exhaled deeply, my heart at once melting and igniting, love overwhelming every part of my being. A lifetime would not lessen the effect of those eyes upon me. It was why I had spent part of what was left of the royal armory in forging her first sword last year. If only there was enough left for all the weapons she wanted to try!

"Yes, Malika," Riqeta said, giving me a smile as well, "but we

212   EPILOGUE: THE WISDOM TO RECOVER FROM THESE …

must learn to respect this sword so we know how to respect one that does have an edge when we are older."

"Yes, Ammi," Malika said obediently. Her lovely little face scrunched in concentration as she executed a perfect downward swing. "Was that good, Ammi?"

One bare lightweight sword held in one hand, Riqeta walked around Malika, examining her form. Then her rose lips spread in a grin, revealing her dimple. "Wonderfully done, Malika. Now, can you show me the upward swing?"

Malika bobbed her head. Then suddenly she dropped her sword and threw her arms around Riqeta's waist. "Thank you for teaching me, Ammi!"

Tears brimmed in Riqeta's eyes, the affection overwhelming her as it did me, as she cast aside her sword and hugged our daughter back. "Of course, Malika, my heart." Fierce love burned on her face, washing away, for a moment, the deep creases that now framed her amber eyes, her pert nose, her rose lips, the place where the dimple emerged on her cheek... Her face was, as always, the most beautiful I had ever beheld, but I abhorred the sight of those crinkles as I did the heavy streaks of white and gray in her walnut bun. Our troubles wore away at her, as they did me, and how I wished that were not so. How I wished her happiness was not burdened by the uncertainty of our future...

Riqeta glanced up from the cap covering Malika's red-gold head and met my gaze.

Attuned by thirteen years of marriage, aided by the intertwined strands of our monarchs' bonds, we read our thoughts in each other's eyes.

The sorrow I felt for her burdens was matched by hers for mine. Like her, my face bore wrinkles that far exceeded what a man still not yet in his middling years should have. My mustache and beard, once a paler version of Malika's red-gold tresses, were now more gray and white than red-blond. Age hunted us with nearly as much intensity as Hisalir plotted our downfall.

My lips quirked in a wry smile.

When Riqeta and I had told Malika in the moon of Lushatte that we would not be able to properly celebrate her sixth birthday, she had replied, seriously, sweetly, unmarred by a single complaint, that all she wanted was a few days of time around her birthday with only our family and a few lessons on the use of the sword.

It had been a pleasure to agree—and a necessity, for she needed to know how to defend herself and her brother should the worst happen to her mother, her uncle, her staff, and me. Indeed, preferably, no one save us would know the extent of her skill.

For that reason, as well as her request, in the last week the palace had been empty even during the day, with Raman, Leoma, and Colan guarding the doors of whichever room Riqeta and I chose. Riqeta taught Malika, resuming her training, while I attended to Arafan's needs.

Riqeta offered a wry smile in return, before glancing down as Malika drew back.

"Ammi," our heart began, sounding worried, little gold brows drawing together, "are you better now?"

Those smiles turned affectionate. "Oh, Malika," Riqeta said, easily swinging her up into her arms, cuddling her close, "I am much better now. Helping your brother into the world was a bit difficult, but the Almighty has restored my strength."

Malika nodded, seeming thoughtful. "I am happy that you are better, Ammi. And I am happy we have Arafan now." Turning, she ran to the dais, bounced up the three steps, and rushed to my side. "Can I kiss him, Abbi?"

"Of course, my darling," I said, unable to help a grin as I tilted my son so that his little face was visible.

Arafan smacked his lips. Then his little eyes opened, the little rosebud of his mouth stretching into a toothless grin as he looked up at his elder sister.

"Arafan!" Malika sang, sprinkling his face with kisses. "Hally! My baby Hally!"

The little baby giggled, unmistakable adoration in his blue eyes.

Malika placed another kiss atop his nose, hugged my neck in a blaze of warmth, and then skipped back to her mother and picked up her sword. "Do I do the upward swing like this, Ammi?"

Riqeta flashed me a happy smile before assessing Malika's form. "Not quite, my heart." She retrieved her sword and slashed upward. "Be careful of the position of your feet..."

I sighed, still smiling, and glanced down at Arafan, who was starting to fuss a little. With a brief redirection of my farsight, I checked his diaper.

Almost ready for a change...

As I continued to rock him, I remembered how wondrous it was that Riqeta had given life to this child so safely.

After Malika's miraculous birth, despite how easy it was, Riqeta and I had not expected to have any more children. But, somehow, the Almighty had blessed with another son... and, though carrying and birthing him had been full of even greater pain than the healers had foreseen, she had not only brought him into the world but also managed to recover in only four months.

In four months, even as she nursed him, she was already wearing armor and wielding her weapons, returning to the rigor of fitness she had maintained through all of our years together.

"Arafan," I whispered, cuddling the baby, before standing and laying him down on my throne in preparation for changing his diaper. With quick, efficient, practiced movements, I swapped the soiled cloth for another, crooning to him all the while, and then gathered him back up and placed him in his favorite spot on my shoulder, his face resting against my neck.

Arafan wriggled a little before falling back asleep.

"Truly supreme," I murmured, unable to lift my eyes from the reddish walnut fuzz lining the edges of his cap. The Guardian of Names had given him his name, sending a letter in the claws of an eagle, so I knew he truly would someday be his name. Just as Malika would... "Fulfillment and supremacy." My lips curved, my mind turning to the discussions that Riqeta and I had had many times over the last six years. "I wonder whose the child named Beneficence is... Perhaps one of those four couples? Princess Diyana?"

A shout from Malika drew my attention, and I glanced up to see her chasing Riqeta across the room, socked feet sliding across the floor, both of them laughing, drawing laughter from my lips as well.

With a flick of concentration, I turned my farsight from the back of the palace around the southern wall to the front of the city.

It was clear. Not a single person stirring. The remnants of the late snowfall from yesterday melting on the gate and roads, while the bright flowers of spring sprouted on the surrounding mountain slopes.

I started to withdraw my farsight.

A boot crushed a flower.

A shadow blackened the blue sky.

Then, rolling out over the hills like the unveiling of a bleak, moonless night across the heaven, appeared an army...

The mass of armor, streaked with scarlet, bearing the insignia of a carmine skull, seethed, rippling like the blinks of an eye, a monster's eye, a chasm staring at Samaha as though it intended to devour her whole.

At the head of that army stood a man wreathed in shadows.

The air around him shrieked in agony, a vow of the torment he would inflict on all whose path he crossed, stealing them from life in the most brutal of ways.

Hisalir.

"Riqeta," I whispered through numb lips. "He is here!"

In my physical vision, Riqeta halted mid-step. Her expression froze, then turned hard.

Realizing her mother was no longer behind her, Malika skidded to a stop and turned, confusion twisting her precious face.

Sneering as though aware I was watching, Hisalir clenched a fist and raised it over his head.

Creaking heavily, the gates swung open.

"Riqeta!" I cried, leaping to my feet. "He is coming!" My heart felt as though it would collapse, so I screamed, "Dalaaneman!"

Riqeta strode forward, sheathed her sword, and grasped Malika's little hand. "Raman!" she called. "We need you!"

One of the grand doors to the throne hall flew open, and Raman rushed inside, closing it behind him. "What happened, Sister!" he exclaimed.

At the sound, Leoma and Colan dashed inside from the antechamber.

"Hisalir is coming!" I screamed. The high noise roused Arafan, who began to wail. Instinctively I started to rock him, but my attention remained on Riqeta's stern face. "Is it time for our last plan?"

"Last plan?" Malika echoed, clutching her mother's waist, little sword falling by her feet.

Though hugging her back, Riqeta cast away all the gentle air she carried in privacy, transforming into the warrior who had slain hundreds in accordance with the laws of the Quest. "Yes," she declared. "It is time."

Raman's face blanched, Leoma's cheeks lost all gloss, and Colan's plates stilled, terror sweeping over them in the monarch's bond.

Our daughter's expression crumpled with an anguish no child should ever feel.

The same terror dragged at me as well, but, with all of Riqeta's training, I focused my mind. "Leoma, Colan, there is a boon I must beg of you." Though Riqeta and I had told them that we had a final plan, we had not given any details, for we knew they would protest.

Our maid and valet of thirteen years hurriedly knelt in front of me. "Please, your Majesty," Leoma said, "we will do anything for you. There are no boons between us."

"At your command, my king," Colan added, cupping his hands up in the gesture of entreaty.

I forced a grim smile. "I must ask you to flee with Arafan. Few know of his birth—it was possible to conceal the birth of a second prince as was not for the crown princess—so there is a chance he may survive this, if you leave now."

Both Leoma and Colan dipped their heads. "At your command," they both murmured. Then Leoma asked anxiously, "What of your Majesties?"

I glanced at Riqeta.

While I had been speaking to our staff, Riqeta had said to Raman, "Brother, there is one last boon I must beg you to grant us: fleeing with Malika, as far from here as you can. The enemy will target her, so you must give all your years of skill and strength to protecting her."

Malika pressed her little face into Riqeta's neck before looking up at her uncle.

"At your command, your Majesty," Raman immediately replied, dipping a reverence. Then he hesitated. "But what will you do, Sister? Will you not escape with us?"

In my farsight, Hisalir was striding boldly down the central avenue, already halfway to the palace, his deputies nowhere to be seen.

His army was pillaging the city, dragging our citizens from their homes before inflicting the worst violations upon them, and setting fire to the towers and turrets. Besmirching the sacred stone with smoke, vice, and blood.

Our soldiers were joining the black wave of his army.

My arms clenched around Arafan, who was now shrieking against my chest. "We cannot, Raman."

"No!" Koroma's last loyal vassals cried. "What are you saying, your Majesty!" "You cannot mean to stay!" "Oh Dalaaneman!"

Malika gasped, beautiful blue eyes as wide as the moon.

"We must slow his approach," Riqeta stated, donning her gloves, "and I must be the one to confront him. Both for your and our children's sakes and for Koroma's." She moved her lieutenant monarch's signet ring to the chain around her neck.

Raman, Leoma, and Colan opened their mouths, intent upon protest, upon finding some other solution.

"Please," I whispered. "I beg you in Dalaaneman's name. There is no time."

At the anguish in my tone, the three of them dipped their heads, pain twisting their faces.

Riqeta nodded. "May the Almighty reward you richly." Then, bending her head, she tilted Malika's chin up. "My heart, Abbi and I need you to go now with Uncle Raman."

Malika's lips quivered as tears slid down her cheeks, so painful to behold. But she only said, "I love you, Ammi. The Almighty will bring us together again." She reached up and kissed her mother's mouth.

"From your lips to the Almighty's blessing," Riqeta whispered, a single terrible tear spilling from her eyes even as her expression remained stern. She pressed a kiss to Malika's forehead. "I love you, my Daughter. Always serve the Quest Leader. Blessings for your sixth birthday. May the Almighty bless you."

Walking toward them both, I kissed Arafan's wet face. "I love you, my darling. Serve your sister well, my Son. May the Almighty bless you." Then I offered him to his mother, who closed her eyes and held him one last time, pressing him to the chest that still brimmed with his milk—of which he would never have another sip.

The moment I did so, Malika threw her arms around my waist. "I love you, Abbi," she whispered.

Unable to help my tears at those most precious words, I lifted her into my arms and kissed her forehead. "I love you, Malika. Never forget, my heir, that you have all of your mother's strength and more. Let no one steal your voice, my Daughter. Blessings for your sixth birthday. May the Almighty bless you."

Malika pressed her face against mine and nodded. "The Almighty is with us," she said in the sacred tongue, in the tone of a promise. Then she kissed my nose.

Suppressing a sob, I picked up her edgeless sword and sheathed it in the scabbard hanging from her little lilac belt. Then I gave her to my brother.

Raman clutched her to his chest, as though she was all that was left of his world. He gazed at me for a final moment, tears dripping down the careworn face that was so much like mine.

"I love you, Brother," I said. "May the Almighty be pleased with you."

His lips tightened, unable to speak any words of farewell. So all he did was bow to his sister and me, trusting my bond to tell me of his heart, and, balancing our daughter's weight, drew his sword. Then he turned and ran for the antechamber.

In my farsight, Hisalir was reaching the doors of the palace.

Retaining her battle-focus despite the devastation in her gaze, Riqeta kissed her crying son's forehead, her farewells spoken in the mysterious language of mother and child, and gave him to Leoma.

Both Leoma and Colan bowed and ran for the antechamber, Arafan's wails echoing behind them as they trusted more in speed than stealth.

My arms immediately felt empty, both of our children gone, now beyond my reach.

We would never see them again...

The agony of that truth reflected in her beautiful golden eyes, Riqeta rose onto her toes, cupped my face, and pulled me into a kiss.

Passionate, full of love, deep and satisfying, yet tasting of the salt of tears.

"I love you," we whispered to each other, embracing. "May the Almighty bless you. May Dalaaneman be with us."

Then Riqeta stepped back and drew both her lightweight swords. Her features hardened further, all emotion disappearing, and she pivoted to face the door, sword raised, socked feet spread, ready to attack.

Her body still retained some of the softness of pregnancy, her chest swollen with milk, a slight pouch over her middle visible even through her armor.

It only increased the grandeur of her glory.

Mother and warrior both, the most powerful in all of Icilia.

And the weapons that she wielded, my courtship gift, like the silver wedding circlet around her signet ring, were the proof of our love.

I dipped my head to her. Then, steeling myself for battle as Riqeta had taught me, moving my own signet ring to a chain, I drew my own sword and stood before the thrones, in front of the door that led to where our family was escaping through the palace corridors.

Hisalir tore open the doors of the throne hall.

Lifting the blades still stained with his blood, magic glowing around her fists, Riqeta leapt up into the air.

I steadied my breathing and waited.

If anyone could defeat him, she could.

She was the only person who held a chance.

But we did not expect to win.

Only to slow his approach.

Giving ourselves as living barriers.

Praying to save our daughter and our son...

Unto their hands—unto Malika's hands—the Almighty had bestowed the wisdom to recover from these evil times.

They had to escape to free us all.

Supremacy.

Fulfillment.

Beneficence.

Lucian! Malika!

Aalia! Manara! Naret!

Dalaaneman!

EPILOGUE: THE MONSTER'S VISAGE

Perspective: The Blood-soaked Sorcerer
Date: Eyyésal, the eighteenth day of the fourth moon, Likberre, of
the year 483, C.Q.

Hisalir, the Blood-soaked Sorcerer as he now instructed his followers to call him, grinned as he paced Koroma's throne hall, his boots leaving bloody marks on the hallowed floor.

"I have waited almost thirteen years for this day, you know," he said casually. "You dared to humiliate me, and I had to slaughter all of my followers because of that. Well, all of them except for that traitor Khonatir." Briefly abandoning his easy tone, he spat the name of his once-brother. "You set my plans back by almost two years. Although it did turn out acceptably—I went to places I didn't expect to, and I found deputies of higher quality. Still, though," his tone hardened, as did his shadow-wreathed fist, "I will make sure to extract every drop of suffering from your virtuous souls."

His enemies, Riqeta and Naman, the only royal pair to actually pose a threat to him, writhed on the floor, screams squeezed from their throats. Still living, his magic disallowing the relief of death, despite the blood pooling around them, the monarchs stared up at him, eyes wide in unnatural horror.

The Blood laughed, loud and scornful, before changing to the sacred tongue: "You defeated me once, Riqeta, but my power has grown beyond your mortal imagination." A flex of his fist drew out a scream. "No will, no matter how sacred, can withstand mine." Another flex, another scream. "It does not matter that you choose to not fear me—I will teach that fear to you." He smirked, enjoying their shock at the perfectly formed syllables of the sacred tongue that poured from his lips. "Even the Divine will fall before me."

The royal couple writhed again, the hot, luscious flare of agony burning both their bodies and their souls.

Grinning, the Blood directed his slow, unhurried prowl to the left, where Riqeta's swords had fallen.

They still gleamed with the stain of his blood—the only blood anyone had drawn from his veins since his twenty-second year.

The utter humiliation of having to beg—actually *beg*—for his life blazed fresh within his mind.

How could he, who possessed greater conjury than any of the old conjurors, have been *defeated*? And that, too, by a *woman*? By a ridiculous little virtuous *princess*?

It had been an embarrassment.

One further compounded by having to wait for Khonatir to undo the spells on his armor and later by that same boy's betrayal.

"You stole my most loyal servant from me, you know," he commented. "He always admired you too much." He shook his head, almost absently flexing his fist for another scream. "If only I had killed him when he snuck away one of your abandoned hilts. But, then, he was valuable, if not as valuable as he could be, until the night he ran away to you." He glanced at Riqeta's and Naman's broken bodies, frozen in place as his own had been. "There is no end to what I plan to punish you for. You represent everything I hate." With those words, he ground his heel into one of the swords marked with his blood, then the other, crushing them into dust, hilt and all.

Then he strode back around. "By the way, excellent work in trying to slow me down. I suppose Riqeta intended to fight me till death before you tried, Naman? Her attacking while you remained fresh so that there would be two barriers between me and your child? Though you do realize you only saw me when you did because I wanted you to?" He purposefully addressed his words to only the fallen king, relishing the petty slight. "As if I would let that happen. There is too much pleasure to be had from you." His lips split open over teeth that were sharpening into fangs. "I don't intend to ever let you die."

Riqeta's plates cracked, shattering beneath the pressure of his magic, cutting into the exposed pink of the underlying skin. Blood exploded from Naman's translucent cheeks. Their crowns and signet rings fractured into countless razor-sharp shards of precious metal and jewels.

The Blood tilted his head back, savoring the heady draught of pain.

As they screamed, blood pouring into their mouths, the antechamber door opened.

His favorite deputy, Suvona, dragged in a little girl, one dressed in blood-drenched silver robes with a lilac belt. An edge-less sword was clenched in the child's hands, and she swung it at Suvona, repeatedly trying to hit her despite the conjuror's blood-drawing grip on her arm.

"Your Viciousness!" Suvona called. "The king's brother put up quite a fight, but I caught him and grabbed the brat. His fear before he died was quite a feast, a real boost to my power, but this one seems entirely resistant." The thin, tall Nasimih woman curled a lip, disappointed at losing the chance at first torture. Then she threw the little princess at the Blood's feet.

Her parents screamed, this time unprompted by conjury, bloodshot eyes weeping at the sight of their daughter in the Blood's clutches.

The child they believed would save all of Icilia.

The Blood-soaked Sorcerer snickered, amused both by his enemies' pain and his subordinate's attempts to take more than what he allowed her. Then he caught the brat's wrist as she raised her sword to strike him.

"Let my parents go!" the little crown princess yelled. Grief filled her vivid, sky-bright blue eyes at the sight of her parents' ruined faces and writhing, bleeding, broken forms, but not a single drop of fear. Not even physical pain.

Utterly immune—her blessing holding strong, the fathoms-deep well of her magic frothing in her defense.

Eager to dim those blue eyes, the Blood chuckled and tore the sword from her hand, leaving bruises on her fingers. Then he yanked her head back so she met his gaze.

Malika stared back, unafraid.

On her lips was the sacred title of the first Quest Leader.

The title he intended to eradicate from Icilia's memory.

The Blood let the mask of his Mutharrim face drop. Revealing the monster's visage beneath.

In a burst of utter gratification, his cream cheeks and nose swelled unevenly into a black wolf-like snout, his green eyes darkened to sinister black flames set in gray sclera, his full mouth stretched into a lipless gash over a cavern of blood-red fangs—a beast's head atop a man's body.

Her eyes full of grudging admiration, Suvona smirked, letting her own monster's face loose.

Riqeta and Naman shrieked at the sight, so close to their daughter, but Malika did not flinch.

The Blood-soaked Sorcerer laughed, this time his voice not smooth and unctuous but coarse, grating, like the screech of claws scoring living stone.

"You are not scary!" declared the crown princess, scion of both the woman he despised and the civilization he disdained.

Laughing again, the Blood tightened his grip on her wrist,

crushing the delicate bones. "There is no one coming to save you, little *princess.*" He sneered the name of the rank.

"The Almighty is with me!" Malika declared. "Dalaanem will never leave me!"

He tossed her into his deputy's bruising grip, then took a step toward her parents, preparing himself for the deliciousness of desecration. "You do not know fear, daughter of Riqeta."

"The Almighty is going to save us!" Malika asserted. "Dalaanem is going to protect us!"

The Blood-soaked Sorcerer smiled darkly. "So I will teach you the meaning of fear, Malika."

Riqeta and Naman screamed.

Then so did Malika.

SIXTEEN YEARS LATER...

The story of King Naman aj-Shehenkorom and Queen Riqeta naj-Shehenkorom continues through that of their daughter, Malika, in *The Lord of Freedom*.

The first chapter of the first book, *The Bell Tolling*, follows...

CHAPTER 1: CIRCLING ENDLESSLY

Book: _The Bell Tolling_
Perspective: _Malika_
Date: _Eyyéqan, the ninth day of the fifth moon, Marberre, of the year 499, C.Q._

Gratitude to the Almighty. I dared to breathe again as the soldier turned back to his comrades, dismissing the shuffle of a pebble on sand that had almost stolen my hard-earned freedom.

I waited a moment, then crept forward through the shadows cast by the last of the tents.

A few steps more... I chanted within my mind.

The soldiers' encampment stretched to the north and the south in a limitless ocean to rival the desert itself. Erected overnight, it was intended for a single goal: my recapture. For what else could explain the presence of a contingent of Ezulal soldiers, who required copious amounts of water to live, in the deserts of Zahacim? Routine patrols were composed of women and men of the Areteen; these Ezulal troops, once members of my own loyal forces, were here to torment me.

How many times I had been forced to watch the Blood-soaked Sorcerer overthrow their free will by pouring water mixed with black spells down their throats. How many times they had subsequently aided the Blood in committing unimaginable violence against me.

The memories brought caustic bile to my mouth, further searing my achingly dry throat. Sharpening the quintessentially Ezulal longing for water to an almost unbearable degree. Far greater, though, was the ever unquenched desire to care for my people.

If only I could free some of them...

But, after those many years of abuse, I could not be certain whether breaking their contrived loyalty was at all possible. And, if I chanced an attempt, and it failed, I would never have another... I needed to disappear. Until he next found me.

After nearly seven years in the desert, I had abandoned trying to understand how the Blood repeatedly calculated precisely the direction in which I would travel next and sent soldiers after me. He had never relented in his pursuit. I would never be rid of him, never escape this endless dash for survival.

Despite my thirst, tears welled in my eyes as I disappeared behind a pair of sand dunes. My memories were the grounds of nightmares...

I had been the Blood's most closely guarded prisoner, for I was his prize, the Heir to Koroma, the nation whose fall marked the death rattle of Icilia's resistance. He had stolen me from where I had knelt sobbing in the blood pooling around my parents' desecrated corpses. As he dragged me from the throne room, he had laughed at my pleas for pity and mercy. Though I was a child of only six years, all alone, my parents dead and my baby brother missing.

In the months that followed, he crushed every wisp of my spirit, suppressing my magic (whatever it had been), tearing away my dignity, and shattering my mind. There had been little at all left of me. And yet he continued to endlessly torment me, relishing in my pain for nine years. I had lost all thought of escape.

Somehow the thought returned to me when he casually mentioned that I was near the age of majority. Trapped for so many years in a nightmare, I had immediately known that he had designs on my womanhood, a torture he had delayed in inflicting so that he might better savor it.

Somehow, a fire ignited in my heart: I would not suffer this one torture, though I had not saved myself from so many others.

With that spark providing animation to my movements, I gathered strands of my hair, day after day. When I had enough strands, I used the dirt and grease from my own person to stick them together into a lock-pick. With much struggle, in quiet moments between patrols and his visits, I unlocked my manacles. With the heavy chains I overpowered the next guard, who had come with the trickle of sustenance that was the Blood's only attempt to stave off starvation, and crept out of the fortress.

My pale skin had been so filthy that the shadows easily concealed me. With hunger and pain weakening my every movement, my escape was the Almighty's blessing, and my survival thereafter even more so.

Stumbling over mountains and neglected fields, I had fled northwest at first, desperate to simply leave the Blood's capital territory behind, even if that meant never returning to my own nation. But, as his soldiers pursued me, I realized that the old border between Koroma and Bhalasa, though defunct because the Blood tyrannized all of Icilia, was too heavily guarded. Despite the vast distance and thick forests, I had a better chance of passing into Zahacim, the eastern border of which with Koroma had sparser patrols, if I was desperate enough to brave the desert. And I had been certainly so desperate.

I was still no less desperate seven years later.

How low the noble are brought, I thought grimly as I slipped down another dune toward an Areteen caravan. I was the last Heir to Koroma, raised from birth to rule with a pure, kind heart and all virtue, but the Blood had turned me into a thief and a fugitive. I had only a filched dagger, a poorly constructed bow, and a pair of dull arrows, and I had not been raised to hunt in Zahacim. To survive, I had to steal from people who had little more food and security than I did.

Since the Blood had a military presence with even tiny, settled caravans, I could not shelter in the same area for more than a few days at a time. Because a terrifying number of soldiers guarded the northern and western borders and no passage south out of Icilia existed, I could not leave Zahacim. So I circled endlessly.

I, Malika tej-Shehenkorom, was going to die on these dunes. My life, my promise, was wasted.

FOR THE FULL STORY...

Begin reading *The Bell Tolling* today!

The Bell Tolling: Book One of The Lord of Freedom is the first book of the primary *The Lord of Freedom* series.
The Resonant Bell: A Complement to The Bell Tolling can be read alongside or subsequently.
The Bell Tolling & The Resonant Bell: Anniversary Edition combines the chapters of both books in the author's recommended reading order.

For full summaries and options on where to read these books, please visit https://amenajamali.com/books/.

PRONUNCIATION SUPPORT

This guide is for selected names. For the sake of brevity, short glossary notes are only given for those who do not directly appear in this volume, as well as the names of the five kinds.

The Quests

The Shining Guide—
The representative sent by the Almighty who is the founder of Icilia's civilization.

Aalia— Aaah-lee-ah
Lady Queen Aalia the Ideal of Light, the first Quest Leader, of the Muthaarim, who spread Icilia's civilization to all five kinds.

Manara— Muh-naa-ruh
Graced Queen Manara the Exemplar of Truth, the Second of the first Quest Leader, of the Muthaarim, who established Icilia's arts and sciences.

Naret— Naa-ret
Honored King Naret the Exemplar of Love, the third Potentate of the Quest of Light, of the Muthaarim, who established Icilia's customs and traditions.

Lucian— Loo-see-uhn
Lord Lucian the Ideal of Freedom, the second Quest Leader, of

the Muthaarim, who returns Light to Icilia amid the evil of the Blood-soaked Sorcerer. *The Lord of Freedom* is his story.

Malika— Maa-lih-kah
Graced Malika the Exemplar of Wisdom, the Second of the second Quest Leader, of the Ezulal, who returns Light to Icilia amid the evil of the Blood-soaked Sorcerer. She is the daughter of Riqeta and Naman. *The Lord of Freedom* is her story.

Family, Guardians, and Vassals (those with repeated mentions, in order of appearance)

Riqeta sej-Shehenzahak, *later* Shehenkorom, naj-Shehenkorom—
Rih-keht-uh sehj-Sheh-hen-zah-haak, *later* Sheh-hen-koh-rohm, naaj-Sheh-hen-koh-rohm
('ket' is said with particular emphasis, the 't' is pronounced with a hard click)

Serama sej-Shehenzahak— Seh-rah-muh sehj-Sheh-hen-zah-haak

Naman sej-Shehenkorom, *later* tej-Shehenkorom, aj-Shehenkorom—
Nuh-muhn sehj-Sheh-hen-koh-rohm, *later* tehj-Sheh-hen-koh-rohm, aaj-Sheh-hen-koh-rohm

Raman tej-Shehenkorom, *later* sej-Shehenkorom, Shehenkorom—
Ruh-muhn tehj-Sheh-hen-koh-rohm, *later* sehj-Sheh-hen-koh-rohm, Sheh-hen-koh-rohm

Colan— Co-lahn ('Co' rhymes with woe)

Leoma— Lee-oh-muh

Doman aj-Shehenkorom— Doh-muhn aaj-Sheh-hen-koh-rohm

Edana naj-Shehenkorom— Eh-dah-nuh naaj-Sheh-hen-koh-rohm

Basima qia-Kafalira— Bah-see-muh qee-uh-Kuh-faa-lee-rah

Falan Shehenkorom— Fah-lahn Sheh-hen-koh-rohm

Countess qia-Mutanacera— qee-uh-Moo-tuh-naa-ceh-rah

Captain bi-Himacer— bee-Hee-mah-cehr

Lieutenant Gatiemt— Gaa-tee-ehmt (the letters for 'ehmt' are all pronounced together.)

Duke Falahan Theriett— Fah-lah-haan Theh-ree-ett (the 'ett' is pronounced with a hard 't')

Talan Iqrarie— Tuh-lahn Ik-raa-ree (the 'Ik' is pronounced with a hard 'k')

Sergeant bia-Donacera— bee-uh-Doh-naa-ceh-ruh

Diyana sej-Shehasfiyi— (Dee-yah-nuh sehj-Sheh-haas-fee-yee) the third princess of Asfiya, of the Mutharrim, a dear cousin of Riqeta, Naman, and Serama, who is known for her magical power, scholarship, and skill in war. She is reputed to be the most powerful warrior of northern and western Icilia.

Beres sej-Shehasfiyi— (Beh-rez sehj-Sheh-haas-fee-yee) the consort of the third princess of Asfiya, of the Mutharrim, who is known for his magical power and gentleness.

Bolana Shehenkorom— Boh-lah-nuh Sheh-hen-koh-rohm

Arafan sej-Shehenkorom— Uh-ruh-fuhn sehj-Sheh-hen-koh-rohm

Enemies

Count Flirien— Flih-ree-ehn

Misleta tej-Shehenzahak— Mis-leh-tuh tehj-Sheh-hen-zah-haak
the crown princess of Zahacim, Serama's eldest sister in Zahacim,
who harbors great anger and jealousy toward Riqeta, once her
possible future lieutenant monarch.

Count Hilaserie—
Hih-laa-seh-ree

Charan Theriett— Chah-ruhn Theh-ree-ett (the 'ett' is
pronounced with a hard 't')

Khonatir bi-Mutanacer— Khoh-nah-teer bee-Moo-tuh-naa-cehr
('Kh' is pronounced with a rasp in the throat; the 'teer' is
pronounced with a slight emphasis)
Although Khonatir later returns to the service of the Quests, his
name is included in this section because of the primary role he
possesses in this volume.

Hisalir— Hih-saa-leer ('saa' is pronounced 'tha')
No title or surname is given for Hisalir because of the horrors
uncovered about him in this volume.

The World (in rough order of appearance)

Athar—ut-hur ('ut' has the same sound as 'but', 'hur' sounds
similar to 'her')

Icilia—Ih-sill-lee-ah ('sill' has the same sound as sill)

Muthaarim— Moo-thaa-rihm (spoken lightly)
the first people of the Shining Guide, who were specially attuned

to athar, had jewel-bright eyes, and glowed silver with their emotions.

Mutharrim— Moo-thuh-rihm (the 'r' of 'rihm' is rolled, giving a heavier sound)
the descendants of the first people but considered fallen from their high holiness though still somewhat attuned to athar; physically, they are a little over six feet tall and possess jewel-bright eyes, bright hair, and creamy skin marked with little chips of colored light that glows silver when overcome with intense emotion.

Areteen— Uh-rut-teen (the 't' is emphasized in both syllables)
the kind attuned to the earth; physically, they are a little under five feet tall and possess dark or amber eyes, dark hair, and darker brown skin that in places is segmented into plates (like hard, flat scales that are part of the skin rather than atop it); the vibration of their plates shows intense emotion.

Ezulal— Eh-zoo-laal
the kind attuned to water; physically, they are about five and a half feet tall and possess blue or hazel eyes, dark hair with a glossy shine, and pale, peachy white skin that is nearly translucent in places that blushes when overcome with intense emotion.

Nasimih— Nuh-see-meeh ('meeh' ends abruptly after the enunciation of the 'h')
the kind attuned to the air; physically, they are a little under six feet tall and possess blue, gray, or brown eyes, thin, wispy pale hair, and light brown skin that glosses when overcome with intense emotion or touched by the wind.

Sholanar— Shoh-laa-naahr
the kind attuned to fire; physically, they are a over six and a half feet tall, have wings commensurate with their height, and possess golden, red, or amber eyes, thick, curly dark or red hair, and dark

brown skin that in places is scaled (the scales are atop the skin instead of part of it); each of the Sholanar has a unique scale color and, when emotional, those scales glow a brighter shade of their natural color (or, conversely, become a duller shade).

Zahacim— Zah-haa-sim

Khuduren— Khoo-doo-rehn ('Kh' is pronounced with a rasp in the throat)

Bhalasa— Bhuh-lah-sah

Etheqa— Eh-theh-kah

Nademan— Naa-deh-muhn (the accent is on 'deh')

Asfiya— As-fee-yah ('As' rhymes with 'mass')

Koroma— Koh-roh-mah

Incé— een-seh (because of the noted accent, 'seh' is pronounced with particular emphasis; see the Glossary of the Sacred Tongue)

Dalaanem— Duh-laan-ehm (see the Glossary of the Sacred Tongue)

Dalaaneman— Duh-laan-ehm-uhn (see the Glossary of the Sacred Tongue)

Koroya— Koh-roh-yah (the address for Koromic women; equivalent to Miss or Misses)

Koroyi— Koh-roh-yee (the address for Koromic men; equivalent to Mister)

Koroma's cities and villages (north to south)

Rifom— Rih-fohm (province)

Samaha— Suh-maa-huh (capital)

Atafom— Ah-toh-fohm (province)

Hafébunna Cliffs— Haa-feh-boo-nah (the cliffs themselves; because of the noted accent, 'feh' is pronounced with particular emphasis)

Ináma— In-aah-muh (city; 'In' rhymes with 'kin'; because of the noted accent, 'aah' is pronounced with particular emphasis)

Hilaserios— Hih-laa-seh-ree-ohs (county)

Fliriene— Flih-ree-eh-neh (county)

Hurom— Hoo-rohm (province)

Mutanacere— Moo-tuh-naa-ceh-reh (county)

Walom— Wah-lohm (province)

Maqom— Mah-qohm (province)

THE GLOSSARY OF THE SACRED TONGUE

The people of Icilia speak two languages, Alimàzahre and Siléalaah. The first is the sacred tongue, given originally by the Shining Guide to the Muthaarim, and the second is the common tongue, given by the Quest of Light to the five kinds. Alimàzahre is the language of religion and magic, while Siléalaah is the language of politics and society. That is why spells and rituals are always recited in the first, while pledges and speeches are announced in the second.

The fascinated reader may consider the entirety of this Edition to be translated from Siléalaah, save for the volumes' titles, which are given in the Author's Note and the Acknowledgments in Alimàzahre.

For the sake of easing the reader's transition into the world of *The Lord of Freedom*, this volume contains only a few words from Alimàzahre.

Common Words:

Incé

A word used in Icilia that combines the meanings of "mortal" and "human" and is used to refer to all five kinds

Dalaanem; Dalaaneman

The formal address in the Sacred Tongue for the Quest

Leader; translates to "my Lady" and "my Lord"—"my Leader," truly, as the same address is used for Lady Queen Aalia the Ideal of Light and Lord Lucian the Ideal of Freedom (literally, "my guide")

Dalaaneman is a form of this address that translate to "our Lady" and "our Lord"—the people of Icilia use this version when they feel they are among the likeminded devout.

Of all the words in these appendices, this is the most important, as it is the name invoked by the people of Icilia in times of great need—or at least so was the custom before the Blood-soaked Sorcerer destroyed it, and so will it be as the wonder of Lord Lucian's ascension sweeps across the land.

Hanny and Hally; Hanlaëm

The words for Sister and Brother used in Zahacim, derived from the sacred words for the same, hanla and hanli. As an indication of greater reverence, Honored Arista at times refers to Graced Malika as "Hanlaëm," my Sister.

Ammi and Abbi; Ambele

The words for Mother and Father used in much of Icilia, derived from the sacred words for the same, amba and ambi. In the title given in the Author's Note, the word Ambele translates to "parents."

Titles:

a'Makalle é a'Ambele é Fidaana Malika a-Haséalaah

The title given in the Author's Note for this volume is 'The Witness of the Parents of Graced Malika the Exemplar of Wisdom.'

a'Silómizze é a'Raah-é-Fazze

The title given in the Acknowledgments for this set of volumes, the *The Lord of Freedom* series, is 'The History of the Quest of Freedom'—more exactly, 'The Connection to the Past of the Quest of Freedom.'

ACKNOWLEDGMENTS

At the fulfillment of the first preliminary to a'Silómizze é a'Raah-é-Fazze, the Archivist proffers gratitude to the Almighty, to the Lady of Icilia, and to the Guardian of Names for the blessing of this chance to behold the glory of the Quest of Freedom. May the Lord of Freedom be pleased with this praise of his name.

* * *

My first and greatest thanks are to the Almighty, Whose blessing of creativity in writing the Quest of Freedom's story flows greater and greater with every passing day. Such has that gift been that it has engendered in this story wisdom and prudence beyond that of which I am capable. Thus, I proffer all my gratitude to the Almighty and, under divine auspice, the Lord who welcomes into his shelter all those who desire never to be parted from Divine Light.

My second offering of gratitude is to the Princes of my community, who have supported my endeavors at every footstep. Their praise and encouragement brighten the path spreading out before my feet. Gratitude to the Almighty for them. I have no less appreciation for my mother and my father, who are the inspirations for the heroes of this story, Riqeta and Naman, the mother and the father of Graced Malika the Exemplar of Wisdom.

Third is my praise for Mary Reid, who has gladly championed the crafting of this book through her friendship and editing prowess even though it was unplanned. No less do I honor Lee

Contreras, who has advised me on the design of this book's cover and happily listened to hours of discussion on the themes and plot of this story.

Fourth is my tribute to my friends—Janice B., Matthew P., Montrez, Mubaraka P., Rukaiya D., and Whitney M.—whose encouragement has heightened my own passion to shared this story, though unplanned, with the world. I also equally extol Mariella Hunt, the friend who both read this story early and offered a commendation for the back of this book.

Fifth is the regard I hold for the Women's Society of Cyberjutsu, who have supported me in numerous areas, from my writing to my career to my confidence as a woman. Their enthusiasm for my achievements has been poured into the personalities and actions of my heroes.

Sixth is my recognition for all those who have purchased copies of my books. No less is my recognition for those friends on social media who have liked and shared my posts about all of my books—their activity, while but a few seconds' work, has done much to bolster my hope for the success of this story. Particularly do I recognize those readers, both advanced and thereafter, who have posted reviews for this book.

If I have forgotten a name in these lists, I ask that you forgive me. My thanks remain true, regardless of mention.

Seventh, I thank you, dear reader, for deigning to peruse this book. I pray that this story meant something to you, that you gained both adventure and inspiration from the writing, and that you felt wisdom sparking in your heart as you witnessed the joys and trials of Riqeta and Naman. May that wisdom help you behold the truth amid the troubles of this age.

In particular, I thank those who have understood that they are the recipients of the dedication of this book.

Lastly, I voice my gratitude for Riqeta and Naman. By striving to discern the coming of evil and learn the truth, they reveal for us the glory of the Light even in the blackest times. Through their fervent desire to protect their people, they offer witness on the nature of evil and the harm rendered by ignoring its spread. Amid that passionate prayer, the greatest proof of their wisdom and prudence is that they cling to their faith despite the suffering that befalls them. For such faith, in their name is freedom someday bestowed upon the world. And, as the heirs of their glory, in many ways it is for Lucian and Malika, and alongside them Elian, Arista, and Kyros, that this book was written. May the second Quest be pleased with the praise of their name.

And above all, may the Almighty bless all of us.

AUTHOR'S BIOGRAPHY

Amena Jamali lives a life animated by the coolness of shrewd logic, the vibrancy of ambitious passion, and the exaltedness of deep morals and philosophy. Her lenses of choice for viewing the world are faith, gratitude, empathy, love, and clear-sighted rationale and strategy. She is many things: devout Muslim, dutiful daughter, patriotic American, thoughtful political activist in the making, blossoming cybersecurity professional, and—not least of all—a writer of epic fantasy.

That last, her epic fantasy writings, holds the essence of all of her hopes, ponderings, and dreams, the substance of her musings about philosophy, and the explorations of her ideas about politics. As her writing evidences, she cares deeply about the power of truth, respectful and reverent discourse, and the formation of a truly inclusive and empowering society that values free choice and the pursuit of virtue for all.

Because of what this story means to her, it is her wish that her books are found to be a source of hope and enlightenment. She prays that every reader falls in love with her characters, as she has, and that their story sets her readers free.

To learn more about Amena's books and to connect with her, please visit www.amenajamali.com. There one may find links to the social media platforms that Amena uses, a form for subscribing to her newsletter, and bonus chapters!

In addition, please support Amena's publication of the books of *The Lord of Freedom* by leaving a review of *The Way It Would Become* on Amazon and on social media!

AUTHOR'S WORKS

Previously Published Books in *The Lord of Freedom* series:
Book One—The Bell Tolling (2021)
A Complement to The Bell Tolling—The Resonant Bell (2022)
Anniversary Edition—The Bell Tolling & The Resonant Bell (2022)

Upcoming Books in *The Lord of Freedom* series:
Book Two—The Reverence Chosen (2023)

Made in the USA
Middletown, DE
10 March 2023

26550713R00156